## "Happy Christmas,"

said a quiet voice behind her. Jasmin turned in surprise to see Benedict Bredon, in a black coat and a white silk scarf and carrying a wrapped bottle and a brightly colored paper bag, coming up the stairs. There was a crazy bubble of joy inside her, as though she had lied to herself when she hoped he wouldn't come. She obeyed a foolish impulse to kiss his cheek.

"Merry Christmas," she said.

Ben put an arm around her. "Is there mistletoe?" he asked.

"Sorry, no mistletoe tonight." She was light-headed, as if she'd drunk on an empty stomach.

"Ah, well, we must do without," he said. He bent and kissed her softly on the lips, and Jasmin felt the heat down to her toes. When he released her, she blinked and leaned against the wall behind her, smiling. For some reason, everything seemed different tonight.

Dear Reader,

The holiday season is here, and as our gift to you, we've got an especially wonderful lineup of books. Just look at our American Hero title, another "Conard County" book from Rachel Lee. *Lost Warriors* is the story of a heart that returns from the brink of oblivion and learns to love again. That heart belongs to rugged Billy Joe Yuma, and the saving hand belongs to nurse Wendy Tate. To learn more, you'll just have to read the book. Believe me, you won't regret it.

And here's another special treat: Judith Duncan is back with *Beyond All Reason,* the first of a special new miniseries called "Wide Open Spaces." It's set in the ranch country of Alberta, Canada, and will introduce you to the McCall family, a set of siblings you won't soon forget. More miniseries news: Marie Ferrarella completes her trilogy about the Sinclair family with *Christmas Every Day,* Nik's story. And the month is rounded out with books by Christine Flynn, a bestseller for Special Edition, Alexandra Sellers, and a second book from Julia Quinn called *Birthright.*

So from all of us to all of you, Happy Holidays— and Happy Reading!

Yours,

Leslie Wainger
Senior Editor and Editorial Coordinator

# A GENTLEMAN
# AND A SCHOLAR

## Alexandra
## Sellers

# Silhouette®
# INTIMATE MOMENTS®
Published by Silhouette Books
**America's Publisher of Contemporary Romance**

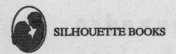 

**SILHOUETTE BOOKS**

ISBN 0-373-07539-1

A GENTLEMAN AND A SCHOLAR

Copyright © 1993 by Alexandra Sellers

This edition published by arrangement with Harlequin Enterprises B. V.

® and TM are trademarks of Harlequin Enterprises B. V., used under
license. Trademarks indicated with ® are registered in the United States
Patent and Trademark Office, the Canadian Trade Marks Office and in
other countries.

Printed in U.S.A.

**Books by Alexandra Sellers**

Silhouette Intimate Moments

*The Real Man* #73
*The Male Chauvinist* #110
*The Old Flame* #154
*The Best of Friends* #348
*The Man Next Door* #406
*A Gentleman and a Scholar* #539

---

## ALEXANDRA SELLERS

used to force her mother to read to her for hours. She wrote her first short story at ten, but as an adult got sidetracked and didn't get published until she was twenty-seven. She also loves travel; she wrote one book in Israel, and began another in Greece. She is currently living in London, but that could change at any time.

To my tetragrammaton

# Prologue

The old woman bent over the child and adjusted the shining fold of fabric that fell around her black hair, then stood back. "There, my darling," she said. "Aren't you beautiful?"

The child gazed at the reflection of herself, transformed into mystery by the exotic fall of the cloth. "You put the necklace on my forehead!" she said in wonderment.

"Yes, my darling, just like the picture. See how the stones match your eyes? My father had green eyes, and we inherited them, you and I. They show your ancestry, and you'll never forget it, will you?" said the old woman.

The child, enchanted, as always, moved her head and watched how the magical image in the mirror reflected the movement. "Am I a princess, Grandmother?" she asked, believing it.

"Oh, yes, my darling. In a country far, far away they would dress you in gold cloth and obey all your commands."

"Would I live in a palace?"

"In a great fortress with walls! Oh, my, how high the gates would seem to you! As though they reached heaven."

"What would I sit on, Grandmother?" she asked, as she always asked, for between young and old the ritual of repetition is a world of delight.

"On a carpet with beautiful pictures on it, of birds and flowers, that they spread over thick cushions for you. It would be as soft as the softest bed," the old woman answered, as she always answered. "And in summer they would bring you iced sorbet to eat, in your own special dish, the sweetest, coolest taste, my darling, and you would like it very much..."

"Would I have maids to undress me, Grandmother?" she asked, when the dreaming was at an end, and the beautiful things were taken off, one by one.

"Oh, yes, my dear, maids to dress and undress you, every piece so carefully, and while they did they would tell you how beautiful you are, and argue over who was to comb out your beautiful black hair. You won't ever cut your hair, my darling, for my sake."

"No, Grandmother. Did they comb your hair?"

"They combed it with a gold comb, all down my back, just like yours, and they scented it with jasmine, for my name. And everywhere I went, I smelled it. Nothing ever smelled as beautiful as that, jasmine in the mountain air."

"Will you take me there, Grandmother?" said the child, as the precious things were packed away till the next time.

"One day, my child, we'll go. Or perhaps you'll go by yourself, when you're older. You'll go to the king, and explain who you are, and ask where your family is. You'll do that, won't you?" said the old woman.

"Yes, Grandmother," the child promised.

# Chapter 1

Jasmin Shaw stood in front of the wide mirror staring blindly at her reflection through her tears as she dragged a comb through her long black hair. *It doesn't get any worse than this,* she thought dully. The washroom was packed with students, and the air charged with their excitement and the sense of new beginnings in the new academic year. An hour ago Jasmin had felt that excitement, and a happy sense of returning home, but now their high, frantic voices were giving her a headache.

Or maybe it was just the effort it took not to cry. Jasmin bent her head and gave her attention to a tangle in her waist-length curls. Using her hair as a screen, she squeezed her eyes shut and tried not to think. It was no good going over and over things in her head; it was no use crying. She must get calm somehow and plan.

"Jasmin! Hi! You're back!" A small blonde with a soft German accent and rather sleepy eyes had pushed through the door and now made her way toward the sink beside Jasmin. She delivered a kiss into the air on each side of Jasmin's face as Jasmin turned to greet her. "Wonderful to see you! How was Kurdistan?"

"Kurdistan was fine," Jasmin said hastily, but the damage was done. She could feel a tear spilling over and down her cheek, and gave up the effort at control. "Andrea, you had to change universities in the middle of your doctorate, didn't you? It's not a complete disaster, is it?" And then she burst into tears.

Andrea's mouth opened in dismay, and she stared at her friend for several frozen seconds. "Change universities? You? Jasmin, what's going on? What's happened?"

But Jasmin was incapable of reply. She leaned on the edge of the sink and wept as though her heart would break. Gently Andrea took the comb from her fingers and slipped it into Jasmin's handbag, then took her arm. "Come on," she said, leading her into a corner where she let Jasmin cry for a minute or two. "Now, tell me what's happened," she said when the flood began to abate. "Your research didn't go well? What happened on the dig? Did you fight with Fellowes or something?"

Jasmin breathed deeply to calm her sobs. "No, nothing like that," she said. "It's Professor Hazlett." At the mention of his name her tears started again. She groped in her bag for a tissue, but in vain. Andrea slipped into a cubicle as another girl came out and pulled a length of paper from the roll, returning to press it into Jasmin's hand.

"Thanks," said Jasmin, blowing her nose. "Oh, God, Andrea, what am I going to do? I can't bear it. I won't be able to stand it. I don't even like being in the same room with him! What shall I do?"

Andrea stared at her. "You don't like being in the same room with Professor Hazlett? What's going on? You *love* Professor Hazlett, or am I crazy?"

Jasmin made a sound that was midway between laughter and a sob. "No, no, not him!" she said. "He's had a heart attack. Oh, God, Andrea, what am I going to do?"

Andrea looked at her for a moment. "First," she said, "you are going to wash your face in cold water. Then we'll get a coffee and go out into the sunshine and you'll tell me all about it. Okay?" She led Jasmin to the sink, and the practicalities of washing her face and blotting up the mascara on her cheeks had the effect of calming her at last.

"Ready?" asked Andrea, when she was presentable, and Jasmin followed her to the door.

"Everybody knows I can't stand him," she muttered, as though Andrea knew all about it. "I can't understand why they're even making the suggestion."

The lobby of the School of Asian and Eastern Studies was jammed. There were lines of students extending from temporary registration desks in the assembly hall, as well as clusters at the cloakroom and in front of the coffee shop and the elevators. A fog of cigarette smoke danced in the sunlight over their heads.

"You go out and get some air," Andrea commanded her, as they fought their way through the crowd. "I'll get us some coffee."

Jasmin obediently moved through the wide doorway and out into the sunlight. The air was clean and fresh with the smell of fall, and the autumn sun bathed the gray stone of the steps with the distinctive gold of late September in London. Away to her left, she could see the trees of Russell Square, russet and yellow against the blackened old brick of the university buildings; ahead, even the Bauhaus white stone shape of Senate House was softened by the golden glow. Sprawled on the steps at her feet, as always on fine days, students lounged, smoking and chatting.

She heaved a sigh. It had been her spiritual home for the past five years. Now, suddenly, it was a hostile environment. It had always seemed to be her protection. Now it threatened her. She would have to leave, not because she wanted to, but because she was no longer safe here.

"Jas!" a voice called from just below where she stood. "Hello! Welcome back!"

She glanced down. A familiar form was leaning on the steps below her, one arm up to shade his eyes from the sun as he looked at her. "Shahdeen!" Jasmin called. She flung herself down beside him, exchanging kisses on both cheeks in greeting. "How are you? How did your summer go?"

"It was very good," he said. "New York Public Library is excellent. I was amazed. And I haven't had a cigarette in six weeks." Jasmin exclaimed over these successes, but when he asked, "How about you?" she stopped smiling.

"Things couldn't be worse," she said, and swallowed. "Did you know that Professor Hazlett has had a heart attack?"

"No," said Shahdeen. "He's your supervisor?" Jasmin nodded. "Bad luck—very bad luck."

"It happened two months ago, and of course I didn't hear a thing about it. He's taking early retirement." Jasmin knew she didn't have to explain the horror that statement implied.

Shahdeen rubbed his cheek and pursed his lips in sympathy. "Ouch."

"It's going to kill me," she said. They sat in silence for a moment.

"Can't he supervise you from retirement?" Shahdeen offered then. "It has been done."

"Hi, Shahdeen. If I'd known you were here I'd have brought you some coffee," called Andrea, as she threaded her way through the students sitting on the steps above them.

Jasmin reached gratefully for her coffee and took a sip. "That's the worst of it. He says—according to the head of the department—Professor Hazlett says he can give me some help, if I've got someone else actually supervising me."

"That's all right, then, isn't it?" Andrea interjected, picking up the thread with no difficulty as she settled herself beside Jasmin.

"But there aren't many people in your field here, are there?" asked Shahdeen.

"There aren't *any* people in my field here, besides my professor. So guess what they're suggesting?" They both looked at her expectantly. "And if I don't do it, I'm going to have to go to Toronto to work with Charpentier or Chicago and work with Fellowes." She lifted her hands and dropped them. "They want me to work with Benedict Bredon."

She had the satisfaction, if that was what it was, of seeing that she had shocked them. "Oooh," said Shahdeen, on a long, drawn-out note, his eyes opening wide at her news. Andrea said nothing, but merely sat with a surprised look on her face.

"And Professor Hazlett thinks it would be a good idea, or so they tell me," Jasmin said helplessly. "I can't believe it."

There was a short silence while they absorbed it. Then Shahdeen made an apologetic face. "I know you don't like him much, but—" He shrugged. "He's got a very good reputation, hasn't he? Couldn't you—" At the look on her face, he started again. "Won't it be worse for you to give up the continuity of some supervision from Professor Hazlett than to work with this man?"

"No," she said baldly. She added nothing to that. She knew there was no way to explain her feeling. Everybody knew she disliked Benedict Bredon, and most of her friends thought they knew why. But no one knew, because she scarcely knew herself that she was also afraid of him. She did not like being in his presence, and she felt under threat when he was near. But she ignored her fear and fanned her anger, taking refuge in dislike. "I'm hoping that I might be able to get a supplement to my grant, so that I could come back from Toronto once or twice a year to work with Professor Hazlett. My grant is from RSOS, and Professor Hazlett is the president. He might be able to arrange something, don't you think?"

"That's a lot of money to be throwing around. I wouldn't count on it," said Shahdeen, who, like most research students, had constant difficulties making his grant money stretch to meet his needs.

"This is impossible," Andrea said firmly. "You are a fool if you think you can make the shift so easily. Believe me, it's a last resort only. You don't know what you are talking about, Jasmin. This man we all know you hate so much—is he any good? Does he know anything about your field? Be honest."

"I know he has some background that's relevant to what I'm doing," Jasmin admitted. "From that point of view it's— But he disagrees with everything Professor Hazlett says. He thinks the whole idea of symbolism in the iconography of Sassanian art is a crock! I know he does! And I know he'd spend his time trying to force me to change my mind."

"Maybe he wouldn't," said Andrea, refusing to be drawn from her purpose. "How well do you know him—academically, I mean?"

"I know him, all right," said Jasmin flatly. "I did classes with him from the first year of my undergraduate degree."

"What marks did he give you?" Shahdeen asked.

"All firsts, for what they were worth."

Andrea stared at her. "You've never told me that! You're crazy! What's the matter with you? Go and talk to him at least! If you can get firsts from him, you can work with him! Be careful, Jas! You don't know what it's like to change institutions, countries, in the middle of your research!"

"At least talk to him," Shahdeen agreed.

The pressure of their opposition caused any remaining control she had to explode. "I can't! I hate him!" Jasmin burst out. "And I know the feeling is mutual! The only reason he's offered to supervise me is because he knows how close I am to Professor Hazlett. He thinks he can get at him through me. He'll try to get me to attack Professor Hazlett's ideas! I know it! And the only reason Professor Hazlett doesn't know it is because he's too much of a gentleman himself to think of such a thing! How the hell can I work under those conditions? I'd rather not get my doctorate!'' Her voice rose. "I'd rather teach art history to *engineers* than work with Benedict Bredon!''

She spoke into a kind of cosmic silence at the end. For some reason conversations all around them had simultaneously died, and then Jasmin felt an unmistakable ripple along her spine. She turned her head; her eyes fixed on the casual shoes a few feet from her and traveled upward.

Dr. Benedict Bredon stood on the step above her, tall, slender and aloof, and she should have known better than to talk about anyone—particularly Dr. Bredon—anywhere in the School's precincts. The familiar mix of fear and dislike she felt for the man uncurled in her stomach and crawled through her system.

Benedict Bredon looked at her for a long moment, as if debating whether to speak to her. Jasmin could feel herself blushing, and it was only by the greatest force of will that she did not drop her eyes. He raised his hand and adjusted his glasses in a characteristic gesture, then slipped his hand into his pocket. He had an attractive, rather aristocratic face, but as usual he was looking somewhat rumpled in a tweed jacket and corduroy trousers. Women generally found him charming, but whenever he looked at Jasmin, his eyes never held charm. His look for her was always dark, always measuring, as though assessing an enemy.

"I was looking for you, Miss Shaw," he said at last. "I understand you've talked to Dr. Harding. I think you and I should discuss this matter privately. Are you free?"

It was impossible to refuse after what he had overheard; it would be a terrible confession of weakness. She had to rise to his challenge, even though the thought of facing him tied her stomach in knots.

She swallowed. "I'll be free in a few minutes," she said.

Bredon consulted his watch. "Shall we say my office, then, in a quarter of an hour?"

Jasmin nodded without speaking, and he turned and continued down the steps, striding off in the direction of Russell Square.

"Was that him?" Andrea demanded in a hoarse half whisper. "My Gott, Jasmin, was that Bredon?"

Jasmin nodded slowly, her lower lip caught between her teeth. "Oh, boy, how I do put my foot in it," she said, forcing her tone to a lightness she did not feel. "That man is *always* creeping up on me when I'm bitching about him! What am I going to do now?"

As if in sympathy, a cloud that had been playing tag with the sun suddenly obscured it completely. A few drops of rain began to freckle the concrete steps. Andrea shrugged. "I think you're going to find a job teaching art history to engineers," she said with Germanic gloom.

# Chapter 2

Jasmin had not always hated Benedict Bredon. Coming late to scholarship after ten years as a model, she had arrived at the School of Asian and Eastern Studies full of intellectual excitement, and from their first meeting she had been ready to like him. She had planned to study the history, religions and art of Afghanistan, with particular emphasis on the modern era, and she had been quite content to discover it was largely his area.

In her first year she took a course with him in the modern history of Central Asia, which, of course, included Afghanistan. His subject was water in the desert to her, and her brain, starved of intellectual stimulus for ten years, drank greedily. She had liked him from the first, for although he was shy and sometimes remote, she felt they shared a sense of humor, and was easy in his presence where others were not.

Believing that he understood her joy in his subject, she had begun to make demands on his time. She went to his office out of class time, asking questions, wanting to discuss with him the sources she was reading. She did not understand why he rebuffed her, but she had taken the cool discouragement personally. She had been first baffled, then hurt. Then it occurred to her that as he was attractive, straight, unmarried and thirty-five, he might be imagining that she was less interested in the Khyber Pass than in the color of his eyes, and she was angry. She backtracked then, but it was nearly impossible to distance herself from the man without it affecting her approach to his subject. She lost pleasure in what she was learning, and blamed him bitterly.

It was not that she lost interest in modern Afghanistan. It was merely that being so discouraged on the one hand, and so encouraged on another, she had gone where the encouragement was.

She was also taking a course with Professor Hazlett in the earliest history of the area now divided under the names Iran and Afghanistan. Jasmin had worked very hard for her first essay with Professor Hazlett, because he was well-known to be a stinker and because the course was tough. He had ripped it to shreds. He had slapped her down for every undefended assumption, every unattributed idea, her improperly footnoted quotations and her use of secondary sources. He had given her the lowest mark Jasmin had ever been given on anything in her life and told her she must learn scholarly method.

To say that Jasmin fell in love with the great professor in that moment would be a lie. She had two emotions then—shock and outrage. Shock because of the low mark, and outrage because he seemed to give her no credit whatever for all the hard thinking that had gone into her work. But she never, ever thought, "I'll show him!" in so many words. She merely discovered, when the next essay came along, that she was working on it to the exclusion of nearly everything else.

She had never realized so many of the classical authors of Greece and Rome had discussed the great empire of the Medes and the Persians—she had scarcely realized so many *existed*—as she read in the two-week period when she researched that essay. She read them thoroughly. She rigidly excluded assumption. She checked up on every secondary source. She footnoted meticulously. She found it all tedious and irritating, but she got an A on the essay, and the penciled comment, "A very commendable effort." Following on Benedict Bredon's sudden remoteness, it felt like the highest praise she had ever had in her life.

It soon became apparent that, unlike Bredon, Professor Hazlett considered an interest in his subject something to be encouraged, and Jasmin herself well worth encouraging. From the day she appeared at his office door to ask a question he treated Jasmin as scholar-in-the-making, and he never resisted the growing intimacy of the student-teacher bond, as Benedict Bredon had done.

Many months later, in difficult search of a quotation that would support a theory, Jasmin made a discovery: she was enjoying herself. The irritation that used to settle on her during such painstaking work had been replaced by pleasure in the mental discipline. In that moment what she felt was a burst of gratitude to the man who had taught her the discipline. She gave her heart into his hands then, sure that she was safe.

Meanwhile, she established an attitude of indifference toward Benedict Bredon. She learned to ignore him except during the two hours a week of his lecture. She did good work for his courses, without any sign of the brilliance that Hazlett fostered in her, and scarcely recognizing her own resentment over this. Bredon never encouraged her. He gave her good marks, but he was sparing to the point of miserliness in his praise, and Jasmin never learned to understand his cryptic comments.

When she submitted her course choices for her second year, Bredon had called her to his office to ask why she was switching the emphasis of her degree. She had looked at him in blank astonishment; she would never have imagined that he even noticed her, let alone kept track of her courses. Af-

ter a moment she had reminded him of the story of the man
who was looking for his house key under a street lamp.
'Where did you drop it?' asked a passerby. 'At my front
door,' said the searcher. 'Then why are you looking for it
here?' asked the passerby. 'Because this is where the light is,
stupid!' the searcher replied. Jasmin had smiled at Bredon
after she related the tale, and shrugged. "Professor Hazlett
is where the light is," she'd said. She was surprised at the
look which passed over Bredon's face.

After that, curiously, there was a certain edge to their relationship. It became difficult to maintain her attitude of
indifference. She felt under threat when he looked at her,
without knowing why. He sometimes spoke as though she
accepted some of Professor Hazlett's more controversial
theories too slavishly, and they exchanged sharp differences of opinion in class.

Late in her second year, when her admiration of Professor Hazlett had moved into adoration, he delivered a controversial paper at a conference. The generally observed rule
at such moments, as far as Jasmin's experience had informed her, was that politeness was the better part of
scholarly valor. People who disagreed even violently with
each other, would, at conferences, put forth only the gen-
tlest of questions, delicately pointing to the body of fact that
made nonsense of a colleague's claims. They saved their
vitriol for print.

At that conference, Dr. Benedict Bredon broke this un-
written rule. The questions that he put to Hazlett after lis-
tening to his paper were clearly impatient, even hostile,
although perhaps to no one but Jasmin did they actually
appear savage. Worse, in Jasmin's eyes, was the fact that
Professor Hazlett was thrown by the hostility, and did not
answer competently. A rage of protectiveness descended on
her. When Bredon finished she jumped to her feet with a
leading question, giving Hazlett the breathing space he
needed to marshal a response to Bredon's challenge.

Jasmin still remembered the look she had exchanged with Bredon then. In that moment the edge hardened into dislike. She never forgave him. Not because he had exposed any weakness in her hero that she was unaware of—Jasmin had never been so naive as to imagine her professor was perfect—but because it was unnecessary, and unfair. And it had looked to her like a matter not of scholarship but of ego. Curiously, the dislike she now felt for Bredon seemed not to be new, but the crystallization of a host of unrecognized feelings she had had for some time. And it was a surprising relief to allow herself to express definable feelings toward him.

She began producing essays that attacked all his own favorite views, whether she agreed with him or not. She hoped to force him to mark her down on the basis of her opinions, because that would have been a victory. He made it clear that he disagreed with her, but he never gave her the satisfaction of marking her down. As long as the essay was well researched, and well reasoned, she got the marks. That made her even angrier. She *wanted* him to take it personally.

Then, in an obscure journal, she had stumbled across an old review written by Benedict Bredon of the controversial, ground-breaking book by Hazlett on symbolism in Sassanian rock sculptures. It was the most vitriolic, unforgiving critique she had ever read. It had been published years ago, before Bredon had gained his Ph.D., and she could see that he had begun his career in the tried and tested fashion of savaging an important figure.

That was the seal of her loathing. From that moment she ceased even to make any attempt to hide her antipathy. She spoke her dislike of Bredon aloud, and told herself she didn't care when it happened—as it must, in such an intimate environment as that of the School—that he had overheard. She was sure that it made him angry, for the atmosphere between them became increasingly uncomfortable.

She graduated with first class honors, and there was no question but that she should continue in an academic life, if she could find the money in a recession to do so. Glowing references from Daniel Hazlett had secured her a study grant, and it was widely recognized within the confines of the School that Professor Hazlett had found another of his rare protégés.

He suggested a subject for her master's thesis that bridged modern and ancient Afghanistan, and it was necessary to sign up for one course with Bredon. The other two courses and her thesis were to be under Hazlett's tutelage. She was being drawn further and further into an interest in pre-Islamic Iran and Central Asia.

To her utter amazement, in the first week of term, before her course choices were final, Benedict Bredon took her to the Senior Common Room for drinks, over which he suggested that she should take another of his courses instead of one of Hazlett's, and mentioned areas of research she might undertake for her thesis that would bring it more into his field. He reminded her of her early interest in modern Afghanistan and urged her not to drop it entirely.

Jasmin was surprisingly shaken by this evidence of his continuing interest in her career in spite of their mutual hostility. For two days she thought about nothing but Benedict Bredon and what she should do. Someone with more intellectual arrogance might have imagined that he wanted the kudos of such a protégée, or even that he felt his field would benefit if she were to enter it. Jasmin had no such pretensions. Someone with more sexual arrogance might have imagined that he was trying, belatedly, to make a pass. It would be a cold day in hell before Jasmin believed that. Someone with a taste for conspiracy theories might have imagined that, to pay off some old debt against Professor Hazlett, Bredon was trying to draw the great man's favorite student away. The moment this possibility occurred to her, Jasmin knew she had hit on the truth. Her protective urge flooded up. Hazlett was the one who had believed in her from the beginning; he was the one who had taught her everything she knew. If Benedict Bredon hoped he could use her to get at his enemy, he could think again.

That year her classes with Bredon were hell. Every time he looked at her she felt burned; every time she looked at him the violence of her feelings was nearly overwhelming.

She received a coveted "with distinction" for her master's work, and was immediately taken on as Daniel Hazlett's teaching assistant, a post that included a research grant for three years of doctoral study. Hazlett drew her securely into his own period for her doctorate. She was examining the symbolism on the silver ware of the dynasty that had ruled Iran from 250 to 650 A.D., the four centuries immediately preceding the Islamic invasion: the Sassanians. That had removed her finally and entirely from Benedict Bredon's orbit.

Until today. As Jasmin and her friends stood and moved back up the steps into the School in the lightly falling rain, she glanced over her shoulder in the direction Bredon had gone and grimaced to herself. She did not want to work with Benedict Bredon. It was not only loathing; she also felt a deep inner apprehension. She did not want to get any closer to him. She did not want to be under his power in any way. As a graduate student she knew she would be very vulnerable. She had been entirely safe with Daniel Hazlett. She did not want to work with Benedict Bredon, because she felt, deep in some primitive part of her self, that she would not be safe in his hands.

# Chapter 3

He was not in when she got to his office. She waited by his door, marshaling her determination and her arguments, and the fact that he kept her waiting fueled her nervous discomfort. Seven minutes after the appointed time she heard a peculiar, rhythmic squishing noise in the hall around the corner, and Benedict Bredon arrived, soaking wet. A few minutes after he left her on the steps, the bottom had fallen out of the sky, and the rain was still pouring down. He had obviously been caught in the worst of it. His hair was plastered to his head, water dripped down his face, his gray tweed jacket was nearly black, and the squishing noise came from his sodden shoes as he walked.

This sudden transformation of the devil of her thoughts into plain mortal flesh and blood shook her out of her carefully constructed attitude of defensive defiance. Jasmin gasped and laughed aloud. "Why on earth didn't you take shelter and wait it out?" she demanded, completely forgetting the scene on the steps, and even her own dislike. Then she bit her lip and waited for the rebuff.

But he laughed, too, taking off his glasses to shake the water droplets from them as he unlocked the door. She decided it was his signal that he was going to ignore what he had overheard. "If there had been shelter, I might have done," he said. "As it happened, I was in the middle of the square."

Jasmin followed him as he strode into his office, and closed the door behind her. Bredon tossed his keys and a wet paper bag onto his desk and began to struggle out of his jacket. The rain was beating against the window, and the office was shadowy under the dark sky. Underneath the jacket his shirt was damp and sticking to the skin over his shoulders, and his trouser legs clung wetly to his thighs. He bent down to pull a towel from a sports bag under his desk, and with one hand began to rub it over his hair. "Sit down," he said.

Jasmin hesitated. "Would you like me to come back later?" she asked uncomfortably. Soaking wet like that, he seemed unfamiliarly human. A man, instead of...

He eyed her quizzically. "No, why?"

She couldn't explain, even to herself. Perhaps she had imagined he would want to take his shirt off, but of course he would not. She shrugged. After a moment she slipped into the chair in front of his desk.

When he was through with the towel, his fair hair was tousled, and he rather absently ran his hands through it from front to back. A lock escaped to fall, as always, over his forehead, but the rest remained slicked back, and in the gray half light the shape of his skull and his facial bone structure were suddenly prominent. He made an interesting piece of sculpture—a broad, high forehead, large, chiseled nose, strong cheekbones and a surprisingly full mouth. It was a strong face, but shadows under his eyes made it curiously vulnerable.

"Do you mind if I smoke?" he asked, picking up his jacket again to feel through the pockets. She shook her head, and he extracted his pipe from an inside pocket and dropped the jacket again. As he crossed to sit behind the desk, his shoes squelched. He sat down, rolled up his shirt cuffs, and switched on the desk lamp. The pool of light cast a halo of intimacy around them that left Jasmin feeling defenseless. In her first year at the School, she had sometimes come to see him here, but that was before he made it clear she was unwelcome. She was not used to being alone with him.

He pulled the disintegrating, soggy paper bag away from a blue-and-silver pack of tobacco, opened it, and began to pack his pipe. In the warm lamplight Jasmin watched his fingers separate a portion of tobacco and press it into the bowl, and slowly became aware that his eyes were not on his task, but on her. For a moment they simply looked at each other.

"I understand you've discussed this with Dr. Harding," he said then. She nodded. "He gathered that you are quite decided against remaining here to complete your research." He didn't say "under my supervision," but she could see the unspoken words in his eyes. The memory of what he had overheard on the steps flickered between them.

Jasmin looked away. "Well, I should probably go and work with someone like Fellowes or Charpentier, shouldn't I?"

He smiled briefly. "I suppose that depends on your point of view." He struck a match and put the pipe into his mouth; there was the sudden odor of burning tobacco, which in spite of everything she found not unpleasant. "From the School's point of view it is certainly preferable that you should stay here."

"Is it?" she asked.

He drew in sharp puffs on the pipe, sucking the match flame down into the bowl. "I am sure you can see that to lose everyone on the pre-Islamic side at short notice is not very desirable. Daniel was scheduled to teach half a dozen courses, some of which certainly ought to be covered this

year, and you, if I'm not mistaken, are down for tutorials as
well as teaching a full course."

"I don't think I could teach anything without Professor
Hazlett's support," Jasmin said stupidly. The shadowed
room, their isolation, seemed to have robbed her of common sense as well as her defenses.

"Nonsense," Bredon said abruptly, as if that irritated
him. He waved the match out with a short snap, picked up
the towel again, wiped his glasses on a corner of it, and put
them on.

Jasmin felt the welcome stirring of anger. "I don't think
this discussion will get very far if you're simply going to
dismiss everything I say as nonsense."

Bredon took his pipe out of his mouth. "Do you expect
me to take seriously an assertion that you are incompetent
to teach your course in the absence of Daniel Hazlett?"

Somehow she had already lost control of this damned
conversation. There was no winning answer to that; they
hadn't been talking three minutes and she was cornered. The
fact that it was her own stupid comment that had caused this
defeat did not help her mood. "I expect you to understand
that I'm feeling shaken by what's happened!" she said.

His elbow was resting on the desk, and he held his pipe
half an inch from his mouth. "However shaken you are, no
end will be served by my catering to any feeling of inade-
quacy on your part."

"It wouldn't hurt *you* to cater to any feeling that's going," Jasmin retorted, and then blinked. She had never
made a personal remark to him before. But her surprise was
nothing compared with its effect on Benedict Bredon. He
had parted his lips slightly for his pipe, but now he simply
stopped there, watching her. He didn't move, he made no
other sign, he simply went still, but somehow she had hit
home. Whatever "home" was.

After a moment he lowered his arm and set his pipe carefully in the large ashtray always on his desk. She was sure
that he was very, very angry. "What feeling, exactly, would

you like me to cater to?'' he asked gently. She sensed a threat in his tone as well as in his eyes, but it was not in her nature to back away from confrontation with him.

She said, "You dislike me. It might help if you admitted that."

A little burst of involuntary laughter escaped him, and again she was disconcerted. He relaxed back in his chair and looked at her with raised eyebrows. "I do not dislike you, Miss Shaw. And if I did, what possible purpose would be served by my telling you so?"

Which was as good as saying he did. "I'd know what I had to deal with in making this decision."

"You will not have to deal with any feelings of mine, I assure you. You should make this decision on purely practical and academic grounds, as Daniel would be the first to tell you."

She wanted to challenge that first statement. But somehow when she opened her mouth the words didn't come. "On academic grounds, it seems to me that I'm better off going to work with Fellowes or Charpentier. It's not really your field, is it, pre-Islamic art?" she said instead.

As the conversation steadied back on course, she had the odd conviction that they had just avoided a very dangerous...something. She shifted in her seat, uncomfortable without knowing why. As he picked up his pipe and struck another match, she sensed in him, too, a kind of restlessness.

"It's not my first field. I expect to take over one or two of Daniel's courses this year until a replacement can be found, but certainly I haven't his background."

"I've only just done my field research. I'll need a tremendous amount of help organizing it."

"For a woman of your rather remarkable abilities, you seem astonishingly dependent," he said. "I'm surprised to learn that Daniel has coddled you in such a way. It's not what I would have expected from him."

His apparent respect for her professor caused her to drop her guard yet again. "He doesn't coddle me," Jasmin assured him with a rueful grin. It was the first time in years she had smiled at Benedict Bredon. "He throws me in at the deep end. But I've got . . . I think I've got so I'm dependent on *that*. If he's not there, I'm afraid I'll stay in the shallows."

It was quite a confession, but Benedict Bredon only smiled back at her and drew on his pipe. "I will not allow you to stay in the shallows. But I will expect you to find your own way to the deeps. Does that reassure you?"

It did and it didn't. She was still feeling uncomfortable, and it took her a moment to discover that it was because of the sudden, unfamiliar ease between them. She wondered suddenly if this was how he would get to her—pretend admiration for Hazlett and slowly wean her away from his ideas. Well, there was one way to spike those guns. She asked, "Do you know what my thesis is?"

He blinked and frowned. "Of course I know what your thesis is."

"You disagree with it." Her normally pleasant voice turned suddenly flat, a not unusual occurrence in his presence, and she saw him move his shoulders as if he, too, were coming out of a trance.

"How can I possibly disagree with something that hasn't yet been written?"

"You must know that I'm going to argue for extensive symbolism in the iconography. I know that you don't accept that position. I think we should discuss the question of your supervising me from that point of view."

"I beg your pardon, you know nothing of the sort." He spoke over her last statement, so Jasmin repeated it.

"I think we should discuss this in the light of your own position on symbolism."

"I don't propose to enter into any discussion based on what you take to be my position on anything," he replied roughly.

"I know you disagree with me."

"Since I have heard nothing and read little from you on the subject, nor ever discussed it with you, you know no such thing."

She was angry now. Why wouldn't he just admit it? Then they might be able to address the problem of whether he could effectively supervise her from his hostile point of view. She said, "Well, I've heard you criticize Professor Hazlett on the subject of Persian Mithraism."

"What has that got to do with anything?" he demanded, in a louder voice than she had ever heard from him.

"I'll be including Mithraic symbolism in my thesis."

"You will certainly have to deal with the subject if you are going to give a comprehensive treatment of the scholarly opinion. How is that pertinent?"

"Well, you disagree with me."

"I have disagreed in the past with Daniel Hazlett. If you do not consider that a significantly different matter from disagreeing with *you,* it would be my duty as your supervisor to point out to you that a doctoral thesis ought to include original research *and* original thinking." His hand came down on the desk with a little thump, cradling his pipe, as he looked levelly at her.

There was a powerful undercurrent to everything now, but Jasmin couldn't grasp what it was. To her it was generalized as anger. "And does original thinking necessarily mean disagreeing with Professor Hazlett?"

Bredon was clearly annoyed. "No, it does not," he said. "It means looking at your evidence with as open a mind as possible, and following it to reasoned and well-supported conclusions. It means not accepting someone else's ideas as a substitute for thinking. I think you know this. If you want to convince me—and, incidentally, your examining board—that your views are correct, you will have to base your arguments on evidence and sound scholarly method."

She knew she had gone too far. Yet, somehow, she couldn't stop waving the red flag. "I expect to argue that

Roman Mithraism was an offshoot of a Persian Mithraic cult.''

"Well, then, I hope you will find better ways to support the theory than have previously been offered."

Here it was. Jasmin leapt into the argument. There were two opposing schools of scholarly opinion on Persian Mithraism, and they met nowhere. And until and unless some significant discovery proved to a certainty that there had once been a cult of Mithra within the Persian Empire, they never would. The issue was a charged one, and it lost none of its charge in Benedict Bredon's office during the next five minutes.

"There *are* no Mithraic temples in Persia proper!" Jasmin protested at one point, telling him nothing he didn't know.

"And you intend to ignore that pertinent fact?"

"But after the Muslim invasion the Mithraic temples must have been destroyed. The Muslims—''

"Whatever the Muslims destroyed, you are not entitled to assume the existence of something of which there is now no trace."

"I don't intend to *assume* it!"

He said, "What evidence have you that Persian worship of Mithra involved a mystery cult like that of the Romans?"

"Phillips thinks the earliest pre-Zoroastrian creation myth entailed Mithra sacrificing the bull, and that's the most important attribute in the Roman cult, isn't it—the bull-slaying?"

His still disheveled hair was drying, and another lock fell forward over his left eye. "Yes, perhaps. It's a long way from pre-Zoroastrian creation myths to first century Persia. You will have to link it up."

It was clear he would admit nothing. "So, as far as you are concerned, the Mithra connection is untenable. If I'm working with you, you'll expect me to challenge rather than support it," she said at last, heaving an angry breath.

He looked irritated, as though she had missed the point. "I'll expect you to base your conclusions on your evidence," he said impatiently. "And I'll expect to point it out to you whenever I perceive that there is insufficient evidence for your conclusions. I haven't said there isn't room for new work on the subject."

Angry as she was, it was with a good deal of pleasure that Jasmin realized that she might actually make Benedict Bredon lose his temper. That would be a first!

"And what about inspiration?" she said deliberately.

"What about inspiration?" he countered, frowning.

"People do have attacks of inspiration, especially around ancient artifacts, don't they?"

She could see that the naiveté of this goaded him. "They do, but if they are scholars, they must find the evidence to support their inspiration, or abandon it. A doctoral thesis is not the proper venue for psychic revelation."

"Thank you," she said coldly, quite forgetting that she had deliberately inspired this derision.

Benedict Bredon pointed his pipe at her. "You are a very beautiful woman," he said, "so it's not surprising that you have got into the habit of blinking those green eyes and asking stupid questions when you want to get away with something. I warn you not to expect that technique to get very far with me. With me you will be required to use your brain, and you will not be allowed to insult your intelligence—or mine—with the kind of coy stupidities I see you use to some effect elsewhere."

He had never gone so far before. Jasmin's mouth fell further and further open as this speech progressed, and by the end of it she was incoherent. "What?" she demanded. "How...when did I...you—" She stopped, closed her eyes, took a breath, and then another. "That is absolutely unjustified!" she said, when she thought she had regained some control.

"Is it?"

But she was not in control. The injustice simply swept her away. "You—I suppose you mean Professor Hazlett! Is that who you mean? I have *never*—that's how you think I get my marks, is it? Professor Hazlett has *never* . . . !" She wanted to hit him. She actually had to force herself to remain in her seat by sheer willpower. Of all the men she had met in her life, Professor Hazlett was the one who never, ever dealt with her through the medium of her looks. It was one reason he had inspired such love in her.

"Please don't put words in my mouth. I did not mean Daniel, as it happens."

"Or *you!* I knew you thought that! Believe me, you'd be the *last* man I'd ever—! Blink my green eyes! How dare you? All I wanted was to know about your subject! That is all I ever wanted from you!"

"I am aware of that," said Bredon. "I think—"

"I don't want to hear what you think!" Jasmin was on her feet and shouting, neither of which actions impinged on her consciousness. "If you think I got my marks because of my looks, how is it I got firsts from you? Was that because of my looks? You were smitten, is that it?"

"I did not say you got your marks for your looks!" It was the first time she had ever heard Benedict Bredon shout, but Jasmin was beyond feeling triumph, or even noticing.

"Every mark I got, I earned!" she carried on over him. "*Especially* from Professor Hazlett! He is the hardest marker I've ever met in my life, and I worked my butt off for those marks! With you I got away with slop! But never, ever *once* did he let me get away with anything! He is *impeccable,* and he wouldn't have cared if I had doorknobs for eyes! Don't talk to *me* about soundly-based arguments! I've written stuff for you that Professor Hazlett would have chopped me up in pieces for! But they got by you!"

"That is ridiculous!" he said loudly.

"But probably you couldn't be bothered reading them, so you wouldn't know! What is it—just green eyes that get past you? You actually read the essays of women with brown eyes?''

"Will you sit down and shut up?'' Bredon shouted. He was on his feet, too, but neither of them could have said when he got up.

"No, I won't! How dare you offer to supervise my work when you have this kind of opinion of me?''

"You have no idea what opinion I have of you.'' Bredon stopped shouting abruptly and fought for calm. "Stop talking nonsense!''

Jasmin bent over and picked up her bag. "I'll stop talking altogether. And I'll remove myself from your presence. Thank you for your offer, but I think I'll be better off in Toronto. I'd be better off in Podunk Polytechnic, come to that!'' She flung open the door and strode out, almost careering into someone in her fury.

Benedict Bredon stood behind his desk, gazing at the empty doorway for some seconds after she had disappeared. Then he dropped his hand to pick up his pipe and, moving to the window, lighted it again. Rain still thundered against the glass. There was nothing but his own reflection and the bright burst of the match's flame, but he seemed to see something that made him frown.

## Chapter 4

"Mind how you go, love," the bus conductor advised, as Jasmin prepared to leap off the back of the double-decker bus while it slowed for a turn. Jasmin smiled, hanging out of the platform with one arm, her long body making a graceful V with the chromium-plated pole, her blue-black hair a cascade almost too heavy for the wind to move. The bright flowers she held drew attention to her own extremes of color. Jasmin had the unconscious knack of making herself a picture against any background.

"I will," she promised. The conductor blossomed in her sunshine. Jasmin's voice was by nature intimate; it sounded as though she were speaking to the one person in all the world she wanted to be with. Most men couldn't see their hands in front of their faces when she spoke, and the bus conductor was no exception. He wanted to say more, wanted to prolong the closeness, but by the time he had marshaled his confused thoughts Jasmin had gone, leaping to the pavement with her own peculiar symmetry—"the sort of grace that gives the term *catwalk* new meaning," as one

gushing fashion columnist had once called it. A car coming
around the corner in the wake of the bus had to brake momentarily, but as Jasmin tossed her head to shift her hair she
smiled her apology. The woman driver grinned back; Jasmin charmed women, too.

That had been the root of her early success as a model.
Women did not just want to *be* Jasmin; they wanted to be
her friend.

She was one of those women who are blessed with the
right figure at the right time. Just when fashion had begun
to demand it, Jasmin's young body had blossomed into that
rare combination of long legs, slim hips, fine bones and full
breasts that would mark the eighties as the flat, thin, boy-
ish figure had marked the sixties—a shape that caused
women born with more ordinary figures to despair, since no
amount of diet, exercise, self-control or even surgery could
produce it. You were born with such a shape or you were
not, and few were.

She had also inherited a head of thick, lustrous, mid-
night-colored hair from her father and, from her paternal
grandmother—the same lady who had doubtless given her
her fine slender bones—an unusual and very individual face,
green eyes and porcelain skin.

Jasmin had gone into modeling at seventeen. Her father
had died young, and her mother worked as a secretary. The
income from Jasmin's work had given the family the first
real financial security they had felt for years. Her mother
had deplored the waste of Jasmin's brain. Jasmin was
blessed with intelligence, and her mother knew, and said,
that she should go on to university. But Jasmin also had a
will stronger than her mother's. She had signed with an
agent while her mother was still wringing her hands.

The next seven or eight years had gone well for Jasmin,
though not brilliantly. She worked constantly, without ever
becoming a generation's icon. Her face had launched a new
perfume without the news of the contract making head-

lines. She earned enough to allow her mother to retire, but not herself, not for life.

She had reached the age of twenty-five with foreboding, because her career would almost certainly soon begin to wane. She changed agents, and her new agent found her two small film parts. A more aggressive man might have tried to introduce her with a much larger part, and if things had gone well, Jasmin might have made the transition without thinking. But those small parts left her on the outside, and gave her time to observe without being involved, time to think.

The American star of Jasmin's first film was thirty-six and famed for her beauty. The day that Jasmin discovered that that beauty was considered to be "in decline," and that the star was generally felt not to have "managed" her looks carefully enough, she had gone home to stare for some time into a mirror.

There it was. She was attractive, unusual, striking; some might call her beautiful, especially, she told herself cynically, if she got larger roles. Did she want to spend the rest of her life "managing" her beauty? Did she want to go on in a life where everything of importance to her was this side of her own nose? She had spent nearly ten years starving herself, avoiding the sun, making up, cleansing her pores, and doing spot-reducing exercises in every spare moment. In the next ten years her palette of preoccupations would no doubt expand to include cosmetic surgery and other more complex rituals.

Of course, if she had a great talent, she might be allowed to age more naturally. But the part she was cast in demanded nothing of her, and Jasmin wasn't at all sure that if it had, she could have fulfilled the demands. She was in the film to look beautiful and mysterious and to be gorily murdered after fifteen minutes, and the more she saw of the work of the real actors, the less confident she became.

Jasmin decided it was time for some other career. Modeling had given her a certain amount of freedom; she had managed her finances well, and so could afford the luxury of taking a few years off from earning. Modeling had also introduced her to a variety of countries and cities, and it was London she loved.

She had always known she would return for her missed university education one day, and her other interest was there waiting for her. Her first love, since her childhood, had been the mysterious East. That interest had been packed away in a satin-lined box in her mind for ten years, but once the lid was off, it came out in all its exotic splendor, with scarcely any dust. Before either of her films was released, Jasmin had moved to England, bought an apartment and enrolled for an undergraduate degree at the world-famous School of Asian and Eastern Studies.

She loved the East because she was of the East. The grandmother who had bequeathed Jasmin her unusual beauty and her name had been half Afghan, raised in England; the grandmother's brother had been, so the family legend said, an Afghan tribal chieftain who fought against the English in the Third Afghan War. Their father had been a diplomat sent to the West late in the nineteenth century by the great king of Afghanistan, Abdur Rahman Khan. He and an English earl's cousin had fallen shockingly in love and, in the teeth of violent resistance from her family, had married. A daughter had been born to them in England before he fulfilled her family's fears and returned with his wife to Afghanistan. There, within a few years, he had died in a skirmish, and his grieving wife had returned to her family in England with her daughter.

The son who had been born to her in Afghanistan she left behind. The boy was her fierce husband's only son, and although she knew that without her husband's support she herself could not live in Afghanistan, she knew, too, that his son must not be removed from his father's homeland. There must be someone to inherit the family estate and take on the duties of the head of the family.

So Jasmin's grandmother had been raised in the stuffy confines of Victorian England, while the brother she scarcely knew was raised as a prince in all the ferocity of a tribal, warrior society, thousands of miles away.

They never met again. When she grew up, she married the most adventurous man she could find, and together they emigrated to Canada, where few of their expectations of adventure had been fulfilled. She never tried to return to her father's country, but her childhood years had marked the woman forever, so that her tales of her life there had enriched the family tradition, and the knowledge of the connection had never been allowed to die.

Jasmin had been fascinated by her heritage from an early age, poring over the few photos her grandmother had, demanding to hear stories of life in the tribal chief's court, delighting to be told that she herself was, in her looks, an Afghan of the great Pathan tribe, like her grandmother, like her great-grandfather. Jasmin's grandmother had been a "princess" in her father's house, although she had never known with certainty how deserved the title was. A diplomat traveling on the important mission which Jasmin's great-grandfather had been given in that period would almost certainly have been a member of the Afghan royal family at some remove, and his daughter had been nearly sure she remembered him being called by the title "prince." From there it was a short step to imagining for her young granddaughter's sake that the title would have been passed on through the generations; and such was Jasmin's charm even then that it had not been difficult for her young friends to believe that she was "a princess in another country."

Jasmin, of all the family, had felt those distant bonds to be real. Before her grandmother's death, she had promised one day to travel to Kabul and try to pick up the traces of the family from the few bits of information there were. Later, without telling anyone, she had determined to go to Afghanistan as soon as she finished high school. But fate and the Salang highway intervened. In December 1979, six

months before Jasmin's graduation, the Russian army drove
its tanks along the highway it had built through previously
inaccessible mountains, killed the Afghan president in his
palace, and then said that he had invited them in. There was
no one to say otherwise.

In the years that followed, it sometimes seemed to Jasmin that the brave and heroic war of resistance which the
Afghans waged against the invaders was of interest to no
one in the outside world but herself. Grain was embargoed,
the Olympics were boycotted, and then...silence. She took
her first job modeling and waited for the war to end. She
read the scanty coverage given to the terrible war in Western newspapers and waited for the storm of outrage that
never came. She pored over a map of the country, trying to
discover from those minimal news reports whether the area
of the country where her cousins might live was being badly
damaged; read all the names of resistance leaders to see if
the family name was among them. And she waited.

It was perhaps not surprising, though she didn't connect
the two events at the time, that she gave up modeling the
same year that the Russians finally declared that they had
been defeated by the Afghan people and prepared to with-
draw. By the time the last Russian troops had left the country, Jasmin was halfway through her first year of university.

She had had no clear plan in mind, unless it was that one
day, when the shooting was finally over, she would go out
to help rebuild her grandmother's country. But that day
seemed longer and longer coming. The tribal skirmishing
that had always marked Afghanistan had been given a fear-
ful impetus by the invasion and the resulting supply of
modern arms to various factions.

Nowadays, Jasmin knew less about the modern country
than its ancient history, and she was determined to add to
the world's knowledge of the area. But it would doubtless
be many years before any archaeological team was granted
permission to dig a site in Afghanistan, and doubtless, too,

there was less to uncover now than there had been before ten years of punishing bombing raids.

One day Professor Hazlett had shown the class slides of an Afghan museum, which he had visited before the invasion. Soldiers had guarded the museum, he told the class, and he had had to pay an entrance fee. Then, to his astonishment, when they saw him taking pictures of the exhibits, they had demanded a photo fee for every picture he took. In some indignation, Professor Hazlett had refrained from taking any pictures at all. He had only the external shots of the museum, and one of a silver ewer. He told the class, "I don't suppose it's even standing today. Certainly none of the exhibits are left. Since then I have always taken pictures. Always take pictures, wherever you are."

The tone of sorrow in which he had spoken had made Jasmin feel the connection between them to be that much stronger. He felt real, human pain for his lost chance to record this small part of a country's lost history. Jasmin had felt tears start in her eyes both for her grandmother's country, and for the man who loved its past so much. It was that moment, perhaps, as much as anything, that drew her into his field.

Now she had found her way through the streets to his home, and she put her hand on the front gate and gazed toward the white house with its pillared porch and its broad, sweeping windows.

*Let him be well,* she prayed with quick fervency. *Whatever happens to me, don't let him be...*

She meant *diminished,* though she did not know it.

Professor Daniel Hazlett looked not unlike the imposing coin portrait of the first Sassanian king of Iran. It was Jasmin's secret delight. When she wanted to speak of Hazlett within the precincts of the School—always a perilous undertaking—she called him Ardashir. She liked, among her friends, to list his attributes: Big, Bearded, Beaked, Benevolent, Brilliant.

Sitting in a large stuffed armchair beside the living room fire, he hadn't changed; he only looked tired. Jasmin's heart beat in heavy jolts, tolling doom, but her smile was bright and warm as she approached the chair. "Good afternoon," she said.

"Good afternoon, Jasmin," said the professor. "Gillian said you were coming. I'm afraid this is not very good news for you. Do sit down."

They did not shake hands, and such a salute as a kiss on the cheek was unthinkable. Anything not strictly intellectual seemed to die on the vine in Hazlett's presence. Jasmin stood awkwardly in front of the great man. "How are you feeling?" she asked.

"It wasn't all that bad, you know," he said, smiling at her. Then she sat in the armchair opposite him across the fire. "I expect I'll be able to give you quite a bit of help. You're going to be working with Ben Bredon, I take it? That won't be easy, but you're perfectly capable of coping."

She bit her lip. "I'm not sure about it. Who suggested it?"

"Philip Harding and I discussed the possibility, and I believe he asked Ben whether it would be feasible," Hazlett replied, in some surprise. "I understand Philip to say that Ben was happy to do it. Am I wrong?"

"No... he... he's agreed. But I don't want to work with Dr. Bredon!" Jasmin said, horrified that he could even dream her capable of this kind of betrayal. "It would be..."

"It won't be ideal, of course. But I should think you would find it a better option than going to work with Gabrielle at this point, although I expect she would take you on." Gabrielle Fellowes was one of his old students.

"I thought, if I could get a supplement to my grant, I might be able to work there most of the time and come here for work with you now and then," Jasmin said, rushing her fences.

"Ah, I see you've forgotten the way your grant stands," he said unhappily. "The fact is, as far as money goes, you have no choice."

"Here we are!" said a low, pleasant voice, and Gillian Hazlett appeared with a tray in her hands. "Your tea, Daniel. I've put Jasmin's flowers on the tray for you. Aren't they lovely?" She crossed the room and set the tray down on the glowing walnut table that stood in a pleasant window embrasure to one side of the fireplace. "If you'll pour, Jasmin, I'll leave you two to your business."

"Yes, of course," Jasmin answered automatically. The professor's last statement had, it seemed, killed off large numbers of her brain cells. *"You have no choice."?* A small tea table was moved forward, and when Gillian Hazlett had left the room, Jasmin dutifully picked up the teapot and a cup.

Then she set them down and looked at her professor. "What do you mean, the way my grant stands? Is there a problem with...?"

"The Royal Society of Oriental Studies grant is restricted to students registered at a university in the United Kingdom. It has always been the case, and there will be nothing I can do the change it. It's part of our charter," Professor Hazlett said, and she did not doubt his word. "If you want to go abroad now, I'm afraid you'll have to find other funding."

# Chapter 5

"I see. What made you change your mind?" Benedict Bredon raised his eyebrows by two point five millimeters, which, by translating, she knew meant utter disdain. He didn't move any other face muscles at all. It was going to be worse than she had imagined.

This was not the time to tell him that she had decided to face out her demon—him. Jasmin said, "I've discovered that my grant isn't transferable outside the U.K."

He leaned back in his chair. "I thought you were a wealthy woman. How much difference can a few thousand pounds make to you?"

"I own an apartment in Hampstead," she admitted dryly. "Is that your definition of wealth? It isn't mine."

"I thought famous model-actresses could retire for life."

She was certain there was an implied insult there, if only she were English enough to understand it. "I suppose they can," she said, opening her eyes at him to indicate that the expression didn't apply to her. "I, however, am going to need a job eventually." It was Professor Hazlett who had pointed out how foolish it would be to give up her position at the School in the difficult economic climate. "Besides, if I give up my grant and my job now, I'll have to pack up my things and rent out my apartment."

His eyebrows rose by another millimeter. She wished she hadn't given him the last reason, because it sounded frivolous. But to her it wasn't. Giving up her home would be a terrible necessity. "And this has changed your mind about a decision you were firmly set on."

He was really, really angry. He was so calm, so unmoved, and sounded so reasonable that he must be absolutely furious. Jasmin's heart started to hammer.

"I wasn't exactly firmly set on it. I have also discussed it with Professor Hazlett. He advised my to stay and work with you."

"Ah," said Bredon. "That had sufficient weight."

He said it without expression, but somehow she got the message. That was the worst of dealing with a man like Bredon; he rarely said anything she could challenge directly, but everything seemed loaded with deprecatory innuendo. Jasmin wondered if he were deliberately trying to get her angry so that she would storm out and he would be relieved of a task she was suddenly sure he no longer wanted to take on. The practicalities cooled her righteous indignation.

"Have you changed your mind? Is the offer no longer open?" she asked.

There was a long, difficult pause. Dr. Bredon sucked thoughtfully on his pipe, but it was dead, and he pulled the large crystal ashtray toward him and made a business of knocking out the dead ash. "I certainly now see the force of your earlier conviction that it would not be easy for us to work together."

Jasmin closed her eyes and took a deep, silent breath. Well, she had no one to thank but herself. She bent her head and rested her chin in her hand, looking up at him from behind the mask of her spread fingers. She opened her mouth, but finding she had nothing to say, closed it again.

"Have you changed your mind about that?" Bredon prompted.

She could have lied, but honesty forbade it. Nevertheless, she did not meet his eyes when she answered. "No," she said with a little shrug. She looked at him and away again, fixing her gaze on her hands in her lap. "I don't think we've ever worked easily together, and I don't really imagine we'll start now. But it will be extremely unpleasant for me to leave, and I think it's sure to damage my career prospects, and I see now that you knew that and offered to work with me in spite of the fact that..."

Having got herself into a verbal corner where the only way out was some variation of "we can't stand each other," Jasmin simply faded out.

But Benedict Bredon made no move to fill the silence. She was forced to look at him. "Didn't you?"

He had abandoned his pipe and, with an elbow propped on his desk, rubbed his cheek as though his beard shadow irritated him. Then he dropped his hand onto the edge of his desk and pushed himself back into his chair. "I thought that it would be very much better both for you and the School if you were to complete your work here, and I saw only one way for that to happen. Your own priorities seemed to be rather different."

"No," she said softly. "And I'm very grateful you were willing to...I just hadn't absorbed the shock of learning about Professor Hazlett." It was all perfectly true, but Jasmin had the unpleasant sensation experienced by those who are selling out, and she didn't know why. Was it beyond her to speak a kind word to the man? Was her dislike so powerful she couldn't bear to tell him a pleasant truth?

Well, of course it was. She knew that, though she had never called it by name before; but what else had it been when she had submitted essays challenging his theories even though she agreed with them?

There was another long pause, while Bredon thought and Jasmin sat nervously awaiting the verdict.

"Well," he said at last, "I'm not going to turn you down now. But a certain amount of self-control is going to be needed, if we're going to work together successfully. I hope you've already taken that into consideration before coming to me, but if you haven't, you'd better give it some thought."

"I do know," said Jasmin. She was unexpectedly feeling a little ashamed of herself.

He bent forward and pulled his diary toward him, picking up a pen. "All right," he said. "We'd better book you an appointment. I'll need to take a look at what you've done and get some idea of the work as a whole."

Jasmin was grateful for his calm disinclination to punish her further. She was even more grateful that he was still willing to work with her. Yet she couldn't shake the feeling she had, as they booked a time, that Benedict Bredon was a man with a secret agenda.

For all her trepidations, it was a relief to have things settled and turn to her work. In spite of Professor Hazlett's rigorous training, Jasmin was not by nature a methodical worker; there was a danger that too long a delay, or too much stress, would cause her to lose certain ideas and connections that were at present only in her head, or written down in a shorthand so elusive she might forget them.

She also had some field research to attend to here in London, in the form of a private collection, if she were lucky enough to be allowed to see it. Toward the end of her first meeting with Benedict Bredon, a productive two-hour discussion of what her field research had produced not only on Gabrielle Fellowes's dig but also during visits to other sites and to museums in Russia and the States, she mentioned it.

"I think I might have the chance of getting to see Dominic Parton's collection. I'm hoping to hear from him."

Bredon looked up from his examination of a photo of a silver bowl that had been found on the dig.

"Dominic Parton has never let anyone see his collection. Do you have some reason for expecting him to make an exception in your case?"

She smiled, because it really might be a coup, and she was thrilled about it. It was true that Dominic Parton's private collection had never been published, never been seen by anyone in the academic community—or if they had, they weren't talking. But because of the amount he bought at public auction, and his rumored spending on private purchases, it was generally assumed that he had one of the most significant private collections of ancient Iranian silver in the world. To be the first scholar to examine it officially, and especially to be the one to publish any previously unknown pieces, would make her thesis an important contribution to the literature as well as giving Jasmin her doctoral qualification.

"One of the American backers came out to the dig for a few weeks," she began to explain. "We really hit it off, and then it turned out we had a mutual friend—a man who was assistant director on a film I did, and she had financed him for an independent production shortly afterward. He's very hot now...." Jasmin paused. Jude Halloran's cinema success was not the point of this story, except in that it had served to set the seal on her friendship with Liz Marshall. "She knows Dominic Parton very well, and she promised to mention me to him. She said she could arrange a meeting this autumn, and then I was on my own as far as getting a look at the collection. But I have the feeling she means to do a bit of politicking on my behalf."

If she had expected him to look interested, she was disappointed. "And what would be the point of the exercise?" he asked.

Jasmin smiled in astonishment. "Well . . . he's got a huge collection. What if I found something really important to my thesis?"

"What, indeed? Is he likely to let you publish it?"

"He might, mightn't he? If I found something really important?"

"Why should you succeed where so many others have failed?"

This stopped her, not because she thought he was right, but because she was confronted by her own secret belief that she *would* succeed where others had failed. Men generally did what Jasmin wanted them to do, but she had never had to look at it head-on before. "I don't say I will," she began lamely. "I only mean— Well, Liz, his friend, said she thought I might be able to convince him." What Liz had in fact said was that if anyone could, Jasmin could, but under Bredon's ironic blue gaze Jasmin felt an extreme reluctance to say so.

But he seemed to get the message, anyway. "It sounds like the basis for an extremely unpleasant scenario. You'd better leave it alone."

"What do you mean by that?" Jasmin asked, ready to take offense. Dominic Parton was commonly labeled London's most eligible bachelor by the tabloid press, where he was said to have an eye for beautiful women.

"I mean several things, none of which ought to have to be spelled out to you. But if they do, I am certainly willing to spell them. For a start, Dominic Parton is not a man to do anyone a favor without getting something in return."

"You think I might sleep with him to get a look at the collection, is that it?" Jasmin said, with deceptive calm.

He raised his eyebrows. "I have insufficient insight into your character for a judgment of that nature. In any case, your moral integrity is not my concern. Your academic credentials are."

This was unexpected and, she was sure, completely unwarranted. He was only changing tack because she had forestalled him by plain speaking.

"Are my academic credentials going to be under threat from Dominic Parton?" she asked, opening her eyes wide.

She was determined not be swept away by her own anger. She would beat him at his own game.

"The very fact that a large part of such a reputedly important collection has never been seen is enough to indicate that all is not as it should be. There is also no evidence that it is as large as is generally believed."

"Don't you think it's a bit unfair of you to judge him without a hearing? You haven't seen the collection yourself, have you?" She couldn't believe that he was dismissing the chance of such a coup so thoroughly.

"A faint chance exists that I do him an injustice. But I am less concerned with doing Parton justice than with supervising you safely through this thesis. You could find yourself in deep water, and it is by no means an appropriate time in your career to take such a risk."

She wondered whether this was professional jealousy, a factor not unknown between supervisor and doctoral candidate. Perhaps he thought it was an appropriate time in *his* career. "What risk, exactly?" she pursued.

"Use your head," he said irritably. She counted it as one point to her that he had cracked first. "He's an amateur, more interested in possession than in accuracy. Suppose you were to discover a piece that supported an argument, and your examining board decided it was a forgery?"

"Well, you would see the photos first," she pointed out, and Bredon laughed.

"Don't expect me to be able to spot a forgery from a photograph! It's not my field, and if it fooled you it might well fool me. And there are other risks. The antiques market attracts the criminal mind, and collectors get greedy. This particular collector apparently feels no shame in hiding from the world a large number of artifacts which might be of historical significance. Do you imagine he feels shame on other grounds? Suppose you were to see or publish a piece that was stolen or had been removed illegally from its country of origin? Where would that leave you?"

Jasmin's mouth fell open. "Are you saying Dominic Parton is a *thief*?" she gasped.

Benedict Bredon took a deep breath, and in the pause which followed she realized he was fighting to stay calm. "I think you know what I'm saying," he said at last. "Parton does not pay sufficient attention to the provenance of what he purchases." Although it was indirectly put, it meant that he thought Parton knowingly purchased things that had been acquired in a dubious manner. In the antiques trade, legitimate offers for sale were accompanied by a history of the object offered. An object that had no history might be either stolen or smuggled out of the country of its origin in defiance of that country's export laws. Then it could only be sold privately, for the large auction houses published all the items they offered in sale catalogs, and these were regularly examined by governments whose ancient treasures were likely to be the target of smugglers and thieves. "Although that doesn't make him a thief himself, he, like anyone who is willing to purchase without asking questions, contributes to the illegal traffic in antiques. You do not need me to tell you this."

Not in general, perhaps. "I've never heard anyone say it about Dominic Parton," Jasmin said challengingly.

"No, and you won't. He is a very rich and somewhat powerful man, and he is shrewd. And there are far too many people who stand to benefit from turning a blind eye to any irregularities. You are not one of them, and I advise you to keep out of his way."

Something in his tone didn't ring true. She asked, with real curiosity, "Do you know Dominic Parton personally?"

His hesitation would have been imperceptible, she thought, to any ears but her own. "I have certainly met him. He has a small collection of Islamic glass." Bredon, she knew, had a particular interest in Islamic glass. That would mean they ran into each other at places like Sotheby's when there was an auction. Maybe at lectures. And maybe there was more to it than that.

"Do you dislike him?"

"He isn't what I would call a deep man." Bredon delivered this remark in a surprisingly open way, considering how close the two of them had just come to drawing their daggers. "And his use of his wealth to hide knowledge from the world seems to me to indicate some basic weakness of character." It was as if he had dropped all his defenses, and for a moment of extraordinary clarity, Jasmin saw the essential honesty of Benedict Bredon's nature, captured as it was in a moment of fastidious withdrawal from the unscrupulous. This had the curious effect of calming her righteous indignation, even, almost, making her like him. She opened her mouth to tell him she would have nothing to do with Dominic Parton. But there was a knock on the door, and her time was up, and once outside his office, she felt a kind of relief.

Jasmin went to the library to look up Parton in *Who's Who*, but she didn't find much she didn't already know from the newspapers. Dominic Parton was forty years old. He had a degree from Cambridge University, where he had been on the rowing team; he had sailed solo across the Atlantic at the age of thirty-three; he was on the board of two charities; he was a member of one of London's most exclusive men's clubs, and another called The Eccentrics; he had never been married; he had a country address with a rather grand name, and a town address in St. James's, which probably translated into extreme wealth; and with a certain charm he listed himself as the owner of Bellissimo, one of the great Thoroughbred racehorses of the eighties, now at stud, whose name even Jasmin knew, and the yacht *Quinquereme*. His hobbies were polo, sailing and collecting Middle Eastern antiquities.

Not exactly a person you would cross the street to avoid meeting. Jasmin closed the volume and pushed it thoughtfully away from her. From the papers she knew that he was a rugged, wiry, good-looking man with a thin face, darkish hair and tanned skin, who was rarely caught smiling. Over the years he had dated a succession of women who were beautiful, intelligent and successful, not necessarily in that order, and the lifespan of each relationship tended to be about two years.

*He isn't what I would call a deep man.* Benedict Bredon had spoken in that curiously defenseless manner, exposing more of himself than of Parton with the statement. The honesty she saw had shocked her out of her anger; it was not something she was used to from him.

Or at least, not recently. As she slowly turned the incident over in her mind, absorbed by it without being able to see why, Jasmin found herself remembering, bit by bit, that five years ago her first impression of Benedict Bredon had been that he had an essential, old-fashioned goodness of character. And then she remembered one particular incident that she had not thought about for years, although it had impressed her at the time.

One day in her first year she had been reading in the library when a classmate had come over to her with a back copy of an academic journal, and had pointed out a book review Bredon had written. It was the first of his writing she had seen, and she read it with great interest. She was not familiar with the subject, but from the second sentence she knew that Bredon had hated the book, and that he was not going to say it in so many words. Between the lines of what was on the surface a balanced review, she found the firmly suppressed academic disdain for the bizarre theory at the book's center so funny that she laughed out loud.

It never occurred to her that she might be alone in seeing it. On the last day of term before the Christmas break, having dropped into his office to ask him about the holiday reading list, she mentioned to him that the review had made her laugh. He professed surprise; he had not meant it to be amusing.

"Well, it was the way you didn't like it, but were bending over backward not to say so," she explained. He had looked at her in astonishment. "Come on," she said rallyingly, for in those early days she hadn't yet learned to control her natural friendliness or the assumption of easy intimacy, "you hated that book. You thought he was a jerk."

To her amazement, he was really shocked, even shaken. "I did hate that book," he admitted simply. "But I thought I'd written a balanced review. A friend read it before I submitted it and assured me that it was fair and I hadn't been scathing."

He was disturbed by the thought that his review might have been unkind—not, she had already learned even then, a common trait among academics. "Oh, well, I know you," she had said, to reassure him. "I could hear you saying it. It was you speaking in that really dry voice."

Of course, it would have been easy for him to deny the truth of what she said. The combination of honesty under pressure and a disinclination to be unkind had impressed her with the feeling that he was a man to be trusted.

That was before she had read his review of Daniel Hazlett's book, and by that time she had forgotten the moment. Now, for the first time, it occurred to Jasmin that there was some kind of contradiction that she had not noticed before. She puzzled over it for a moment and then shrugged. No doubt, like most people, he was honest sometimes, and perhaps he didn't like savaging people unless he considered them a threat.

Anyway, she had probably not thought of it again from that moment to this. In the term after New Year's, there had been no more easy rapport, no more visits to his office, no more chance to observe any innate honesty, or imagine she was safe with him. In that term she had learned that her breach of Benedict Bredon's idea of academic discipline was going to be summarily repaired. She had stopped trusting him in anything except an academic way, and eventually she had lost even that trust.

If she had trusted Benedict Bredon now the way she had at first—with an instinctive rather than a reasoned trust— she might have felt more inclination to obey his injunction to avoid Dominic Parton. Or if she had had that one extra moment in his office in which to give her word on the matter. But she had not promised him anything, and when she thought about it she was glad, because she should not trust him very far. Whatever sudden bursts of inspiration she might feel, her reason told her that he disliked her and had some secret agenda that would do her no good.

So a few days later, when someone who said he was Dominic Parton's assistant phoned and invited her to a dinner party at the St. James's address, Jasmin accepted with a kind of defiant joy.

Since she probably only had one chance to make an impression on Dominic Parton, Jasmin gave a good deal of thought to what she would wear. Not since her modeling days had she paid such attention to her clothing. But thinking was going to do her little good; after five years in academia she had very few things in her wardrobe that might pass muster at a dinner party in St. James's. Jasmin gave some consideration to her bank balance and the probability of London having a hard winter. The apartment cost a great deal to heat, but if necessary she could keep the bills down by working in the School library instead of at home during the days. She settled on a sum and went out shopping.

She came home again empty-handed. Any outfit that had the desired impact cost far too much, and she wasn't going to spend the winter's fuel money on anything merely simple but smart. She would "cobble it together," as the English saying went, from what she already had in her wardrobe.

She spent an evening rummaging about with dresses and scarves. Most of her things, although very good, had been in fashion five years ago or more and were too obviously

dated. Jasmin limited her attention to several items she had
that were timelessly smart and had been doing sterling duty
at any number of events since she became a student. At last
she came up with something acceptable, but miles from
what she would have gone for, given a decent budget. Her
model's soul rebelled, but what could she do?

The next evening Andrea came over for dinner, and on an
impulse Jasmin asked her advice. Andrea had a certain off-
the-wall glitzy charm, and probably a fashion sense Jasmin
could trust. Andrea's reaction on seeing what she had come
up with was enough market research for Jasmin. "It's all
right, it's very smart, but . . ." She shrugged.

Jasmin sighed at this putting of her instinct into words
and slumped onto the bed. "Let's look at what else you
have," Andrea offered cheerfully. "Maybe you missed
something, or maybe we can cut something up. I can sew a
little, you know?"

The new possibilities this opened up made Jasmin attack
the problem with fresh courage, but at the end of another
hour the bedroom was a chaos of discarded clothing, and
she was dressed in an outfit that had marginally more impact, perhaps, than the previous one.

Andrea shrugged again, making a face. "You know, it
would be all right for some people. But it's so . . . it's *ordinary*, Jasmin, and you are many things, but you are not ordinary. Also, this is a man you want to impress, yes? You
want him to notice you and remember you, think you're
special. If you just look like any beautiful woman, he'll
maybe want to take you to bed, but will he want to show you
his silver collection?"

"I can't afford to buy an outfit. I can buy something, you
know, shoes or a scarf or some earrings . . . but anything really terrific is just way above my budget," Jasmin said unhappily.

Andrea shook her head. "Forget about a designer dress.
Can't you find something in a shop that sells old clothing,
or a charity shop, for example?"

Jasmin had naturally already gone to several "second-time-around" shops, but aside from the fact that in the recession women were hanging on to their good stuff, suppose she turned up wearing a castoff that someone at the party recognized? It was a thought that had put her off the idea in the end.

Andrea shook her head patiently. "No, Jasmin, I mean very old—I mean antique, you know, something from the thirties. Or, you know, you have that Eastern look a little. Why don't you do something like that? Try to look like somebody in one of those miniatures he collects. You could go out to Ealing Broadway and get, not a sari, but they make dresses, too, or a pair of those Indian pajamas which can be very beautiful, and much cheaper than a designer dress! And you could—"

She stopped because Jasmin was standing staring at her, her eyes getting wider and wider as an idea took hold. Then she bent and kissed the top of Andrea's head. "You're brilliant!" she exclaimed. "I wonder... I wonder if I could?"

Before Andrea could answer she dashed across the room to the carved wooden trunk that sat under a window and, opening it, began to lift out sweaters and cardigans, setting them on the floor beside her. Then she bent inside and carefully lifted out a rustling, plastic-wrapped package and carried it over to the bed, where she gently set it down.

"My great-grandmother brought this back from Afghanistan when she came," she told Andrea, sliding a large mass of tissue out of the bag. An exotic scent of sandalwood and something else crept up around them, reminding Jasmin with sudden clarity of her grandmother and magical, long-ago afternoons. "I don't know whether she wore it as a wedding dress at a second ceremony there, or was merely given it as a wedding present, but my grandmother said she always treasured it, even though she never wore it after her return to England. What do you think?"

Out of layers of yellowing tissue, she lifted a treasure that made Andrea gasp: a heavily gold-embroidered tunic with

long sleeves and a round neck and a background of midnight blue silk.

"My Gott, it's absolutely beautiful!" Andrea breathed,
reaching out a tentative hand. "Is it pajamas? Does it have
the pants?"

"A *shalwar kamees*," said Jasmin. "Yes." She lifted out
the delicately draped trousers and held them up. The lower
legs were thick with embroidery in the same heavy gold
thread enclosing bits of midnight blue stone that caught the
light.

"I'm afraid to touch it," said Andrea softly. "How did
you get it?"

"My great-grandmother gave it to my grandmother, and
when she died she left it to me in her will. But everybody
knew it was mine, anyway. I was the one who cared
about...that side of the family history. I had it relined so
the silk wouldn't tear." The scent of the Orient was over-
powering now; Jasmin could almost hear her grandmother's voice, telling her she was a princess.

"This must be worth a fortune," said Andrea. "Is this
real gold, the thread?"

"I don't know. But look at this. This is..." Without trying to describe it, Jasmin pulled out the last piece, the
matching stole, which, even after all this time, was a mira-
cle of night sky and stars. The fabric was the gauziest imag-
inable silk, and the embroidery was almost fantastically
delicate.

Andrea made an exclamation of delight and then sat
back, shaking her head in amazement. "And does this fabulous thing fit you? You can wear it?"

"I think so. My grandmother let me try it on when I was
fifteen, and I didn't grow much after that. I'm probably
taller and bigger than my great-grandmother was, but with
a *shalwar kamees* you can get away with being the wrong
size, can't you? Anyway, the cut is generous. Look how full
the legs are."

"You never wore it since then?"

"My grandmother always said I'd know when to wear it. For a while I used to think I'd wear it on the night I collected an Oscar. What do you think?" she asked, carefully slipping her legs into the trousers for the first time in over fifteen years, and tying the strips that held the waist together. This method of construction, and the loose tunic overdress, were what made it possible for her to wear it, in spite of being bigger than her great-grandmother. "Is it too much for a dinner party?"

"My Gott, now I believe you are an Afghan princess," said Andrea, when, the tunic on, Jasmin picked up the gauzy stole and draped it, Eastern fashion, over her shoulders, the two ends floating behind her. "I think you should marry a—what do they call it?—*mujahed* commander and wear this at your wedding. What will you do with your hair? Will you wear it down?" She jumped up to pull off the band that held Jasmin's hair in a loose bun and turned her to face the mirror as the weight of black hair tumbled over her shoulders and down her back to her waist.

Andrea swore in awe. "You look like someone in the *Arabian Nights,* Jasmin. I've never seen you look so fantastic."

"It's too much, though, don't you think?"

Andrea stood back and examined her silently for a moment. "You know, on some women it might be too much," she said at last. "You have to be able to carry it off. But, Jasmin, I think you know how to carry something like this off. If you don't, who can?"

"This was made by someone with amazing style," said Jasmin absently, examining herself in the mirror. "Look at the way the pant leg is draped to fall around the ankle. Have you ever seen anything so feminine in your life?"

"Oh, well, you've decided," said Andrea, grinning. "If you're talking about the wonderful cut, of course you're going to wear it."

# Chapter 6

She knew she had made a hit when one of the other women followed her into the powder room, a large one with two basins and a makeup table, which led off the toilet.

"Oh, poor thing," the woman said to her in overdone commiseration. A blonde, and dressed in smoky green, she had an extremely "right" accent and apparently worked for a posh fashion magazine. She was also clearly on the waiting list as Dominic Parton's next of kin. "Did you think it was a fancy dress?"

Jasmin glanced up at the reflection behind her in the mirror, where she was repairing her lipstick. The implication was that she was dressed in costume. She smiled lightly. "No," she said, "did you?"

The woman made a moue of well-bred indignation. "Of course not!" she said. She tried again. "But you surely have no...ethnic background, have you?" Although it couldn't have been proven on her, her attitude was clear from her tone.

Jasmin smiled again, slowly, but with glinting eyes, as she closed her lipstick and slipped it into her bag. "Oh, yes," she assured her, getting up. "My great-uncle fought against the British in the Third Afghan War." She glided smoothly to the door, opened it and turned. "The British lost that one, too," she informed her sweetly, and went out.

Jasmin looked fantastic, and knew it. She had bought a small navy blue silk evening shoulder bag which had cost a fortune, and a pair of gold sandals which had cost a little less, and it was going to be a chilly apartment this winter. After a great deal of discussion, Andrea had carefully unpicked the million tiny stitches some long-ago craftsman had used to attach the sleeves to the tunic and hemmed the openings, so Jasmin's arms were bare. It had taken Jasmin an hour to do her very subtle, understated makeup. Her hair was drawn smoothly back into a simple heavy knot that lay against her back and neck. She wore large antique hoops of textured gold in her ears, a heavy gold bracelet on one arm and gold bangles on the other. As Andrea had said, she was a Persian miniature come to life: haughty, sensual, compelling. She had never looked better in her life.

She was pretty sure the blonde was angry because she imagined that Jasmin had made a late entry into the Dominic Parton sweepstakes. It seemed likely, from comments that had been made, that Parton and his latest woman friend had very recently parted company, and Parton was not the sufferer. To Jasmin's experienced eye it seemed likely the blonde in green had not only known about this, but had been waiting for it to happen for some time. And, coming late to the party, she had planned to make a kind of entrance. But she had come just that little bit *too* late, and it was a small group—nine altogether—and the room was already established in its conversational groups by the time she arrived. She had been greeted and introduced, but she had not taken center stage. She blamed Jasmin for this, but whether that was justified or not it would have been difficult to say.

Jasmin had certainly not been foolish enough to arrive late; she had only with difficulty restrained herself from coming before the stated time. She had been the second guest, and the first was apparently a visitor staying in the apartment with Dominic Parton. It was unfashionable, perhaps, but she had as a result had nearly fifteen minutes to talk to Parton undisturbed, and she had not wasted the time.

He was certainly built for show. One look told her he was a man with great dress sense, and she doubted very much if he let any woman decide what he wore. He was wearing a black double-breasted dinner jacket and bow tie that he somehow made look casual. His hair was thick, and threaded through with early gray. This gave him such an air of distinction that Jasmin stopped admiring him for not touching it up and began to wonder if it was even natural.

"Jasmin Shaw," he had said, taking her hand as she introduced herself. "Yes, Liz has told me a great deal about you. Thank you for your note. How lovely that you've come in good time, so that we can have a chat and get to know each other before the others get here."

She had that awful feeling that means someone is seeing through you completely. She smiled in rueful acknowledgment, and said, "Yes, I was hoping for that. Did Liz tell you why?"

"Liz told me everything," he assured her, drawing her arm through his and leading her over to a large chair by the fire. "William, I'd like you to meet Jasmin Shaw, who, along with her many other talents, is currently at work on a doctoral thesis." William looked familiar, but Parton did not offer his last name, and Jasmin's instinct told her not to ask. "Let me get you some champagne." Thereafter the two men gave her their undivided attention.

There was a quality about Dominic Parton that she could not pinpoint. He was watchful, but it was not only that; he seemed entirely in control of himself, but there was more to it than that. Whatever it was, it made her just slightly uncomfortable, even while under his expert treatment she relaxed and opened up.

She made good use of the time. They discussed Sassanian silver and the subject of her thesis, and he was certainly knowledgeable. She did not restrain her enthusiasm for her subject, and tried, with some success, she thought, to draw him into her area of interest. Although she had not asked him directly if he would let her see his collection, she had made it clear that valuable information might be found in any previously unseen pieces. "If it's an important collection," she had said guilelessly, "it could be a gold mine."

Dominic Parton had grinned in a slightly saturnine way, as if appreciative of her subtle attempts at manipulation. Little warning signals had stirred through her then, and she thought that, on the whole, she would be best to keep Dominic Parton at a distance. Just now, she would have told the blonde in green so, but there had been no chance for feminine solidarity after the woman's opening.

She had heard the bustle of the last guest's arrival while she was in the powder room, and hoped it meant they would eat soon. She was famished, being no longer used to eating at ten o'clock. Another time, she told herself, reentering the magnificent drawing room, she must eat a snack before she came. Always assuming there was going to be another time.

Two steps inside the door she stopped, with such an audible intake of breath that everyone in the room turned to look at her. On the other side of the fireplace Benedict Bredon stared at her, too, with a surprised shock on his face that told her he had believed she would obey him when he advised her to avoid Dominic Parton.

Almost immediately she recovered and moved forward, but not before the entire room had clocked the moment. As luck would have it, Bredon was standing right beside the little table that held her glass. Dominic Parton, a bottle of champagne in his hand, was chatting with him, and as Jasmin picked up the delicate tulip glass, he topped it up for her.

"No need to introduce you two, I think," he said.

"No, indeed," said Bredon. "Good evening, Miss Shaw." He saluted her with his glass.

Ben Bredon was wearing a dinner jacket, too, though not with the same air of having been born to it. Jasmin noted that even though the thing was perfectly pressed, he somehow managed to look a bit rumpled, as though he had fallen asleep in it, but standing up.

"Good evening, Dr. Bredon." Jasmin took a sip and looked him straight in the eye. Then she smiled. So this was why he hadn't wanted her to meet Dominic Parton. She was encroaching on his territory. Of course, his interest couldn't be Sassanian silver, but if he wanted a look at all that Islamic glass, no doubt he'd feel he had a better chance of getting it if he were the only applicant of the moment. Her knowing smile did not disconcert him, however. He merely raised an eyebrow at her.

She heard footsteps on the richly polished floorboards behind her and the blonde in green came up to Dominic Parton's other elbow, between the two men. "Hello, darling," she said to Parton, "I haven't spoken to you all night."

"Ah, but the night is young," he replied, and Jasmin saw the blonde go just slightly pink. *He sees through her, too,* she thought, in some fellow feeling. *There was some deeper meaning to that.* "Say hello to Dr. Bredon. Ben, this is Winifred Knowle."

Either Winifred liked what she saw, or she was hoping to punish Dominic Parton for whatever that last remark had meant.

"How do you do?" the blonde asked slowly, taking his hand and looking at him as though he were what she would call "absolutely fabulous," and beginning to chat. Ben Bredon was in general somewhat shy, Jasmin knew, but the woman clearly had generations behind her of the kind of social expertise that overcame that, talking the sort of nothings that made shy people feel safe. It was clear that

Benedict Bredon did. Jasmin wondered suddenly if the stupid woman imagined this was some kind of punishment for *her,* and not Dominic Parton.

She irritably turned her back on the pair as Dominic spoke to her. "You don't know Ben very well, I take it."

She sipped the champagne. Her third glass on an empty stomach. If he didn't feed them soon, she'd be drunk. "Well enough," she said. "He's my graduate supervisor."

For the first time, she had the pleasure of surprising him. "*Ben* is? I thought it was Daniel Hazlett." Of course, this evening she had spoken only of him as her inspiration.

"Daniel Hazlett has had a heart attack and retired. Dr. Bredon very kindly stepped in with an offer to supervise me. Otherwise, I'd have had to leave the country to finish my degree."

"Ben, you didn't tell me this!" Dominic said over her shoulder, so that, to be polite, she had to turn again. "When I mentioned Jasmin would be coming tonight, you didn't say anything about supervising her graduate research."

"It's a very new arrangement," said Ben Bredon, neatly avoiding the point.

Jasmin was looking at him with a frown. So he had known she was coming, had he? But then, why had he looked so shocked when she walked into the room just now? What had that dark look meant, if not surprise that she had disobeyed him? Unconsciously, Jasmin's frown deepened. Even knowing she had accepted an invitation, Ben Bredon had not expected to see her here. Why?

There were six men and four women sitting down to dinner, and the heavy question of who would sit at the head of the table opposite Dominic Parton, and therefore might be considered next in line for the throne, was neatly sidestepped by his placing his friend William there. Winifred Knowle flashed Jasmin a look as though to assess the extent of her disappointment. But Jasmin was happy to see that her own position was on Dominic's left.

"And why don't you sit there, beside your student?' their host suggested to Benedict Bredon, as though in a kind of inspiration. It was impossible to say whether the seating was truly a last-minute decision or had all been previously arranged, but it was certainly something Winifred Knowle, opposite Ben Bredon, would have given a lot to know.

They were well into the first course, and chatting about whether the recent upturn in the economy meant real recovery, when Jasmin made the observation that students were the last to feel the benefit of such recovery, because of the length of time it took to filter through to the area of private grant-giving as well as public spending on education.

Dominic listened attentively to this comment, and then said, "That's true. Now you must tell me why you gave up such a potentially lucrative and recession-proof career as the movies in order to move into an area that is so precarious." Before she could answer he turned to the table at large. "Jasmin was an actress in the movies before her shift into academia. I wonder if any of you recognized her from the scene in *Victim of Circumstance?*"

There were various exclamations from the guests, all of whom apparently knew when to respond to Dominic Parton's direction, and some of whom might actually have seen the film. "Oh, I remember that! That marvellous scene?" said an older woman, on the other side of Benedict Bredon. "That was you?" She leaned in over the table to get a view of Jasmin around Bredon. "But of course it was! So beautiful, but you've been introduced as a scholar, so naturally one didn't connect." Jasmin abruptly realized that the woman was the film critic of one of the Sunday newspaper magazines.

"But that film was ages ago, wasn't it?" Winifred Knowle protested. "Who remembers it now?"

"Only the connoisseurs," Dominic assured her blandly. "Did you see the film, Ben?" he asked softly. Jasmin felt acute discomfort. She sensed a kind of devilish joy just under the bland surface of the question, but what he was looking for she couldn't read.

"Yes, I did," said Bredon, to her complete surprise.

"You did?" she breathed, turning involuntarily toward him.

"Ah!" said Parton, simultaneously, his mouth and eyes open to take in the information. "And what did you think of Jasmin's scene?"

"I thought it was beautiful and erotic and that it clearly did not belong with the rest of the film, which was mundane," Benedict Bredon said, with the same simple directness she had seen in him when he told her, a couple of weeks ago, that he didn't find Parton a deep man. He glanced at Jasmin after he spoke, but returned his gaze to Dominic Parton.

Jasmin was blinking at him in astonishment. It was the first unalloyed praise she had ever received from him, and it moved her more than she could have imagined. It was as though she had been waiting for it, but without hope. How extraordinary that it should come, at last, for her appearance in a film, and not for her academic work at all.

He had never previously given any indication that he had seen the film, although everyone else she knew had. It had been released in England during the summer at the end of her first year, and a love scene she was in was acclaimed by critics on both sides of the Atlantic as one of cinema's "moments." Jasmin read the descriptions of the "intense, moodily erotic" scene with fascinated surprise.

Well did she remember how the scene had been shot. The director, apparently saving his high art for the stars, had been "called away" on the days scheduled for Jasmin's big scene, and left it to his assistant. Jasmin knew this was her punishment for having repulsed the man's advances, and she was certain the scene would end up on the cutting-room floor. That gave her the courage not to put up with the treatment. Her contract had called for the nude scene to be shot on a closed set, with a list of the persons who would be present, by title. The list read "director," and not "assistant director." Jasmin made her stand. She would not take off her clothes unless the director were present. She called her agent, and after an hour's brouhaha, the assistant director, Jude Halloran, who did not intend to miss his chance, agreed to shoot the scene with Jasmin clothed.

Jasmin remembered Jude Halloran primarily for his irritating fixation on lighting and camera angles, and a curious responsiveness in his direction of her. "Just run your hand down along your neck, just see what it feels like," he would say. And, "Kiss the hand beside your cheek. You don't know if it's his hand or yours. You don't care."

And he knew what he was doing. At one point, with the camera close over her face as she lay in profile, someone had suddenly pressed ice against her feet. In the overheated atmosphere Jude Halloran had by then created on the set, this had acted on Jasmin as a full-blown sensual shock, and she had gasped and jerked her head so that, her green eyes dark with what read as passionate surprise, she was looking full into the camera, as if into her lover's face.

She had not expected the scene to make it into the final cut, and when she learned it had, she had gone to see the film with a great deal of curiosity as to how Jude Halloran's vision had translated onto the screen.

Jude Halloran was brilliant. Jasmin gazed with her mouth open at her own transformation into Symbol. Even she could see that it was one of those rare moments when accident produces perfection. There was firelight flickering on translucent skin as her head dropped back, her hair swept down, and her own fingertips, in sensual curiosity, trailed hesitantly down her throat, as though under her lover's ministrations she was made curious about every erotic possibility. There was a man's darkly shadowed hand on a long, golden leg, urgently pushing her skirt up to the hip. But mostly there was Jasmin's face, transformed first by desire and last by complete erotic surprise, and lovingly watched by the camera through all the stages in between.

The cry she had made when the ice was applied to her feet was so erotic on screen that members of the audience gasped with her. That was when Jasmin knew she might have had it all. She had had one of those incredible pieces of luck that happens to very few. If she had stayed with it one more year, this scene, that young director's brilliance, would now have given her all the impetus she needed to launch a real career.

In London the news had gone around among her fellow students, and they had flocked to see the film. Jasmin had rarely talked about her past and no one had realized before how serious her career had been. Some lecturers had seen it, too, and one or two of them had mentioned it to her. But never Benedict Bredon. Jasmin would have sworn he hadn't heard about it—or had ignored whatever he heard.

Dominic Parton was smiling. "So academia does partake of the less intellectual pleasures from time to time!" he said, and Jasmin understood with a little shock that he had been expecting to hear that Benedict Bredon did not know of the film, and would have taken pleasure in the other man's ignorance, and perhaps even in describing the scene to him. What she did not understand was why that would give him pleasure.

"What were you hoping for?" she asked Parton, and his bright gaze fixed on her. He was not slow to understand when *he* had been seen through.

"You're right!" he said. He held up a finger, as though he would get back to that question presently, and returned to Bredon. "And did you know Jasmin was in the film before you went to see it, or was it a surprise?"

Bredon smiled very, very faintly, and his blue eyes glinted with humor. "You're a man who appreciates secrets," he said. "I think you'll have to allow academia to keep a few of our own."

Parton flung up a hand in acknowledgment. "Of course, of course," he said. But Jasmin had the curious feeling he was not used to being thwarted, and did not like it. "And you abandoned your cinematic career before the film was released," he said to Jasmin, sitting back as the second course arrived. "Weren't you tempted to try to make a comeback and ah...cash in on the unexpected success? I don't suppose it would have been all that difficult. Someone must have come knocking at your door."

Jasmin smiled and shrugged. "I think all the knocking was at Jude Halloran's door. There was no one at mine." She picked up a knife and fork and began to attack the food in front of her. In truth, she had thought about it briefly, but he was naive about the movie business if he thought she'd have gotten offers without asking for them.

"It was a fabulous scene, of course," said Parton. "Made my...hair...stand on end."

"It was a long time ago," said Jasmin. "This salmon is fabulous! I wonder if it's Canadian?"

"Louise," Dominic called the woman who was serving, "go and ask Gerard whether this is Canadian salmon." The young woman nodded, set down a plate and quietly disappeared out the door. Conversation at Parton's end of the table died while they awaited the answer for this attempt to change the subject. It was a signal of Dominic's displeasure, and his way of punishing Jasmin. But the film critic was holding forth loudly to William, which reduced the impact.

"It's Scottish salmon, sir," Louise said softly on her return. Dominic Parton opened his hands and bent his head as if presenting the information to Jasmin. He was a difficult personality, that much was clear. On the surface what he did seemed accommodating, as though he aspired to be the perfect host. Underneath, there seemed to be a kind of deliberate manipulation, and a tendency to punish when his wishes were flouted. Jasmin hoped she was imagining this, but she intended to keep on her toes. She was not surprised that he belonged to a club called The Eccentrics.

Winifred Knowle, tired of being excluded from the spotlight, determinedly took up the conversational lead, and since she was assisted in this by both Jasmin and Benedict Bredon, Dominic Parton lost his tight control of the situation, and the conversation settled into more normal lines. She held forth on fashion for a while, and then there was a discussion of why in England the lower classes considered the wearing of green unlucky while the upper classes did not.

"Do you wear green?" Winifred Knowle asked Jasmin sweetly. Fearing what she did, it was foolish of her to let the conversation focus on Jasmin again, even briefly, but she could not resist the impulse to scratch.

"When I can afford to buy it," Jasmin said. She had the pleasure of hearing Benedict Bredon choke slightly in appreciation.

"Of course, what you're wearing now is lovely," said the blonde. The husky overtones of her voice came and went, but she seemed to remember them more often when she was being bitchy. "Where did you find it?" Jasmin loved the subtle emphasis on *find*.

"In the bottom of my trunk," she said briefly. "It belonged to my great-grandmother." It was not the answer Winifred Knowle wanted to hear, since it opened for discussion the fascinating subject of Jasmin's brave great-grandmother, but failure didn't seem to teach her anything. She went on through the meal, randomly searching for holes in Jasmin's armor. Dominic Parton, as was evident to all but Winifred Knowle herself, took a perverse delight in this, and egged her on by paying Jasmin more and more flattering attention. Nothing Jasmin did could deflect the woman from her course for long, and even when, in something like desperation, she took advantage of a lull in the onslaught to start a quiet dialogue with Benedict Bredon, the blonde interrupted them with, "'Dr. Bredon?' You call Ben 'Dr. Bredon'? And what do you call her, Ben?"

"What do I call whom?" Benedict Bredon asked softly. Jasmin began to fear she would end the evening by liking him.

"Jasmin, of course." She was by now a little drunk, but intensely well-bred, for all that. "Your brilliant student."

"I call her Miss Shaw," said Bredon.

"Is that protocol in academic circles? Does everyone use such formality? How charmingly passé." It was not common, of course. They must be the only supervisor and postgraduate candidate in the school who were not on first-name terms.

"It's a habit one gets into," Benedict Bredon said. Which might be true, perhaps, but Jasmin knew he hadn't got into the habit with any other student. They used last names because they disliked each other. She could see where the conversation was heading, and irritation took hold of her. She didn't *want* to call Benedict Bredon by his first name, and certainly not when goaded into it by this woman.

"It's a very useful habit," she said jokingly, disguising her annoyance. "In my opinion, the British are far too casual about the use of first names."

This was, of course, a reversal of the usual knee-jerk British complaint about North Americans, so it caused some laughter. But Winifred, who had sound intuition, if nothing else, had smelled Jasmin's irritation, and pressed her victory home.

"How long have you known each other?"

Jasmin remained determinedly silent. "Five years," she heard Benedict Bredon say. "And you're quite right, it's time the formality was abandoned." He turned to her and held out his hand. "Jasmin," he said.

It was like having ice slapped on her feet all over again, to have that low voice suddenly calling her by name. After five years it seemed an extraordinary stride into intimacy. The shock traveled along her spine and made the hair prickle on her scalp. Jasmin's jaw tightened. The time to abandon the formality was not now; it had passed four and a half years ago, but that was precisely when Benedict Bredon had decided to shut out their budding friendship and retire behind ramparts of indifference.

It infuriated her suddenly that he was now willing—or pretending to be willing—to adopt a friendly manner in order to please a stupid, malicious woman. In fact, it was necessary, since their formality would certainly soon be re-marked upon at the School, but she nevertheless felt a sense of outrage. She disliked him, and he knew it. He disliked her, and she knew it. Why should they change the usage of five years?

In that split second allowed her for thinking before her response, Jasmin's brain worked at superhuman speed, searching for a way to stay on the old ground without making her feelings obvious to everybody in the room, but in vain. She smiled briefly and slipped her hand in his. "Ben," she said, bowing to the inevitable.

Just for a moment, the blue eyes went dark as they looked into hers, the trace of a transient emotion, or one quickly suppressed. Jasmin dropped her gaze and took her hand away. She felt a curious kind of ache in the flesh, as though he had squeezed her hand too hard. It occurred to her then that after five years, it was the first time they had touched.

## Chapter 7

"Have you got a lift home?" asked Benedict Bredon. The party seemed to be breaking up all at once. Jasmin had arrived in a taxi, because she had not wanted to drive herself in the delicate *shalwar kamees*, but she didn't think she wanted him driving her.

Dominic Parton appeared at her elbow. "I'm glad everyone's going at once," he said, just as if he hadn't engineered it. "Do you mind staying on for five minutes? I'd like to have a little chat with you."

Beside her, Bredon stiffened, but said nothing. Jasmin looked from one to the other. In truth, she wanted to be with neither. It had been a difficult evening, and she wanted to be alone. Nor did she like the feeling of being manipulated by Dominic Parton, especially when it entailed offending her supervisor. On the other hand, he had made some mention late in the evening that encouraged her to think he was considering allowing some of his collection to be published.

"Yes, of course," she said easily, because the quicker she agreed, the less she would seem to be submitting to his will.

Benedict Bredon shrugged into a trench coat that had seen better days and said his good-nights without any sign of disapproval, but not so Winifred Knowle. She was just drunk enough to forget the wisdom of discretion, while being far too well-bred to show her disappointment with anything more than a couple of biting comments.

If they both imagined that Jasmin's staying behind meant the opening of romantic negotiations, Jasmin herself knew better. Dominic Parton had no physical interest in her, much as he had labored to give everyone the impression that he did, including Jasmin. Her radar told her, and she accepted its findings, that she had seldom encountered such detachment, even among her gay friends. It bothered her not a jot. Dominic Parton did not attract her, either, although he made her curious about what made him tick.

Of course, it was always possible her radar wasn't able to read such an eccentric, and there were all these witnesses to the fact that Jasmin had remained behind, apparently quite prepared to receive his advances, so she intended to keep her wits about her. It was a relief to see that William showed no signs of disappearing.

When all the guests had left, William went back into the drawing room, while Dominic Parton led Jasmin across the hall to another door. "Pour us a nightcap, William," he called. "We'll be with you in five minutes."

The room had a steel door and two massive locks, including a coded number lock, and by the time the door was open, Jasmin's heart was beating up a storm. Was it going to be this easy? Could it possibly be so easy?

It had the air of a funeral parlor or a bank safe, with a carpet of grass green felt on the floor and pale walls lined with heavy, close-fronted wooden cabinets. Not an artifact of any description was in view. Jasmin was astounded. He didn't even have them displayed in his own home? He just locked them away?

"Don't you even *look* at them?" she asked involuntarily.

Dominic Parton was unlocking a drawer. He glanced at her. "What?" he said. He was changed now; his movements were different, sharper, and so was his voice.

"Your collection—it isn't displayed?"

"Oh. No, I like to look at one piece at a time," he said, and turned back to the drawer. He drew out a small velvet-wrapped item and carried it over to a desk against the far wall. He set it down on the green baize top and switched on a swivel lamp, pulled out a chair and turned to her. "Come and sit down," he said.

Jasmin couldn't believe this. He could not possibly be going to show her his collection, just like that! She crossed the room with her heart thundering in her ears. She had a true delight in her subject, and the thought of seeing something new in Sassanian silver was deeply thrilling to her.

"This is not a part of my collection," he said, unwrapping the velvet with careful precision. "Or not yet. I've been offered it for sale. I wondered if you would just have a look and tell me what you think."

Jasmin sank down into the chair with a small inward laugh. Well, Bredon had warned her that the man never did any favors! "Of course," she said. She wasn't going to turn down any chance to see some Sassanian silver. She opened her bag to take out her glasses, slid them over her nose and, reaching up to pull the lamp to a better angle, bent over the item Dominic Parton had just exposed.

"Bahram Gur," she said instantly. The subject was unmistakable, the theme of stories and songs as well as murals, painted ceramics and, as here, silver plates.

Dominic Parton had pulled up another chair close beside her. "Tell me about Bahram Gur," he demanded softly.

Jasmin stroked the delicately etched face of perhaps the most famous Sassanian king. "Not a very nice story," she murmured, almost to herself, as she bent lovingly over the plate. She was not reluctant to recite the story, though doubtless he was familiar with it. "Bahram Gur's favorite in the harem was a young Greek woman named Azade. He could not bear to be separated from her. One day when he went hunting, he took her up on the back of his camel—he had been raised by the Arabs, and unlike all the other Sassanian kings, he rode a camel to the hunt, so the fact that this king is riding a camel makes the identification certain—and began to show off his prowess.

"To impress Azade, Bahram Gur shot an arrow at an animal that was scratching its ear, and pinned the foot of the animal to its own head. It's depicted on this plate, here." She traced the outline of the unfortunate animal with a gentle finger. "But Azade was not impressed. She said a real hunter should be able to make a male female and a female male—a curious measure of hunting prowess, I've always thought—" Jasmin grinned "—but Bahram Gur took up the challenge, and shot an arrow—this plate shows a special arrow with a crescent head, but some show an ordinary arrow—at a male and cut off its horns. They should be…ah, here they are, rather faint. He shot two arrows into the forehead of a female and thus turned her into a male." Her finger tapped the arrow-horned female just visible at the edge of a jagged hole in the plate. "But when he wanted praise, Azade was too shocked by his barbarity to give it. In some versions of the story she calls him *Ahriman*, the Zoroastrian god of evil. In a rage, Bahram Gur knocked his beloved off the camel and trod her underfoot, killing her. Some pieces show her underfoot, but this, like the Guennol plate, has her still perched on the back of the camel." As though she had been under a spell, Jasmin shook her head a little. "But you know this story," she said, with a self-conscious grin.

"But you like it, and I enjoyed hearing you tell it."

"No, I don't think I do like the story. It's not what you'd call a woman's story, is it? I find it curious, not least because it was so popular, especially with the Muslims after the conquest of Persia. They found it painted on the walls of a Sassanian palace, and they took it up."

"It's difficult to judge the past with the values of the present, especially in the relations between men and women," Parton said.

"Yes, perhaps, but it's still a pretty fragile ego, isn't it, if he had to kill her? Daniel Hazlett thinks it wasn't ego at all. He says Bahram Gur was a secret Mithraist, and the Mithraists had to kill anyone who said Ahriman's name in their presence. That would make this story a signal to other Mithraists that the king was of their number. It would be nice to find a plate or something that could be seen as confirmation of that theory." She smiled. "But I'd better have a proper look at this plate."

Dominic Parton shrugged and smiled, but she knew he was anxious for an opinion. "What's the provenance?" she asked.

He hesitated. "It was brought out of Iran as part of a family treasure on the eve of the revolution."

That might mean anything, and Jasmin did not comment, though mentally she chalked up another point to Benedict Bredon. "It's suffered a lot of damage," she said. She spent some time examining the plate and pointing out the technical details of its manufacture, then said, "The artist's style is good, although perhaps more the style of what some people think were provincial workshops. I doubt if it's of Sassanian manufacture. Almost certainly later, at best a Muslim copy of a popular Sassanian plate, perhaps tenth century. At worst... frankly," she said at last, hoping she had prepared him, "it feels to me more like a very late forgery."

Parton blinked as though it was very unexpected. "Why do you say that?"

She shook her head. "It's mostly gut reaction. But if you want technical backup, I don't think the patina is right. A plate even of the tenth century would have a heavier patina than this." The patina referred to the defects of age that should have been on the plate. It was worn thin in places— there was actually a hole through the middle, obliterating

much of the female deer with the arrows in her forehead—
but to Jasmin's mind the silver itself seemed too fresh. There
was little erosion or pitting of the surface, no encrustation.
It did not feel right. She turned it over.

"No inscription," she said. "An inscription might have
helped to date it, but the lack of one doesn't prove anything."

"But I've shown it to a dealer friend who put it in a provincial workshop of the sixth or seventh century," he protested.

Jasmin shrugged. "Well, there you go. It's not an easy
field." People did disagree about such things, and Jasmin
wasn't going to change her opinion because a dealer held an
opposing view. She held it up. "I don't really like the shape,
either."

"So you advise me not to buy it?"

"It depends on what you want. I advise you not to pay
what you'd pay for an undisputedly genuine plate. I think
you should get other opinions, and maybe get the silver an-
alysed. If some people accept it as genuine, it'll be worth
something, even if it's also disputed by others. If you're not
looking at it in investment terms, but merely want an example of a Bahram Gur plate in your collection . . . it's not
a bad copy of the Guennol plate, with some additions that
prove the artist had seen other plates—he shows the double-
headed arrow where the Guennol does not. But in my opinion it won't be more than a century old. There's a certain
charm in the execution. It's up to you to decide whether
that's what you want in your collection."

"How much should I offer?"

"What are they asking?"

"A hundred thousand."

Jasmin shook her head. "It's too doubtful for a price like
that," she said. "Unless I'm completely off beam, it
wouldn't fetch more than ten thousand at auction, and
that's assuming you have several experts thinking it's gen-

uine. I wouldn't pay anything for it myself, but I could certainly be wrong. You need another opinion."

She wrapped the velvet cloth around the plate again, and stood up, yawning. "And now I've got to get home. I've got a long day in the library tomorrow."

"I'll call you a taxi," he said, ushering her out of the room. She noticed that he didn't stop to lock the door. "Come and have a nightcap with William while I ring."

But that would take another twenty minutes, and she had had enough of Dominic Parton for one day. "I can get one on the street," she said. "It's not that late."

He nodded silently and held her coat for her. For one crazy moment Jasmin thought of the unlocked door to the safe room, and fantasized dashing back inside and locking it, refusing to come out until she had examined his Sassanian collection. The plate she had seen, although disappointing, had only whetted her appetite. As though reading her mind, he said, "Well, I owe you now, don't I? You'll have to come back one day soon and have a look at a few pieces that are more satisfying than the one you just saw."

Jasmin didn't answer. She was too thrilled to speak. Oh, if only Benedict Bredon could have heard that!

The upper floors of the Georgian mansion were served by a tiny wrought-iron elevator. Dominic Parton opened the door and ushered her in, then followed her. "I'll wait till you find a taxi," he said firmly. He pushed the button for the ground floor.

Jasmin noticed the figure on the stairs as they passed the third floor, but they were almost at the ground before she recognized who it was. She felt her cheeks go hot, and wished she dared to push the button that would take them back up to the top. Dominic hadn't seen anything, but when he turned around and opened the door, he certainly noticed the figure of Benedict Bredon standing in the hall.

"Good God, Ben!" he said in astonishment. "What's the matter—did you forget something?"

"I waited to take Miss—to take Jasmin home," Bredon said evenly. A professional mind reader couldn't have said what was behind that statement, Jasmin thought, but Dominic seemed to think he understood. His eyebrows went up and came down again.

"Ah, right," he said. He turned to the doorman. "Jonas, what were you thinking of? Why didn't you find the gentleman a chair while he was waiting?"

"Well, 'e's only just come down, Mr. Parton," said the doorman, aggrievedly. " 'e came as the lift came. I thought it was too crowded, as usual."

"Of course," said Dominic Parton blandly. He looked at Ben again. "Yes, I see." His lips twitched. Jasmin could feel herself going redder with every second that passed. What on earth was the man playing at, hanging around outside the apartment like a jealous lover, or as if she might need him to save her from attack? When the doorman opened the door she almost ran through it. Outside, the night was cold enough to calm her, and she stood on the steps breathing in the fresh air for a moment before turning to say a last goodnight.

When the door closed she was alone with Benedict Bredon and the stars. "What is all this in aid of?" she demanded.

"You're a starving student," he said mildly. "I thought you'd be grateful to be saved the taxi fare."

She almost laughed, but she remembered her anger in time. "What were you afraid of? That I was going to be assaulted?"

"It wasn't entirely beyond the realm of possibility," he said, and there was no arguing that. Worse things happened. Nevertheless, it was a ridiculous situation, and as he led the way to his car, she croaked, "Are you seriously telling me you thought Dominic Parton was going to jump me?"

He opened the passenger door. Suddenly he looked angry. "Get in," he said shortly. "You're too pigheaded to listen to reason, even if I knew how to explain."

It had been a long and difficult night, and suddenly Jasmin's temper went off like a rocket. "Stop being so goddamned English and aloof and autocratic!" she shouted at him. "Tell me what the—"

"Believe me," he began, with a certain reined-in fury of his own, "you would not want me any other way! Be grateful I'm English and aloof! If I were anyone else I wouldn't put up with your nonsense for a second! You should be grateful for my rigorous training in self-control! I've needed it! Now, get in the car, Jasmin!"

Between the unaccustomed sound of her name on his lips, and the fascinating fact that he was *shouting* to her about the virtues of self-control, she was sufficiently distracted to obey.

"You don't seem to *have* any self-control," she observed mildly a minute later, as he settled beside her and leaned to start the engine. Benedict Bredon looked over at her with the most curiously unreadable expression on his face.

"Oh, but I do, Jasmin," he said, with a short breath of laughter. "I do."

She found herself staring into his shadowed eyes as a shiver of some unnameable feeling ran through her. Suddenly there was a huge pressure in her throat. She could think of no way to relieve it, except, perhaps, by screaming some unknown fury at him, or launching herself at him and beating him black and blue. Jasmin closed her eyes and looked away, swallowing hard over the lump. He was still looking at her, and the silence was suffocating.

"I live in Hampstead," said Jasmin.

## Chapter 8

"You were right," she said ruefully, as he steered the car through the bright city. He had chosen the lights of Piccadilly and the West End rather than thread his way through the quiet, dark lanes of Mayfair. Jasmin watched the crowds, still spilling along the pavement after midnight, with a familiar pleasure. "He doesn't do anything for nothing. He wanted my opinion on a plate he's been offered for sale."

The car stopped at a red light, and Benedict turned to look at her. "What was the plate?" he asked. He was frowning slightly, as if his interest were more than casual.

"Oh, a kind of poor man's copy of a plate in the Guennol collection, of Bahram Gur and Azade. Do you know it?" Jasmin replied. "I said I thought it was a forgery. I hope he gets another opinion before he decides."

"Why did you think it was a forgery?"

She told him about the lack of patina. "Anyway, there was something just not right about it. You know, the Guennol plate doesn't show the curved arrow—that kind of crescent-moon-headed arrow that some plates show him having used to take the horns off the male. Yet, in composition this was a fairly close copy of the Guennol. I didn't think of it then, but now it seems to me that it's almost as though..." Jasmin sighed. "I don't know. It's too much like the best of everything. Here's the perfect picture of the Bahram Gur story. I just . . . didn't believe it."

There was a pause as he negotiated the traffic. "How did Parton take the news?"

"I'm not sure. He asked me a lot of questions about the patina, and why I thought it wasn't right, but he wasn't very disappointed, I think. He said he hadn't bought it yet, and I believed him." She turned toward Bredon. "Do you know that he hasn't got *one* of his treasures actually exhibited? He's got them all locked up in a little room that looks like an undertaker's parlor! He says he likes to look at them one at a time! Isn't that—" she paused "—dreadful, really. It's appalling."

Bredon shrugged. "Assuming there's something of real value in those cabinets, it is. You probably know that the Japanese collector who now owns van Gogh's *Sunflowers* wants it buried with him when he dies. It's a kind of mind."

She had not heard about it. Jasmin let out a little breath of astonishment. "It's unbelievable, except that it's not, I suppose. I'm getting so I'll believe anything. What's the matter with these people?" Her antagonism for Bredon seemed to be in abeyance for the moment; tonight he had seemed the only person in the room with any real values, and she had been drawn to him in spite of herself. In the darkness of the car, she was aware of a kind of understanding between them, as though her anger and dislike were a kind of turbulent surface over a deep, powerful current of something else.

"I suppose they know the price of everything," he said.

"It's more than that," Jasmin insisted. "People who know the price of everything want to display it over their names, don't they? Dominic Parton just wants to *have* it. I mean, it's weird, isn't it, his not ever publishing anything from his collection? I'm not sure I even believe him when he says he likes to examine it one piece at a time."

"No, I expect you're right," said Bredon, with an understated conviction.

"Why, what do you know?" demanded Jasmin.

He glanced at her in surprise. "What do you mean?"

"You sounded as though—as though you *know* he doesn't really care for it as art."

"Did I? I don't know him well enough for that, but I suppose, like you, I have a sense of it."

After that they fell silent, and then she realized they were already on Haverstock Hill, and she would soon be home. With a curious sense of urgency, which she tried to disguise, Jasmin asked without looking at him, "What you said about the film tonight—did you mean it?"

It was as though he, too, had been thinking of that moment. "Yes, I did." He did not repeat his comments. It seemed he was a man who said things and expected them to stand.

Jasmin laughed a little, without joy. "It's funny. That's the first praise I've ever had from you, and it's nothing to do with any academic work at all. It's ironic, isn't it? I guess you've never thought much of my abilities."

The car braked a little sharply at an orange light, as Bredon turned to face her. "What on earth do you mean— the first praise you've ever had from me?"

"Well, for my essays and things. You never encour—"

"You have submitted very few essays to me in which you did not receive a first, as I recall. Unless I am mistaken, you also gained firsts in every course you took with me."

"Yes, I know."

"And that's what you call never encouraging you?" The car behind honked and Benedict Bredon let out the clutch with a lack of control that stalled the engine. He started it again and pulled away.

"The next right," she said, "and the second left. Well," she said, a little unnerved by the fact that she had irritated him, but wanting to say it too much to stop, "you never wrote any comments. I never knew where I stood."

"Since you seemed to spend most of your argument on an attempt to antagonize me, perhaps you should be grateful for my reticence," he said grimly. Jasmin gasped in surprise. She had no idea he'd guessed what she was doing. "Is this it?" He stopped in front of her building, so he must have known where she lived all along. He turned off the engine, put his arm along the wheel, and faced her. "What was it you wanted from me?"

Suddenly she felt like a demanding three-year-old. "I guess I wanted some sign that you thought I was ... worth encouraging."

"On average over the years, although it does not necessarily hold for each individual class, eight percent of my students get firsts. This is slightly higher than the School's overall rate of just over seven percent," he said grimly. "Now, that puts you at one in twelve students, and my classes—or they did before the new education policies began overloading the universities—generally average ten students. How special did you want to be?"

The last question was almost gentle, which she found curiously unnerving. Yet if they were going to work together, surely it must be better to get some of the ill feeling out of the way? She wondered if she would ever have the courage to mention his attacks on Professor Hazlett.

She said, "Professor Hazlett always made me feel as if he thought I was brilliant."

"I suppose you *were* brilliant, for him. In fact, I know you were, because I took the trouble to read a couple of the essays you submitted to him, as well as your master's paper. With me, after the first few months of your degree, you showed no signs of incipient brilliance. You were very intelligent and you used your intelligence, for which you got firsts. But you were uninspired."

She felt the justice of it somewhere within. At first she had lost interest, and later she had been too intent on attack to demonstrate the flair she had for finding a new argument and supporting it. He was watching her, as if for her protest, but she could say nothing. She was beginning to feel nervous. Everything seemed to have a hidden meaning. "Why did you read essays I had written for Professor Hazlett?"

"Because he spoke of you as a brilliant student, and was giving you extremely high marks. I was curious, and I wondered if perhaps he was exaggerating in his own mind, to satisfy his need for one last protégée worth his talents." He shrugged. "He wasn't exaggerating. Your work for him had a very different quality. If you want high praise, I can give it to you there. Your work for him had brilliance and individual flair. His subject obviously appealed to you strongly, or perhaps it was the relationship between you that fostered it. Whatever it was, I expect you to produce that sort of excellence in your Ph.D. thesis."

To her utter surprise and confusion—not to mention his—Jasmin's eyes filled up and spilled over so copiously that tears actually spurted from her eyes and landed on her arm. Bredon muttered an astonished oath, putting out an involuntary hand.

In panic, Jasmin shrank away from his touch. His sympathy now would be her undoing. If she really let go, where would she stop? "I'm sorry!" she muttered, groping blindly for the door handle. "I do apologize. Thank you for the lift!" The door swung open, and the means of escape calmed her slightly. "I am sorry," she said, trying to smile through her tears as she slipped out into the fresh air. "Good night."

"Good night, Jasmin," he said, and with a powerful mixture of emotions, she closed the door and went inside. Not until long after she had gone through her front door did she hear his engine start up, and then her tears came again for no reason she could understand.

* * *

She went to see Professor Hazlett. She had some questions about her thesis material, and she wanted to show him the plate that had been discovered on Gabrielle Fellowes's dig. She also wanted to sound him out about Dominic Parton. Ben Bredon had been right about two things: Parton wanted favors, and he was apparently willing to buy things with no provenance. If Hazlett also felt she ought to avoid the collector, she would keep away, whatever the temptation.

That there was going to be temptation, she was fairly certain. Dominic Parton had sent her a gracious little note thanking her for her opinion and telling her that he had decided not to purchase the plate. He expected to see her again soon.

But mostly she wanted to talk to her mentor about the difficulties she was now having in trying to work with Benedict Bredon. She had thought of a dozen ways of bringing the subject up casually.

"How are you finding work with Ben?" Hazlett asked, as soon as the preliminaries were over and they had settled at the table to work, thus making all her inventions unnecessary. The last few weeks had seen a significant improvement in the professor's health, and Jasmin could sense a restlessness in him. She wondered if he now wished he hadn't been so quick to retire.

"I think he's going to be nearly as rigorous as you," she said, with a determined smile. Improved or not, she wasn't going to challenge her professor's health with the truth. If she had thought that evening of plain talk after Parton's party was going to change anything, she was wrong. She and Benedict Bredon seemed to be fighting over everything. At times she despaired of ever being able to complete her thesis under such conditions. She had gone to Dr. Harding, the head of the department, and he had dismissed her fears. She was treading on difficult ground with her thesis, and if she thought her viva would be easy, she was mistaken. If Dr.

Bredon was challenging her at every turn, she should thank him. Her examiners would do it, if he did not, and then it would be too late.

"Good," said Daniel Hazlett now, in unconscious repetition of Harding's view. "You don't want anything sloppy about your work. You have a little tendency to go off the rails, Jasmin, and if Ben is determined to keep you on the straight you may look on it as a good thing. Of course you'll find it difficult."

Jasmin just blinked. Didn't he realize that what Bredon attacked most rigorously—or what she defended most fiercely—were Professor Hazlett's own theories? That was what made it so difficult for her. Her love and loyalty made her respond emotionally whenever one of Hazlett's ideas got challenged. It was always personal.

"He'll give in when your work is sound," Hazlett said comfortably, when she delicately tried to suggest this fact to him. With a silent snort of frustration, Jasmin gave up the battle. She had imagined, when he had told her at the outset that he would back her up, that somehow the team of Hazlett and Shaw was going to put Benedict Bredon to rout in this paper. Jasmin felt like a general on the battlefield who discovers that the king is parleying with the very traitor who is challenging his throne.

"Here's the bowl," she said, pulling an envelope out of her case. "Isn't it beautiful? I brought a couple of slides for your collection, if you'd like to have them. The photographs really came out well."

Hazlett reached for the photographs and bent to examine the first, a shot of the interior, where a scene had been chased and engraved into the silver. He was never more authoritative than when he was examining something. His hands, his whole body, took on a mantle of strength and confidence, as a good surgeon with a sick child, or a great pianist with a grand piano. "Yes, I see. Another one on the Dionysus theme. The artist didn't understand that the chariot was wheeled. He's turned it into a rather uninspired mandala. Probably copied from a Kushan copy.''

They discussed some of the symbolic possibilities of the subject. Daniel Hazlett's eye was utterly expert; others might disagree with his interpretation, but no one would ever dispute the points he raised as to the elements that were matters of particular interest. As usual in his presence, Jasmin was taking notes as fast as she could write.

He set the photograph down and passed on to one of the underside of the bowl, discussing the techniques and the probable method of manufacture with her, asking her questions about the physical properties of the bowl that could not be ascertained from a photograph, and making judgments based on her replies. ''Ah, what's this?'' he said with interest, when he came to the next photograph. It was a blowup of an inscription that was faintly legible around a portion of the outside rim of the shallow bowl. It made the piece of real significance, since it established its credentials very firmly, as well as pointing to a pre-Islamic date. The Pahlavi alphabet had gone out of use within a century or so of the conquest of the Persian empire by the Arab-speaking Muslims in the seventh century A.D.

Jasmin bounced in her chair. ''Terrific, isn't it? It's late Pahlavi.''

''Yes, I see that it is.'' He bent over the photograph. ''It needs to be cleaned a little if it's going to be fully read. 'M, T, R, D, T'—well, that's clear enough, isn't it? 'Mehrdad.''' He read out the unmistakably Persian name and then puzzled silently over the rest of the inscription. ''Now what? Is that *nafshu?*'' The word meant the equivalent of ''owned by,'' and was to be expected. ''I'm afraid it's rather obscured, but no doubt it can be read eventually.'' He set the photo down and looked at Jasmin. ''Gabrielle is letting you publish it, is she? That's very good of her.''

They examined and discussed the piece and her work for far too long, considering his health, and Jasmin was feeling more and more guilty, without knowing how to stop him. Professor Hazlett had always been very generous with his time, and he was also driven by his intellect. Today these two traits caused him to carry on when he should have stopped. She couldn't understand why Gillian, his wife, did not come in to put a stop to the discussion, which must surely be taxing his health. At last, in desperation, she simply put down her pen and changed the subject by main force.

"I have a problem I'd like to ask your advice on before I go," she said.

"I see. Yes?" he said, setting the photos aside and looking attentive.

She told him about Dominic Parton, briefly but in some detail. "I see. He asked you to comment on a plate, did he?" Jasmin nodded. Hazlett snorted. "Well, there is no need for him to impose on you. He's only got to go along to the British Museum if he wants an expert opinion." This aspect of the matter hadn't quite struck Jasmin before. "You thought it was a forgery, did you?"

"It certainly looked very late to me."

"Well, you've got a good eye. Yes, well, if he does want your opinion, there's no reason for you not to give it. You can't go inquiring into the moral credentials of everyone who comes to you for an opinion, or you'd never give it. It will be good practice for you. Others will be coming to you for opinions before long." He leaned back and thought a moment. "As for the collection, he's an enthusiastic amateur, as far as I know, but he is certainly not an expert, and he doubtless will have forgeries in his collection unless he has received consistently good advice and followed it, which is unlikely. But it's by no means desirable, you know, that you should look only at demonstrably genuine pieces. At first, I try to prevent students seeing forgeries because they don't get a feel for the genuine. But your eye is trained now, and the more you see, the better your eye will get. It won't hurt you at all to get the feel of a few forgeries."

She knew that he himself was used to having everyone from West End art dealers and private traders to the British Museum and Scotland Yard's Art and Antiquities Squad coming to him. She wondered if they had stopped coming since his illness, and if he missed the activity. It must be hard to have everything in your career come to a halt at once, especially two years before you were expecting it.

"As far as Ben's fear goes, you need not worry about including any forgery in your thesis. It was proper of him to remind you that he is not an expert in the area, but if Dominic Parton proposes to allow you to publish anything, you will naturally make arrangements for me to see the piece. I am sure Mr. Parton would agree to that." There was the tiniest implication that if Dominic Parton were *not* willing to let Hazlett examine the piece, it could be condemned as forgery outright. "In any case, a genuine mistake in a doctoral thesis need not cost you your degree. We all make mistakes."

"And what about if there's something that's the subject of a claim?"

"There are an awful lot of claims against ancient works of art by one government or another," said Hazlett. "It has even been known for two governments to claim the same piece. Not all claims have the same merit." He smiled at her. "If Dominic Parton has got anything like that in his collection, and he let you publish it, he would not be protected by any guarantee of anonymity you had given him. In the event of any claim, you would naturally disclose your source. He should know this before you publish."

"What if I see something I recognize?"

"Then you'll be faced with a moral and ethical dilemma at that point. But I shouldn't have thought the risk was very high. If Parton is acquiring suspicious items, as Ben seems to think—and I must suppose he's got some information privately, because I've never heard anything—he will keep things of that nature out of your sight. If one were going to be put off looking at works of art because they had been obtained by questionable methods, half the British Museum would have to be boycotted, you know." The professor looked at her with a glint of amusement in his eye. "If he'll let you take pictures of whatever he shows you, I'd like to see them. If not, make sketches and take full notes, even if he's not going to let you publish. It's always a good idea to keep a record of what you've seen, because you may well see them again sometime in the future."

This was tantamount to a command to get a look at Dominic Parton's collection if she could, as far as Jasmin could see. She was happy about it, because the more she saw, the better her thesis would be, but she hadn't felt exactly comfortable acting against Benedict Bredon's advice. Jasmin left the Hazlett house with a heart lighter than it had been for some time, and her head spinning with all the new data she had taken in. The latter was nothing new, after a meeting with her professor. She wasn't sure what had caused the former.

# Chapter 9

In spite of Professor Hazlett's endorsement, she could not get along with Benedict Bredon. It seemed they disagreed over everything. This would not have mattered much, if Jasmin had been one of those students who need only marginal input from a supervisor. But Jasmin was "high maintenance": she liked to talk over every detail, every argument, every scholar's opinion as it contributed to her own. In short, Jasmin needed a sounding board. Daniel Hazlett had been the ideal sounding board for over three years, giving her inordinate amounts of his time and attention, and had thereby increased her expectation and her need. Benedict Bredon was less a sounding board than a punching bag who punched back.

She was working on the chapter of her thesis that discussed the Mithraic element, preparatory to delivering it at a graduate seminar after the Christmas holiday. She would certainly have done better to start with some other chapter, so that they could find a working routine through a less contentious topic. When it was too late to change she real-

ized it was sheer pigheadedness that had urged her to choose
to begin with such a difficult issue. Bredon disagreed with
her basic premise, and the coolly distant manner of dealing
with each other which they had used for four years now gave
way to a turbulent inability to discuss without arguing, or
argue without real loss of temper.

It surprised her to see such loss of control in a man whom
she had always in her heart accused of coldness and hateful
detachment. And Jasmin was not the only one to be surprised. One day, they had left his office to go to the small
departmental library on the same floor to look up a point.
Jasmin was congratulating herself because she was cool even
though Bredon had been attacking what she said.

The departmental library was often untidy, with books
put back on the shelves in the wrong place. Because it was
very small—shelves of only the most pertinent works lining
the walls of one small room—you could usually find the
volume you sought after a short search, wherever it was,
especially if you recognized the spine. But a large table and
chairs in the center of the room impeded access to the
shelves, and any search meant being squashed in against the
shelves with little elbow room. They made their slow way
around the room, struggling past chairs in silence, as they
combed neighboring cases, bending awkwardly sideways to
examine the lower shelving. Jasmin found this close and silent confinement with him unnerving.

"Layard!" she exclaimed at last, with a relief which perhaps sounded more like anticipated triumph. She began to
leaf through the volume toward the middle. She had lost her
reference note and had to search for the passage she wanted,
but she remembered vaguely where it was. Bredon propped
himself against the table beside her and waited. The room
felt overheated, and sweat broke out on her forehead.

"Here! Page 249," she caroled in relief. "He's talking
about the Yazidis. 'The name of the evil spirit is, however,
never mentioned, and any allusion to it by others so vexes

them, that it is said they have put to death persons who have wantonly outraged their feelings by its use.' ''

Bredon had his arms folded across his chest and was playing with the pipe in his mouth, which had gone out. ''And what is the name of the evil spirit among the Yazidis?'' he asked.

''Well, it's Shaitan, of course.''

''But the name of the evil spirit reportedly used by Azade to Bahram Gur was Ahriman?''

''Well, the Yazidis got Islamicized, didn't they? Naturally they changed the name of their evil spirit.''

''And they transferred their old custom to the new name?''

''Yes,'' said Jasmin. ''Well, it's natural, isn't it?''

His eyebrows went up. ''I don't know how natural it is, but I do know you're on very flimsy ground here. What is the connection, anyway, of the Yazidis in Kurdistan with the ancient Mithraists who you suggest had a cult in Persia?''

''Well, the Yazidi religion is thought to be a descendant of the old Mithraic religion, isn't it?'' she asserted.

''Is it? Who thinks it and where's the evidence?''

''I haven't got the exact source at my fingertips!'' she said. ''But I know it's been said. I'll be able to find it.''

''You're going to need more than its having been said,'' Bredon said levelly. ''You've got only the most tenuous of links here, if any. Even if the Yazidis of the last century—of whom we know almost nothing—are said by Layard to have sometimes put to death someone who 'outraged their feelings' by the use of the name Shaitan, you're still a long way from proving to me that Bahram Gur was required by a secret oath among Mithraists to put Azade to death because she used the name Ahriman. Only one manuscript carries the version of the story where she calls him Ahriman, in any case.''

''And how many would it take to convince you?'' Jasmin demanded irritably.

Bredon's jaw tightened. "I'm not saying it's a matter of numbers. But it does mean you have to go carefully. It seems to me you're getting carried away by your own conviction, which is never acceptable."

"Well, if you dispute every source..." It did not help Jasmin's temper to know, as she did, that this sounded childish. She wanted to make her point, not bicker uselessly.

"You have only shown me one, and I do not dispute what Layard says. I merely—"

"You merely dispute any interpretation of what he says that tends to confirm my point," Jasmin said hotly. It was important to her to use this argument, and it infuriated her that he wouldn't see. "You know perfectly well that religions all over the world have shifted the names and attributes of their deities and devils to conform to some new idea or invader religion, and still carried on very much as before! You know perfectly well that with a little research I'll be able to document a dozen parallels!"

"You know nothing about what I know perfectly well," he began irritably, interrupting her increasingly heated flow. "It isn't my job to come halfway to your argument, Jasmin! You've got to do the work!"

*"Halfway?"* she demanded in outrage. In spite of her good intentions, she was lost. "You don't give an *inch!* You won't admit anything!"

"I will admit it when you have sufficient arguments to be convincing!" he informed her loudly. "If you'd spend less energy on fighting me and more on finding your documentation, we might get somewhere. Now stop trying to browbeat me!" She saw that he had well and truly lost his temper. "I have told you that your argument is not sufficient and you should not include it—" he began to thump the desk with his hand to emphasize each word "—until and unless your supporting evidence is—"

"Overwhelming!" she cried.

He overrode her. "Until and unless your supporting evidence makes it a reasonable hypothesis! Now, I am not going to—"

There was a tap on the door, followed by the sound of a key in the lock, and they both turned to look as a lecturer whose office adjoined the library poked his head in. "What on earth is all the shouting?" he began. "I'm trying to—" He broke off as he caught sight of his colleague. "G-good grief, Ben!" he stammered, in obvious astonishment. "Was that *you* shouting?"

"No," Bredon said, and then looked at Jasmin and added hesitantly, "Well... perhaps it was. Was I shouting, Jasmin?"

"You both were, as far as I could hear. It sounded like a rip-roaring debate." The lecturer grinned. "Sorry, I didn't mean to interrupt. I thought it was two students taking refuge in here to have a lovers' quarrel."

A thick, choking silence fell in the library as the lecturer withdrew and the door closed behind him. Jasmin stared unseeingly down at page 249 of Layard's *Nineveh and its Remains,* while Bredon thoughtfully regarded her bent head.

"Jasmin," he said at last. She looked up nervously. For some reason all she could remember was the phrase "lovers' quarrel." If they were going to start saying that she and Benedict Bredon were having the standard supervisor-postgraduate romantic affair, it would kill her. She met the gaze of blue eyes that had gone dark with emotion, and across the back of her mind some thought stirred. Then her body went hot, as though it had blushed without any reference to her conscious mind.

"Yes?"

"Did Daniel never challenge your ideas?"

"Yes, of course he did."

"How did he phrase his... ah, lack of agreement?"

She had to laugh a little. "Usually he just said I was talking rubbish. Or he'd say I was 'going far too far.'"

"And what was your reaction when he did?"

"Of course I was sorry if I really liked the idea. I've had to abandon some pretty interesting possibilities—well, for the present."

"So it's not criticism in itself, but criticism from me that is the difficulty here?"

She took a deep breath and faced him. "I guess it is," she admitted unwillingly.

"You agreed with me at the outset of this undertaking to make a certain effort to restrain your acute dislike of me. We both agreed it couldn't work otherwise. Isn't that so?"

"I don't remember our putting it in so many words," she said, discomfited by his casual statement of her "acute dislike."

"Nevertheless, I think it was the substance of our agreement."

"You agreed to restrain your acute dislike of me, too," she pointed out. "It does take two."

"I did not agree to restrain my dislike, because I do not dislike you, and I did say that in so many words."

She thought he was being cowardly. Fine to force *her* opinion to words, and then quibble about his own. "You don't *like* me, though, do you?" she challenged, looking right into his eyes.

Just for a second his gaze shifted, and then returned to hold hers. "On the contrary, Jasmin," he informed her gently, "I like you very much."

If he had picked up the Layard and clobbered her with it she would have been less surprised. Jasmin swallowed. "Do you?" she asked in disbelief, her voice almost a whisper.

His color was heightened; it had not been easy to say. He smiled in rueful amusement. "Why does it surprise you?"

Oh, if she answered that! "Why are you telling me now?" she countered.

"Because it has occurred to me several times that you may believe I am attacking you personally. If so, I want you to know it isn't true. I like you, and want to see you succeed. I am rigorous with you because your brilliance often leads you astray and it is my role to bridle it, not because I want to kill your inspiration.''

She could think of nothing to say. With an abrupt, ungainly motion she closed the volume of Layard and, turning away, blindly placed it on a shelf. "I have to go," she said, stopping there with her hand on the shelf, her head bent, and her back to him. "I'm meeting someone for lunch.''

She sensed him glance at the clock on the wall overhead. He must know she had lied. It was only a quarter to one and she was careful never to lose a minute of the time he allotted her. She would not have booked a lunch date before one. The silence that followed was terrible to her; she could neither move nor speak, and her mind was in chaos.

At last he said, "All right, Jasmin. See you next week," and that freed her from immobility.

"See you," she agreed, as she opened the door. She went out, still without looking at him. Halfway down the corridor she realized that the burning on her cheeks was tears.

She was not wrong about Dominic Parton. She was summoned to dinner again, this time by a note in his handwriting, which seemed to suggest that he would let her look at something in his collection. Jasmin packed a small camera and notebook in her handbag, just in case. This time she wore a plain black ankle-length dress in cotton jersey, with a jade bracelet that matched her eyes. She looked striking but, if not exactly businesslike, at least formal.

"Ah!" said Dominic, who had opened the door himself, as he took her coat. "Dressed for a working evening, I see!" He was certainly not slow, Jasmin reflected. What a curiously unmasculine insight he had.

"Am I going to be working?" she asked. She thought it worse than useless to pretend his insight was wrong; it could only make him despise her.

"Let's have a sherry first," he said. To her surprise, she was the only guest. Either he planned seduction, or she was going to get a look at some pieces. With an insight of her own, Jasmin realized Parton might perhaps have been prepared to play the evening whatever way she liked. If she had come dressed to kill, would he have taken her to bed? The thought was disturbing. To be manipulated through sexual means by a man to whom it meant nothing must be a supremely distasteful experience. Jasmin was grateful for the fact that she was immune to the charm that he seemed to hold for other women, and for the radar that had told her on their last meeting that he felt no sexual attraction for her, either.

She drank sherry with him in front of a warm fire, relaxing and trying to enjoy the moment as they chatted about horses. Jasmin's experience was entirely limited to holidays on her uncle's farm in Ontario farm country, where, as a gangly, bony child, she had learned to ride bareback—and barefoot—on hot summer days. Dominic Parton was not only used to riding the most beautiful Thoroughbred horses, he was also an owner.

In the middle of a description of a one-year-old that had been sired by Bellissimo and was certain to be a great winner, Dominic Parton laughed and set down his glass. "All right, I can see when it's useless. Would you like to look at a piece before dinner? I've got a phone call I should make."

Jasmin jumped up so fast it made nonsense of her apparent interest in the colt. She nearly dropped her glass. "Yes, please," she said.

"Tell me," he said, as he led her out of the room, "does Ben know you are here?"

"Ben Bredon? No."

He paused at the door to the collection room. "I wonder if I might ask you not to tell him that you are seeing my collection unless it becomes absolutely necessary?"

Jasmin frowned. "Why not?"

He smiled deprecatingly, as though it didn't really matter. "He has been asking me for some time for a look at my Islamic collection. I'm afraid . . . well, I would not want to offend an old friend unnecessarily by letting him know that others have succeeded where he has failed."

Well, she had suspected this. Should she give her word? It might be hard to keep, and in any case, wasn't it disloyal? But Dominic Parton was too shrewd to ask for an answer. He simply turned then and unlocked the door.

This time she entered the little room with something of the air of a novice entering the inner sanctum: she was expecting mysteries to be revealed. On the green baize of the desk, in a glow of light, stood a silver wine cup, its elegant scallops as attractive now as they had been sixteen centuries ago. With a little indrawn breath, Jasmin moved toward the table, drawn to the cup as if it held the sacred *haoma* of the ancient Zoroastrian ritual. Parton waited until she was seated and had picked up the cup before going out and closing the door softly behind him.

She did not notice his going. The cup felt alive under her hand, and she was sure it was genuine even before examining it. A small cardboard slip beside it on the desk informed her that it had been found on a dig in Afghanistan late in the last century, when there were no export controls, and had been in the collection of a Danish explorer. It had gone to an unknown purchaser on the death of the explorer in the mid-thirties. Dominic Parton had acquired it from a private collector three years before.

Jasmin gazed intently into the bowl for a few moments with a curious feeling of recognition, and then gasped lightly. It was not the information on the card that told her what treasure she held in her hands, but the magnificent engraving of the dancing girl, so beautiful it was said she resembled an angel. The cup was not unknown; sketches of the dancing girl had been published early in this century, but no one had ever photographed it. By the time there was sufficient academic interest in such things, the cup's where-abouts were unknown. Some people believed it to be lost.

It was like looking at someone who had come back from the dead. For several seconds, as she held it in her hands and recognized it as the Angel Cup, Jasmin's breathing stopped. It wasn't possible. Common sense told her someone had made a forgery using the published sketches as a guide. Yet even her blood seemed to recognize this as genuine. The delicacy of that figure, which had been the subject of a paragraph by someone who had seen the cup in 1898, could not possibly be a forgery.

"Her sweet, heavenly face, those tempting breasts, the delicate veiling of the scarf which seems to move with her breath..." Victorian tripe it may have been, but the words came back to her mind with stunning accuracy as she looked at the image that had inspired them. Jasmin, forgetting everything, simply sat staring at that image for a length of time she could never afterward determine.

Slowly she came to, and began to examine the cup methodically. Then, remembering Professor Hazlett's injunction, and having no idea how much time Parton meant to give her, she reached for her handbag and pulled out her notebook and pen.

Underneath lay the little camera. She went still, staring at it. Then, like a thief, she glanced over her shoulder. He had not given her permission to photograph it, yet... "always take pictures," she heard Daniel Hazlett's voice saying. He had been talking then about treasures of Afghanistan that were probably forever lost. This was a treasure, also from Afghanistan. Would the world ever get the chance to see it?

Of course, she would not publish any photograph, if she took one. But at least it would exist. If the cup were lost to the world, if in twenty or thirty years Dominic Parton decided to be buried with it... photographs would exist.

It was a treasure of her own grandmother's country. Surely the Afghan people had some rights over the cup that all the wealth of collectors could not take away? It had disappeared for decades. It might do so again.

Suddenly, Jasmin did not care about the ethics of her situation. Benedict Bredon was right, though it had not hit home until she was face-to-face with this cup. It was immoral of people such as Dominic Parton to use their wealth to hide from all view an artifact of such beauty and archaeological importance. Carefully she set the cup in the middle of the green baize, pulled out the little camera, and took photographs from as many angles as she could manage.

When it was over, all the tension left her, and all the turmoil. She had done what was right. Perhaps the pictures could never be published in her lifetime, but at least they *existed*. If the cup remained hidden, she would leave the slides to the Royal Society of Oriental Studies in her will. Let that august body worry about the ethics of publishing them when she and Parton were both dead.

Parton left her alone with the cup for over an hour, during which time she made copious notes and detailed sketches. It was not easy to reproduce an image from a curved surface, especially one of such delicacy. Well could she believe the Arab author who had enthused about the effect of drinking wine from another "dancing girl" wine cup, and watching the "smoothly swaying form" appear and disappear under the bubbles as the wine shifted in the bowl. When Parton at last appeared at her shoulder, Jasmin frowned up at him in faint surprise.

"Yes?" she enquired distantly, and then, "Oh, goodness, Dominic! I'm so sorry! How stupid of me! I was absolutely miles away!"

"I see you like my little treasure," he said softly.

Unconsciously her strong, elegant hands caressed the cup, as though love were ownership enough. "Dominic," she breathed, "do you know that this is the Angel Cup?"

"That's what they call it."

"Dominic, it hasn't been seen for nearly a century."

"It's been seen by me," he told her, and his eyes took on a curiously flat, opaque quality. She remembered how, as a child, she had stepped barefoot onto stone on a cold morning, and her soul danced away from the chill she saw there.

He picked up the Angel Cup, wrapped it carefully, and stored it away in the drawer he had used before. She thought it must be the temporary home of any piece that he was examining. He stood over the drawer for a moment, and then, his back to her, he said, "I wonder—would it be too much to ask you to have a glance at something else for me?"

She had been pretty sure this would happen. "Of course not," she said.

# Chapter 10

"**Y**ou thought you had troubles!" Andrea set down her wineglass and prepared to launch into a story. "You won't believe what happened to one of the students who comes to the stress sessions!" The university ran a counseling group specifically for doctoral candidates, to help them cope with the pressures of their academic work. "You should come to these sessions, Jasmin," she said kindly. Jasmin's eyes were red, but Andrea didn't comment on the fact. Her friend needed time to recover.

"What?" asked Jasmin, grateful for this silent understanding. They were having a meal in the Senior Dining Room, where most of the teaching staff lunched. She had just had a fight with Ben, and it was not the moment, or the place, for getting into her problems. The tables were too close for real privacy, and she certainly didn't want to start weeping in public.

"Now, this is the truth, Jasmin—" Andrea leaned over the table confidentially "—this guy's supervisor told him what data he should collect in his field research, but he never told him why, never said what it was for, you know? So he dutifully went off and collected all the data, and he came home, and his supervisor had *died!* Can you imagine? And he has all this data, but he has no idea what he got it for! He doesn't know what the argument is! He's ready to commit suicide."

Jasmin had to laugh with her, but their laughter was the laughter of shared horror. Both could too readily imagine the student's terror. "My God!" said Jasmin feelingly. It certainly cast Professor Hazlett's retirement into the shade. "What on *earth* is he going to do?"

"Nobody knows. At the moment he's just crying over his fate, you know? He can't see any way out."

"Well, I can understand that."

Andrea kept up a stream of light conversation throughout the meal, but by two o'clock, when afternoon classes began, the room was all but empty. Andrea asked the waitress for refills of their coffee cups and then stopped talking and looked at Jasmin.

"All right, what's wrong?" she demanded gently.

Jasmin wiped her nose on her napkin. "Oh, God, where do I begin?" she asked.

"It's trouble with your supervisor?"

Jasmin looked at her in shock. Did people *know?* "How did you know that?" she whispered.

Andrea laughed. "Come on, Jasmin, everybody has trouble with their work!" Andrea had been working on her thesis a year longer than Jasmin and was within six months of completion. This naturally gave her the air of an expert on the process. "And I remember in October how much you didn't want to work with this man." She paused. "You should be coming to these therapeutic sessions. They really help."

"I know, I know," said Jasmin. But she knew she wouldn't go. Somehow her problems with Benedict Bredon seemed too personal for a public dissection.

"So, what's going on?"

"We're always fighting. I can't stand it. I don't know what goes wrong, but no matter how often I swear to myself I'm never going to get angry at what he says again, it's impossible not to. I feel like a basket case. I'm always either crying or shouting."

Andrea sipped her coffee thoughtfully. "Do you still hate him?"

"What?"

"You hated him, don't you remember? That was why you were afraid to work with him."

So it was. Jasmin blinked. "No, I . . . well, hate is far too strong a word. I mean, I don't suppose it was ever accurate, but I'm . . . I go overboard."

"So . . . what? You like him?"

This was not the conversation she had imagined, or wanted. "Oh, *no!*" Jasmin sighed. "I don't know. I know him a lot better than I used to."

"And?"

"And what?"

"What kind of man is he?"

Jasmin felt stupid and reluctant, as though she couldn't quite think and didn't want to. "Well, he's . . . he's actually what you'd call . . . I don't know . . . honorable? He's kind of got a sense of what's right, and you get the feeling he just wouldn't ever consider doing something wrong or underhand. I admire that. But we just can't . . . agree."

"Mmmm." Andrea was attentive, taking it in.

"I don't mean he's pompous or anything like that. It's very difficult to describe—the whole idea seems old-fashioned, doesn't it?—but it's really an attractive character trait, when you meet it. He's a . . . a gentleman, I guess." Jasmin laughed as the word formed itself on her tongue.

"And he's got this peculiar kind of honesty," she went on, as the gates began to open. "If I ask him something, he just tells me. You know, he seems shy. I know he's not very comfortable meeting strangers and he doesn't like parties, but . . . well, you imagine that goes with a kind of emotional reticence, don't you? But if Ben's asked, he always just . . . tells you. Do you know what I mean?''

Andrea, who didn't, merely murmured something encouraging.

"For example, if I say, 'Do you like this person?', he'll just say, 'No' or 'Yes.' He never fudges.'' Jasmin looked at Andrea and laughed suddenly. "I can see I've lost you!''

"Not exactly, but this doesn't strike me as a sign of openness of character, necessarily.''

"It's because I can't explain it.'' She couldn't explain it because she didn't want to tell Andrea that what she was talking about was the way he had said, "I like you very much,'' believing that she disliked him so acutely. Or how he had told Parton that he had liked the film, leaving himself open to any kind of interpretation. Or how he had so quietly and unobtrusively defended her when that awful woman was having a go at her. "What do I call whom?'' She still remembered his voice saying that, what she called his "damned arrogance'' operating on her behalf . . . or even, how she could get him angry when she argued with him, how he no longer retired behind his English reserve, but just let her have as good as she gave.

No, she couldn't explain any of this.

"So, why do say you don't like him?'' Andrea said, trying to sum the thing up. "It sounds to me that you do.''

But this was going a bit far for Jasmin. "I'm too nervous of him to like him. I see he's not the monster I thought he was, but he . . . I'm nervous of him. There's always something between us. I don't know what it is. I feel as though I'm walking in the dark, every step I take with him.'' Sometimes she got the feeling that Ben was not walking in the dark, that he could see exactly where he was going. Perhaps that was what scared her.

Andrea sat and gazed at her thoughtfully for a few seconds. "You'd better sleep with him,'' she said finally.

This had a whiplash effect on Jasmin. Her head snapped back and came forward again, and she protested in a whispered screech, *"What?"*

"Oh, come on," Andrea said dismissively. "You know it happens. It happens a lot."

"I didn't say I didn't know it happened," Jasmin protested. "I just don't see how you can casually prescribe it as some sort of . . . cure for my difficulties."

Andrea smiled. "That's just what I think. All of this problem, this fighting, is probably just sexual tension. You know, working together on a doctoral thesis is one of the most intimate things you can do, for an intellectual. You share ideas and excitement that no one else in the world can understand . . . and he is guiding you and shaping you—"

"He is not!" Jasmin inserted firmly.

"Well, you resist that, that's the problem. Because he doesn't agree with your first supervisor—you see, you have a loyalty problem that most students don't face. But I know about it. You fell under the spell of your . . . what's his name, and now you don't want to let go with Ben. But you never . . . did you start an affair with Professor . . . ?"

"No, I did not!" Jasmin had to laugh. "Are you crazy? He *never* responded to anything but my brain. He was far too . . . well, I was just totally safe with him."

Andrea nodded, unimpressed. "Good. So it wouldn't be a betrayal of him to sleep with Ben, right? It's different territory. Believe me, Jasmin," she said, as her friend snorted, "you do not know how much sexual tension there is if you're resisting it. I'm sure that's what the problem is."

"Are you sleeping with Henry, then?"

"No. But I slept with Uwe, in Düsseldorf. That was part of what caused the problem. He was married, and we got too involved."

"So your life was completely disrupted, and now you advise this as a calculated course of action," Jasmin observed dryly.

"Ben isn't married, is he?" Jasmin shook her head. "And you are not seeing anyone for a long time, I think." Jasmin remained mulishly silent. She was not normally judgmental, but she didn't like this at all. "So, where's the problem?"

"Do you think that's what he's angling for?" Jasmin asked in sudden horror. Was *that* why he had told her he liked her?

Andrea shrugged. "I don't say that. If he's so shy as you say...but he must have supervised other women. So he knows it can happen. And it's there—I mean, you are very attractive, Jasmin—I don't just mean beautiful, but you know you have some...thing that makes people want to know you, and I'm sure it makes men jump in front of buses for you. And he's a very good-looking man."

"Is he?"

"Don't you think so?" Andrea countered.

"I don't want to sleep with him," Jasmin said levelly. "And if all this really is just sexual tension, I hope I never find out. I don't believe it is."

Her friend shrugged. "You should come to the sessions, Jasmin. You really need to look at this with...how do you call *Abstand*?...with perspective. Everybody has these problems, it's not just you."

For some reason this was not as comforting as Andrea had meant it to be.


Jasmin strode down the fourth floor corridor and turned the corner, right on time, as always. She was never late, and when she was early she hung around in the corridor until the appointed time. This carefulness was a function of the curious tension between them, a leftover from the days when he had made her realize that he did not welcome her casual appearances at his door.

They were emptying Professor Hazlett's office. Jasmin had seen the boxes of books and papers and all his personal possessions go a few days ago, and today the furni-

ture was coming out. Her footsteps slowed and she stared as
two men came out of his office leading a trolley that carried the large glass-fronted bookcase she knew so well. It
was empty, of course, and it looked naked, barren. Jasmin
suddenly remembered all the richness of her many hours in
front of that bookcase, remembered how often Daniel
Hazlett would have recourse to it in the course of a lesson.
The books that bookcase held had been written in Greek,
Latin, Arabic, Persian, German, French...and he read them
all. "I think Mas'udi mentions something about that," he
would say, and down would come a volume of the Arab
historian and the professor would leaf through it and translate for her something she needed for an essay. Once he had
confessed to her, as though it were a failing, that he did not
read Russian without the aid of a dictionary.

Jasmin stood unhappily in the corridor, watching the
progress of the bookcase until it was almost on top of her.
"Excuse us, love," said the leading workman kindly, and
she came out of her trance with a blink.

"Oh, I'm sorry," she said, looking around for some way
to get out of their way. Her voice, husky with emotion, had
a predictable effect.

"That's all right, darlin'," he said. "We're not in any
hurry, are we, Harry?"

Harry, at the other end of the bookcase, could not see
Jasmin, and merely grunted.

They were moving slowly, of necessity. If she led them
back up the corridor to the corner and waited for them to
pass, she would be late for her meeting with Ben. Jasmin
saw the solution and stepped into Ben's doorway, where she
fitted snugly in between the bookcase and the door. "All
right," she said. The workman looked at her.

"Will we get past all right?" he called. "Don't want to
run over your toes!"

"No, it's fine, there's lots of space," she said. It was a bit
of an exaggeration; the bookcase was no more than eight
inches from her nose. Jasmin flattened herself against the

door, clutching her books tightly against her chest, and stood motionless as the massive piece of furniture rumbled slowly past.

"All right?" said the man at the back as he passed her.

"Just fi...ahhh!" Jasmin's words were lost in a sharp breath of astonishment as Ben's door was abruptly opened behind her and she toppled backward into the room. Her books flew out of her arms as she flailed, trying to find her balance, and then she was caught and held against a rough tweed-covered chest, and she knew with utter physical certainty that she was in Benedict Bredon's arms.

"What's going on?" he had asked, but now he was perfectly silent, completely still. Jasmin breathed softly for a moment, but Ben was not breathing. Her head was against his throat, her arms pinned helplessly against her chest, and caught in a firm embrace that saved her from falling, she felt a peculiar, lethargic reluctance to move.

At last she found her feet, and then his grip on her tightened, and the strength in his hands became possessive. With slow certainty he turned her body around to face his own, and of their own volition her palms flattened against his chest; helplessly she felt her fingers spread wide, felt his heartbeat shake her.

That movement reached him; his breath caught roughly in his throat. Jasmin closed her eyes, and emotion flooded up in her, a river of unknown depth. As it spilled over into the field of her consciousness, she began to tremble.

She felt hands in her hair. Her head was drawn slowly back and Ben, his blue eyes entirely black, looked down into her face with the naked helplessness of a man who was starving.

"You all right, love? You didn't hurt yourself, did you?" The friendly voice at the door faltered a little, and then decided to notice nothing. "Here, I've picked up some of your books for you. Where shall I leave them? This all right?"

She felt his hands reluctantly open, his arms let her go, and she blindly turned to face the workman. "Yes," she said. "Thank you, that's fine," with no idea what she was agreeing to. He set the books on a filing cabinet that stood inside the door as Jasmin bent to pick up a few more.

"Right. Didn't mean to knock you over."

"No, that's all right. I didn't fall."

He left finally; she had no idea how long it took. Behind her Benedict Bredon said nothing. Her hair was all around her, getting in her way, blinding her, tangling her efforts to collect her books, but she couldn't stop. She was afraid to touch her own hair for fear of feeling his touch still there.

"Jasmin," he said. She saw his hand reach out and close over her upper arm, felt her breathing shift to another gear. Her response frightened and amazed her. How could this be happening? With his other hand he took the books from her and set them down.

"The door," she whispered, fighting for time.

"Damn the door," said Ben. But he closed it. He was going to kiss her; she knew he was going to kiss her. And she wanted the kiss—her whole body was suddenly crying out for his touch. But it was impossible!—as though she had become a different person between one second and the next.

"I can't take this, Ben," she said. Her head was whirling and her gut was in turmoil, but his mouth was so close, his arm around her. He stroked the hair from her face with an unsteady hand. "Neither can I," he said, with a soft laugh.

"What do you want?" she whispered.

"This," he said, and bent his head and kissed her. When his lips met hers, her mouth felt swollen with wanting, as though she had been waiting for this touch longer than she knew. All the free-floating electricity in the atmosphere collected around their two bodies, and his hands enclosed her head and his arms tightened, and in that moment she gave herself utterly to his embrace, with a trust that made him shake.

When at last they drew apart, his control was fragile, but Jasmin knew hers had broken. "Jasmin," he said huskily, his hand against her cheek, "Jasmin, my God, Jasmin." She looked into his face, and began to panic. This was Ben Bredon. How could he make her feel this way? It was impossible. She struggled in his arms so that he had to let her go.

"I'll just—I'll just—I'll be back in five minutes," Jasmin said, and without waiting for any response she pulled open the door and ran.

In the washroom she ran cold water over her wrists and then pressed them to her temples. What was it? What was happening to her? Never in her life...*Ben!* Ben for whom she felt... How could this be happening? It was as though she'd been turned upside down and shaken, and all her ideas were now on their heads.

*Probably just sexual tension.* She heard Andrea's voice in her head. *You'd better sleep with him.* Jasmin gulped a breath. Was that what it was? This unbearable, overwhelming need she could feel threatening in the pit of her stomach was just the standard response of two bodies in close conjunction unable to resist the obvious?

Hanging onto the edge of the porcelain sink, Jasmin bent her head and tried to breathe long, deep breaths. And it was this that fuelled their arguments. She had never felt anything like it in her life, but having met it naked now, she recognized it as the power that flowed between them when they fought.

At last she drew herself straight. Well, she was not giving in to it. For people who liked each other, perhaps a brief sexual relationship during the course of their work was an appropriate response, but what sort of mess would it be for her, getting involved with a man for whom she had such fatally mixed emotions? Two months ago she had hated him.

How many women had he supervised through a doctorate, anyway? Were they all scalps hanging at his belt? She didn't even *like* the man, she reminded herself fiercely, and that thought brought with it all the comfort of the known, and calmed her turmoil.

He was standing in front of the window when she returned, and she closed the door and leaned against it. "Ben."

He turned as though he had heard it all in the tone of her voice. He said nothing.

"Do you want to have an affair with me?" she asked roughly. "Is that what you want?"

He laughed on a joyless breath, shaking his head. "Jasmin," he began, "I know you—"

"No, please just answer the question. Do you want an affair?"

He rubbed the back of his neck. He looked like a man who was furious with himself, or fate, or the world. "No," he said at last, with peculiar emphasis, "I do not want an affair with you, Jasmin. I—"

She didn't care if he was lying. "I don't want an affair with you, either. I want this to stop right here. Andrea says there's a lot of sexual tension involved in this kind of working relationship, and now I believe her. But I have very mixed feelings about you." He looked at her, and her voice rose, as though he had challenged the statement. "You know I do!" she shrilled.

"Do I?" He looked as though he were about to say something and changed his mind. "All right, Jasmin."

"Maybe now that we know it's there, we can control it better."

Ben laughed again. "Maybe," he said. His eyes were shadowed; he looked bruised. "Why don't we call it a day?" he said then. "I'll see you on Thursday."

"All right." She felt suddenly deflated; in spite of everything she didn't really want to leave. She turned and picked up her books and opened the door. "Goodbye," she said.

But he only nodded. He was already at his desk, bending over his papers. He didn't look up as she closed the door.

# Chapter 11

At her next visit to Parton's flat she wore jeans, and there was no dinner invitation included, although tea was brought to her in what she now called the Inner Sanctum. Dominic was not interested in any comment she had to make on the piece he showed her from his collection, and left her alone; but when she was through, as she fully expected, he was glad of her comments on another piece he had been offered for private sale. On the visit after that, he was not even in the flat when she called. Two pieces sat on the green baize, and beside them a tape recorder for Jasmin to record, if she would be so kind, her estimate of one of the pieces. That was generally the pattern of subsequent visits, although there was no predicting when Parton would be there himself. When he was, he always sat with her for a brief drink and they chatted, generally about her work in progress.

His Iranian collection was, she guessed from what she saw, a very broad mixture of all the varieties of artifact of the Persian Empire from the prehistoric period, well before the time of Cyrus the Great in the sixth century B.C., right

up to the Muslim conquest of the Sassanian King Yazde-
gird III in the middle of the seventh century A.D., and included artifacts from the Kushan and Gandharan kingdoms
which had independently ruled over much of what is now
known as Afghanistan in the centuries before Islam.

Some of what she saw was outside the scope of her thesis, but anything might shed light on it, and all items, of
course, were of great interest to her, independently of her
immediate preoccupation. So she examined the odd seal or
coin or figurine he showed her with as much attention as the
silver dishes that were the subject of her study.

All the items of which he asked her opinion before pur-
chasing, however, were items of silver ware. Jasmin assumed that he took seals, coins and bronzes to someone
whose judgment he trusted in that area, and she further assumed that some expert somewhere was assessing her as-
sessments of the silver pieces, and that this was all an
elaborate kind of audition for the role of Dominic Parton's
tame expert on Sassanian silver.

She didn't really care. It was the sort of thing that spe-
cialists were called upon to do, and she might as well get
used to it. A few years down the road, if she lived right,
more people than Dominic Parton would be asking her
opinion. All she could do was offer her best judgment,
which, after all, she had had only a few years' training to
develop. She knew she made mistakes, and she said so, but
Parton didn't seem to mind. And even Daniel Hazlett, as he
often said himself, made mistakes.

Nothing Parton was offered for sale was up to the standard of the Sassanian royal workshops. Generally she
judged them to be copies from Muslim workshops long after the conquest; for Sassanian silver had been treasured by
the Arab conquerors of the magnificent Persian Empire,
and what they could not find, for many centuries they copied. Such objects were still of value on the art market, of
course. A 1990s' pastiche of a Victorian art form is only a

copy in 1990; in five hundred years, however, it will be a genuine 1990s' artifact.

Some of what he showed her she thought were modern forgeries. Once she even imagined that she detected the same artist's style as she had seen in the Bahram Gur plate. She was fairly sure that Parton had been an undiscriminating buyer in the past, or his source would not so frequently have tried to sell him questionable items.

Parton was never satisfied with a simple condemnation of any item as a forgery; he wanted her detailed reasoning. It was partly this that caused her to assume that what she was undergoing was an elaborate testing period. So, on the occasion when she thought she'd found a second plate by the same artist, she said into the tape recorder, "Ah, I think we have here the hand of the enterprising artisan who was so careful about the details of Bahram Gur and Azade. He is a very good silversmith. He's also got a damaged chasing tool, which might be considered his trademark. This may be helpful in future if the forger was very active."

There she paused. After a few moments, she pressed rewind, and then play. "...ry good silversmith," her voice said. Jasmin pressed record. "We must keep an eye out for his style in future," she recorded over the top of her previous comment. After all, she didn't know who would be hearing this tape. She would keep her observation about the damaged tool to herself for the moment.

The piece she was examining was a small medallion bowl that had fluted sides and, on the inside bottom, the bust of a woman wearing the elaborate ringlets that were the hallmark of Sassanian high fashion. Around the inside edge of the medallion the artist had chased a design of small circles about a sixteenth of an inch in diameter, and it was this tool that was damaged—the circles were minutely flattened on one edge. Without a magnifying glass, she would probably not have noticed it.

Although Parton had made it very clear that he would not allow the publication of anything she saw, after her second visit, not without misgivings, Jasmin had been taking pictures of everything she saw, where possible. Unsure what to do with them, she now had a collection of undeveloped films in the closet of her study. She felt compelled to this action. She knew that she might be the only scholar to see Parton's collection for the foreseeable future. Even if he sold it off in his lifetime, the individual items might conceivably disappear into other private collections without ever being published, especially anything that had a questionable history. Items offered for public auction were automatically published in a sale catalog, but anything changing hands privately was nobody's business but that of buyer and seller. And what had never been published could hardly be claimed by a foreign government as an illegally exported antiquity. They would never see it.

Of course, he owned some things that were well-known and previously published, and he had shown her a few of these, too, rather as a "freebie" at the end of a session. It was a joy to get her hands on pieces which she had previously seen only in photographs and slides, and sometimes her idea of the item changed dramatically because of its physical feel.

She told no one what she was doing, neither Ben Bredon nor Daniel Hazlett. Sooner or later she would have to tell someone, if only because the films in her closet were weighing on her conscience. That in taking pictures without permission she was on morally gray ground, she accepted. But so, in her opinion, was Dominic Parton. There ought to be a record of such precious pieces of human history. Suppose he sold them one day to a madman who melted them down? He must not be the only one to know they had ever existed.

Every year, Jasmin held a Christmas party at which her friends decorated her tree. The tradition had begun when she was a model, and she had carried it on at university because so many of her fellow students could not go home for the holiday, and because in a way they had become each other's family. Many of the students who could not afford the trip home, of course, were not of Christian background, for the School of Asian and Eastern Studies naturally attracted a far higher percentage of foreign students than most colleges of the university. But Jasmin took the position that the tradition of the tree was not restricted to the Christian religion, and nor was peace and goodwill; so every year Jews, Muslims, Hindus, Sikhs, Jains, Shintos and anyone else who was alone over the holiday gathered to debate over the perfect placement of baubles on her tree.

It was the only debate allowed. After a rather difficult time at her first party, Jasmin, who had friends on all sides, made it absolutely clear to everyone that if political, racial and religious prejudice were not left *at* the door, the bearer of such would soon be shown *to* it. Peace and brotherhood reigned, or Jasmin knew the reason why. Thus people who could not bear to come up against any representative of a group they hated simply stayed away. It was a friendly gathering, and those who came regularly looked forward to it. Every year there were sad gaps in the gathering as people who had gained their degrees returned home, and every year there were new people to take their place.

This year, Jasmin was faced with the troublesome question of whether to invite Ben Bredon. Since she was inviting her entire graduate seminar, including their supervisors, if she did not invite Ben it would cause remark. She thought that Ben might understand and even appreciate her decision, but it was possible he, too, might read too much into it.

Set against that were two problems. She had stupidly mentioned the tradition to Dominic Parton at one of their early meetings, and promised to invite him. As Christmas approached, she would have quietly allowed this promise to slide, but Parton actually reminded her, and she had been forced to renew the invitation. And as far as she knew, Ben did not know that her connection with Parton had continued after that first dinner, and quite independently of Parton's request, Jasmin preferred to keep things that way. They were having enough trouble working together without the added weight of her utter disregard of his advice.

The fact was, their relationship had gone right off the rails since the day she had fallen through the door of his office. Not that it had been right before, but if Andrea had seriously imagined that the exposure of the sexual tension would ease their problems, she was wrong. It was like opening a can of some substance that expands on contact with oxygen and then hoping to get it all safely back in the can. Sometimes she thought she would drown in sheer physical awareness of the man.

It was always there; it never let up. Once she handed him some paper or photograph over the desk, and their hands had brushed. Both had snatched their hands back from the contact almost before it happened, but not before she felt a jolt of some force that would have felled a horse. After that, they were careful never to risk such a touch. They learned, too, though they never spoke it aloud, that there was a kind of magnetic field around each of them which the other must stay out of. It was, unfortunately, about the size of an elevator. They were safe enough if others were in the elevator with them, but the first time they traveled alone together in the SAES elevator Jasmin had developed a headache by the time they reached the fourth floor. She wanted to go to him, as though the only relief from the force field that surrounded him was to be right at the center—where he was. The headache was the mark of the effort it took not to do so.

Now they never went to the departmental library together. His office was safe because they always kept the desk between them, but the library with its oversize table had too little room for maneuver. If they needed a book, one or other of them went and fetched it.

They fought less, but their fights were more savage. Sometimes it was a relief to fight, and yet there was always the danger inherent in any free release of emotion, that it might bring others in its train. She did not know why she was so terrified of this possibility.

"What is your point?" Ben said one day, in a scene that was typical of their disputes now. He was bending over photostats of two different photographs of the famous Mithraic hunting scene uncovered by archaeologists in the underground Mithraic temple at a site called Dura Europos. The first had been taken before restoration of the painting; the second after it.

"He's shooting arrows at all these beasts," she said. "Most of them have been pierced by an arrow."

"I can see that, yes," he said, as she leaned forward to indicate the faint black line of each arrow on the restored painting. She was careful not to let her hand get near his, but she couldn't stop her eyes flicking up to his. She dropped them again.

"And one through the wild boar," she said.

"All right."

"Before the restoration, several of these arrows are partly visible, you see? Here and here, here. But there's no arrow visible in the wild boar in the painting *before* it was restored."

"It was in very bad condition when discovered. Do you feel they've taken too many liberties with the restoration?"

She said, "If there is no arrow through the boar, what does that mean, in the context of the picture?"

"Almost anything, Jasmin," he said tiredly, dropping the pictures. "What the hell do you know—what do any of us know—about a mystery cult that flourished two thousand years ago and left us no trace except these damned pictures in underground caves? For God's sake, we have enough trouble sorting out the past when it's written down!"

"Oh, come on, Ben!" she said. "What are we supposed to do? Forget it just because it's not easily accessible?"

Suddenly the air was humming and heavy with subtext, as though that comment were personal. Jasmin heaved a sigh, furiously ignoring the double entendre. "My whole thesis is based on finding history where there hasn't been any. I remind you that you told me at the outset that you were not in principle opposed to my viewpoint!"

"I at no time, however, undertook to swallow leaps of faith in the absence of sound evidence," he said, his voice jumping up in volume, and his middle finger hitting the table once for emphasis.

"This is not a leap of faith!" she squawked, and her own fist hit the desk. "You're prejudiced, Ben!" What a tiresome man! Why couldn't he listen for two minutes together? She wanted to hit him. "I'm not asking you to *accept* the argument!" She was shouting. "I'm only asking you to admit that it *is* one!"

"Don't shout at me," Ben commanded her levelly. They looked at each other, and it was clear that they would both have found coming to blows somehow satisfactory. After a moment he breathed deeply. "All right," he said. "What are you trying to say? If the boar has no arrow in his body, what does it mean except that Mithra hasn't got around to killing them all?" Jasmin was sure he was being willfully obdurate, but she could not afford any more outbursts of anger. She spoke calmly.

"It means the boar is not the *prey,* but the *partner* of the god, like the snake. Look at his position, ahead of Mithra's horse and just beside this animal, as if he were helping to hunt it. And the Zoroastrian god who was sometimes represented as a wild boar was Verethragna, and he is said in Mithra's Hymn to travel with Mithra."

"Ah."

"Now—" she sat back "—isn't that evidence that suggests the Mithras of the Roman cult was the same god as the Zoroastrian god of Mithra's Hymn?"

Ben paused and rubbed his eyes under his glasses. "If Verethragna was represented in Sassanian iconography as a wild boar," he asked, "why do so many of the silver plates show the king killing the wild boar in the hunt?"

"Because they reflected reality," she said. "The kings did kill wild boars in the hunt. That's attested."

"If the kings did so, and I am sure they did, why not Mithra? Is there any evidence that the wild boar at Dura Europos is not the god's prey? And if there is, where goes your belief that the iconography of the royal hunting plates is based on Mithraic scenes such as this? As far as I can see, according to your theory, if the god *is* killing the boar, he isn't Zoroastrian Mithra, and if he *isn't* killing the boar, he's not the model for the kings on the royal hunting plates."

"You're being too rigid," she complained. "Can't you see that the boar sometimes represented Verethragna and sometimes just a boar?"

Ben began to laugh in real amusement. "Ah, Jasmin, what are you trying to tell me? That sometimes a cigar is just a cigar?"

"What does that mean?" she demanded.

"It's what Freud said about phallic symbols, isn't it?" He shrugged. "All right, I'm going to accept that," he said, before she could speak. "Sometimes a boar is just a boar."

"Thank you," she said dryly.

"But you still have got a lot of talking to do."

"You're too damn pedantic, Ben," she said.

"And you have too much of a tendency to leap over chasms," he said. "Among other things. I don't say you won't ultimately be able to use this. But you are going to have to answer every point, and you had better get used now to being challenged on this theory, because it is not popular, as you well know, and your examiners will challenge you on it. It seems to me that this argument runs into the sand on every side. You will have a lot of shoring up to do."

She wished she had never fallen into his arms that day, or that she had not so weakly let him kiss her. She wished she hadn't found out about any sexual tension between them; and most of all, she wished she didn't have to invite Ben Bredon to her Christmas party.

"Don't you think you're overreacting?" asked Shahdeen, when she had decided what she needed was a masculine point of view.

"Am I?"

He shrugged. "Well, what do you think is going to happen? He kissed you once, and he's never made a move since, is that right?"

"Yeeess," she said reluctantly. She was sorry now she'd told him about the kiss, but how else could she get a solidly based opinion?

"And when did he kiss you? He opened the door of his office and you fell into his arms, isn't that it?" Jasmin nodded. "Jasmin, I hate to say it, but, you know, most men would have done the same."

She laughed disbelievingly. "Most men would kiss a woman whom they saved from falling?" she demanded.

Shahdeen grinned. "No, Jasmin, most men would kiss *you* if they got their arms around you. It's just a sort of effect you have. But it doesn't mean anything except that men respond to a certain stimulus which you have a lot of."

For an answer Jasmin tripped and fell against him, and instinctively his arms went around her. He smiled at her in amused acknowledgment and then gently kissed her lips. Warmth flowed between them, and he set her on her feet and took his arms away. "You see?" he said.

She did, more or less. "So how come you've never made a pass in all this time?" she asked jokingly. Shahdeen looked at her.

"Partly," he said quietly, and he was not joking, "because I intend to go home when my degree is finished, and you would not survive in Bangladesh even if you were willing to come."

"Oh." Jasmin felt rather subdued. Then she rallied. "Well, but we could have . . . you might have thought . . ."

"No, Jasmin," he said with a smile. "You are not the sort of woman one imagines casual affairs with. If we had fallen in love, one of us would have had to make a terrible choice next year. You see, in your heart, Jasmin, it was never a joke, that story your grandmother told. You pretended it was, maybe. But in your heart, you are a princess.''

"I am not!" she said hotly, outraged.

He laughed. "You see, the word has been debased. I mean, in the old meaning. You are the Real Princess, the one whom nothing demeaning ever touches. You are the one to whom nothing but perfection can be offered. For you, Jasmin, only nobility of temperament and purpose will do. Tell me I'm wrong.''

"I don't know what you're talking about," she said.

"Tell me about the first time you fell in love."

"I was eleven and there was a boy who used to—"

"No. I mean real love, as an adult," said Shahdeen.

"Oh . . . well, I've never been *in* love, but . . ."

"You see? Thirty-one, and you have never been in love."

"But I've *loved* people! Men, I mean. But . . . do you think that exists? Being in love? I think it's just a fiction, really."

Shahdeen's eyelids dropped to hood his eyes. "Oh, yes. I think it exists. For lesser mortals it's easy. We fall in love all the time. For the princess, locked away in the tower, it's not so easy. She has to wait till someone crosses the moat and climbs the wall to her window. And that can only be done by someone very special. Isn't that right?''

"You're telling me I live in a fairy tale?" Jasmin demanded.

"That's your role, Jasmin, that's what you are."

She decided to get back to the point at issue. "So, what does this lead to? Ben Bredon really feels no attraction for me, and it was just a thing of the moment?"

Shahdeen looked at her assessingly for a moment. "It means . . . you see, to a man you look very expensive, Jasmin. He's going to have to be the best he is, and for most men that's not easy. This isn't necessarily what you demand, but what he demands of himself on your behalf. Unfortunately, you are very attractive, and most men will wish they could just take what they want without paying the price. Some men will try to do that, of course. If Bredon were going to be that sort, he'd have tried it long ago. So, my guess is—he kissed you because you were there. You told him a short-term affair was not a possibility. He accepts that. The chances are he won't come to your party, so it's safe to ask him.''

This seemed full of contradiction to Jasmin, but she knew better than to try to understand the male psyche very accurately. And she didn't like the assessment, though she couldn't have said why.

Nevertheless, she did invite Ben to the party.

"Thank you," said Ben. "It may be too close to Christmas. I expect to go out of town that weekend, but I'll try to come. Should I bring something?"

She breathed again. This was a clear sign that, like so many of the English, he would prefer to decline the invitation a bit later, rather than at the moment of being asked.

In her relief, Jasmin opened up. "A tree decoration, perhaps. It's a tradition with some of my friends, but it's not necessary. As it is, I now have to get a huge tree just to take all the decorations that have accumulated over the years.''

Ben smiled as though the idea charmed him; for once there was no subtext between them. "All right," he said. "Thank you. I'll make every effort to come.''

Oh, fine. So much for the masculine point of view.

# Chapter 12

Jasmin had the second floor—what the English call the first—of a large Edwardian house on a quiet street in the area of London that was traditionally the home of writers and artists—Hampstead. A huge living and dining area went through from front to back, and great bay windows looked out on the street in front and over Hampstead Heath behind.

A tall, fat Christmas tree sat in the front bay window, naked and expectant. On the dining table behind, which had been pushed against the wall to allow free access to the tree, were spread the decorations: strings of colored lights first, then a variety of bulbs, baubles and trimmings from many different countries, tinsel and ribbon and garlands. Light from the period chandelier made everything in the room bright. In the sitting room, the lighting was much softer, and there was quiet music playing, jazz and ballads interspersed with carols and traditional songs. Champagne and glasses twinkled on a low table. In the kitchen, wine and spices were mulling in a large vat, and there were trays of food being laid out by Andrea and Padma, who had come early to help.

Generally it fell to the first man through the door to help Jasmin fix the lights on the tree, since this was a job that had to be done before the decorating proper could begin, and she was waiting in some impatience for the first arrivals. Jasmin loved Christmas, and she loved her "family," and she always enjoyed her own party.

She was wearing the red velvet dress that she always wore for this party, a plain sleeveless scoop-neck bodice fitting snugly to the hips, and then a flared floor-length skirt. She was barefoot under it, and her hair was casually held back with a red ribbon. The effect, somewhat bohemian, was highly individual.

Jasmin laid the last box of ornaments on the table and removed the lid, then picked up the fresh holly wreath which Andrea had brought as her contribution and went into the kitchen. "How's everything? Do you need help?" she asked, rummaging in what she called her tool drawer.

"We're fine," said Andrea. "We don't need any help. You just carry on with what you're doing."

Having located a hammer and something that would serve as a hook, Jasmin carried the wreath to the apartment door, opened it, and began to hammer. The door banged back and forth against the wall with each blow, and the nail, not very straight to begin with, abruptly bent. Andrea, wearing an apron and carrying a ladle, came out of the kitchen. "What's that horrible banging?" she demanded. "For goodness' sake, Jasmin, take it outside and close the door so you can hammer properly. You'll never get it in this way."

Dutifully, Jasmin went out, closing the door behind her. With careful tapping, she might encourage the nail to go into the wood, bent as it was. Next year she must get some kind of stick-on hook.

After a few false starts she got the nail reasonably firmly fixed, hung the wreath and stepped back to look.

"Happy Christmas," said a quiet voice behind her. Jasmin turned in surprise to see Benedict Bredon, in a black coat and a white silk scarf and carrying a wrapped bottle and a brightly colored paper bag coming up the stairs. Behind her, the nail chose that moment to come loose, and the wreath crashed to the floor. Under the effect of this double assault, Jasmin gasped and burst into laughter.

"Shall I?" he asked. He was matter-of-fact, as though there need be no subtext between them tonight. He traded the hammer for the bottle and bag he carried and bent to pick up the nail. He held it up with one eyebrow raised; it was bent at an angle of forty-five degrees. "Have you got another nail?"

"I doubt it," said Jasmin. There was a crazy bubble of joy inside her, as though she had lied to herself when she hoped he wouldn't come.

The door in front of them opened. "Jasmin, someone just rang the be— Oh, you've already arrived. Oh, good, you're a man."

"Your appreciation makes it all worthwhile," said Ben. Jasmin laughed.

"I mean you're the first man, so you can help Jasmin put the lights on the tree. That's traditional." Andrea glanced at the hammer. "Are you fixing the wreath? That's good, I'll close the door. Jas, we hear voices down the street, so I think people will be starting to arrive."

The door closed and Jasmin was left in sudden silence with Ben. The landing in front of her door was about the size of an elevator, but this was Christmas. She obeyed the foolish impulse to kiss his cheek. "Merry Christmas," she said.

Ben put an immediate arm around her. "Is there mistletoe?" he asked.

"Sorry, no mistletoe tonight. My little man in the market said it was in very short supply." She was light-headed, as if she'd drunk on an empty stomach.

"Ah, well, we must do without," said Ben. He bent and kissed her softly on the lips, and Jasmin felt the heat down to her toes. When he released her, she blinked and leaned against the wall behind her, smiling. For some reason, everything seemed different tonight.

He turned and quickly fixed the wreath, and they entered the apartment just as the doorbell rang. Jasmin pressed the buzzer, and led Ben through to the bedroom. "Just toss your coat on the bed," she instructed him, turning on the light. "I haven't got enough room in the closet to hang things. The bathroom's through there."

There was the sound of laughter on the stairs, and she ran to open the door. Shahdeen jumped quickly through the doorway. "Setu tried to beat me up the stairs, but these kids have no energy," he said, amid much laughter from the group. "Am I first man?"

"No chance," said Ben Bredon softly, entering the hallway behind her. He was wearing a black sweater and trousers under his gray tweed jacket. A masculine message passed between Ben and Shahdeen, and the latter grinned.

"And for this you nearly ripped my leg off?" Setu demanded in mock petulance. "I was first up the stairs and Shahdeen grabbed my leg," he told Jasmin. "I nearly broke my neck!"

"Awww," said Jasmin. She kissed him on the cheek. "Did you want to put the lights on the tree?"

"No, I just wanted to beat Shahdeen up the stairs," he joked. "What do I know about putting lights on a tree?" Setu was a Jain. Elegant, slender, brilliant, he was, at twenty-three, on his way to becoming a bright star in international shipping law. "Oh, this is beautiful, this is very nice," he said, looking around. He nodded several times. "I like this . . . do you want to get married, Jasmin?"

Jasmin, busy kissing everyone and directing them to the bedroom, merely held out her hand. "Ring, please," she said.

She was light-headed with the laughter and bustle when at last she turned and picked up the bottle that Ben had brought, and, leading the way into the sitting room, unwrapped it. It was champagne, the best, and it looked very expensive. "Oh, the real thing!" Jasmin sang. "How lovely, I haven't had real champagne for an age!" Suddenly she remembered when she had last drunk it, and glanced up at Ben. She hoped Dominic Parton would forget the party tonight. Jasmin babbled nervously, "Oh, would there be enough to go around if we opened it now before everyone else arrives? I've only got cava." Cava, a sparkling wine from Spain, was her favorite "almost-champagne," but nothing could compare with Dom Perignon.

Shahdeen made a face and shook his head. "Don't be silly. Put it away and drink it later. Don't waste it on us."

"I don't want any," said Setu, in some satisfaction. "I don't drink that stuff."

"But I want some *now,*" Jasmin said plaintively.

Ben took the bottle from her and opened it, putting an end to the discussion. Cheers greeted the subdued *pop,* and he filled several glasses and handed Jasmin one. She could not avoid brushing his hand as she took it, and did not try. The shock of the contact made the glass tremble. On the other side of the table someone opened a bottle of the cava and filled more glasses.

Jasmin raised her glass. "Happy holiday," she said. "And peace on earth, goodwill to all."

Half an hour later, when the lights were fixed on the tree and most of the guests had arrived, Jasmin remembered Ben's little bag. People were admiring the decorations from previous years and displaying those they had brought this year, preparatory to the first bauble being placed on the tree. Jasmin ran out into the hall and found the bag, still sitting beside the hammer on the bookcase there.

"Is this for the tree?" she called to him across the room, holding it up. Jasmin liked paper bags and surprises. Ben nodded. There was a peculiar understanding between them tonight. It had been a strange pleasure to help him put the lights on the tree in her home.

"Oh, how pretty!" she exclaimed, ripping open the little parcel, as the gold of the contents caught the light and glinted among the folds of paper. They were warm gold hoops, each with a red velvet bow and a tiny hook for hanging on the tree. "Aren't they gorgeous!" said Jasmin. Carefully she separated the hooks and laid them one by one on the table as, all around her, friends chatted and laughed. "Five!" she announced, to no one in particular, and then felt the heat slowly and inexorably climb into her cheeks. Her head bent, Jasmin searched the bag for the one that would bring the total up to an unremarkable six, but the bag was empty. She played for a moment with the rings on the table, but in the end she was forced to look up.

He was half the table length away, watching her. Five golden rings. *On the fifth day of Christmas, my true love gave to me...*

"Jasmin, are you going to put the first ornament on so we can get started?" someone who was familiar with all the rituals of the party demanded. Jasmin turned away with her heart thumping.

"Yes, yes, where is it?" They made way for her to get to the tree, now twinkling with lights. There were a few ornaments already hung by someone, but that didn't matter. The "first" ornament was a battered old glass Santa Claus that had been her favorite when she was a child. Among those that her parents had bought on their first Christmas after they were married, it had hung on every Christmas tree since she was born, and from the age of five she had always been the one to hang it. The red paint was much worn, but the heavy white glass had been dropped a dozen times and never broken. When she was fifteen she had repainted the holly the Santa held with green and red metallic nail polish, but no repairs had been effected since then.

By the time the little ceremony was performed, she had recovered her common sense. The five golden rings meant nothing except that Ben understood tradition. Whatever had possessed her to imagine...whatever she had imagined? Jasmin busied herself refilling glasses with mulled wine and taking around a tray of canapés, and when she next looked, the golden rings were all hanging from the tree.

When it was all done, the lights in the dining room were turned out, and everyone stood admiring their handiwork. The tree was magnificent, and the bow window was its perfect setting, and they were all momentarily overcome by its silent beauty. For a few seconds no one spoke.

The doorbell rang; it was at that curious moment that Dominic Parton chose to arrive. "You are looking absolutely ravishing, my dear," he said as he entered, kissing Jasmin on both cheeks and offering her a bottle. Her heart sinking, she led him into the bedroom, where he fished something out of his pocket and then tossed his coat onto the heap on the bed. When they arrived in the sitting room the group admiring the tree had broken up and people were sitting around chatting. In the darkened dining room in front of the tree, two couples were dancing to the soft music.

Dominic Parton paused at the archway between sitting and dining room to stare at the tree. "But I thought the purpose of the party was to decorate the tree!" he protested. He was wearing a blue velvet dinner jacket with an impeccable white ruffled shirt and bow tie, but he didn't look out of place. He simply looked as if he owned the place, and therefore it didn't matter if the others didn't come up to his standards.

"Well, we do that first," said Jasmin, with an ironic grin.

"And I'm terribly late! You must forgive me. I didn't realize how the time was going. May I put a decoration on the tree, anyway? I did bring one."

Jasmin was surprised. "Did I tell you to bring a decoration? I don't remember doing that."

"Well, I brought one," he said. He handed her a little tissue-wrapped parcel, and Jasmin, with an apology to the dancers, turned the lights in the dining room on low. "I thought you'd like it."

She unwrapped the tissue to disclose a small silver disk. She smiled conventionally before she realized what it was, and then she gasped. "Oh, how...how *lovely!*" she exclaimed.

It was a tiny replica of a Sassanian silver plate. The artist was not technically very good, but the intention was unmistakable: a tiny engraved stick figure with a crown and a bow and arrow riding a tiny stick horse and chasing a lion.

"It's absolutely...!" She kissed his cheek. "Thank you, Dominic, it's lovely." She handed it to him. "You'd better hang it yourself, so we can say you had some hand in it!"

He drew her over to the tree with him, and after a little problem in finding a hook and fixing it to the plate, he hung it up. Then he kissed her lightly, on the lips. Jasmin, heady with mulled wine and champagne and Christmas joy, let it happen, and although it was the first time he had kissed her it was casual enough to seem a comfortable habit.

A minute later, coming back into the sitting room with Dominic's arm around her waist, she paused to dim the lights in the dining room again, and caught Ben Bredon's eye. The two men nodded greetings to each other, but his face was stone. He could have no doubts now that she had seen Dominic Parton often since that dinner party in October. Gently, without knowing why she did it, she eased herself out of Parton's light clasp. Two women from her graduate seminar were standing there, and she introduced Dominic to them.

"Tamiko's subject is ancient Persian languages," she said, by way of breaking the ice. When the conversation was under way, she moved around the room, stopping here and there, and neatly avoiding whatever part of the room Ben happened to be in. Finally she sat down by Setu, who was telling a joke. Nearly everyone in the room knew everyone else, and the room was full of voices and laughter.

"So, Jasmin, you have to name the date," Setu said, when the punch-line had been delivered, abandoning his groaning audience and turning to her.

"It's a nice apartment, isn't it?"

"Yes. Oh, yes, I am going to enjoy living here very much."

"Your eyes are going green, Setu."

"Good. Our children will have green eyes *and* they'll understand the value of money. I like that in a kid."

"Speaking of kids, don't I have to wait until you come of age?"

"No, my father will give his permission. I'll show him pictures of this place."

He was capable of talking nonsense till the cows came home, but Ben Bredon was bending over her, and Setu graciously paused. Ben smiled and took her wrist in a loose clasp, but she looked at his hand and felt the heat of his touch roar through her body. "Is it traditional to ask the hostess to dance?" he asked softly. Jasmin's heart was choking her.

"So long as you remember she's engaged to me," Setu told him. "You can have an affair with her after we're married, though. I don't mind, I'm not greedy."

"I see I must remind you that I was first man," said Ben with a smile. He looked at her after he said it, and she knew that the joke was only for Setu.

Setu looked alarmed. "What does that mean?" he demanded. "Does that mean I can't marry you? Can't I live here, Jasmin?"

"Of course you can. I'll adopt you," Jasmin said soothingly, as they moved away.

"Do I like that? Yes, that'll be all right. That way I get my own room, right?" He continued the nonsense as Ben led her into the dining room and took her in his arms. A ballad was playing; there were no fast tracks on the tape except for songs like "Jingle Bells." It was not really dance music, although people were dancing intermittently. Another couple joined them.

She was afraid he meant to ask her about her relationship with Dominic Parton, but he made no move to speak. When the song ended he did not let her go, holding her lazily in the curve of one arm and waiting for the next. A slow, moody number came on, and he drew her more closely into his arms. His hand was a warm, firm pressure against her spine, and Jasmin closed her eyes and let her head fall against his shoulder. He was holding her hand, and he lifted it up around his neck and released it to wrap both arms around her, bringing her body close against him. Warmly, lazily, obediently, Jasmin snuggled into his embrace. There was no urgency, only perfect understanding. He moved, and she moved in response, and then he moved in response to that and they got closer and closer, swaying with the music as their bodies gently, gently fused into one. They even breathed together. She had never felt such security, such sweetness, and as the music stilled and silence fell, it seemed to Jasmin that all questions had been answered and her heart need never ask another. The contradiction of feeling this for Ben Bredon hardly got her attention. It simply felt right.

"Frosty, the snowman, was a jolly, happy soul..." They broke apart with soft reluctance and smiled at each other in the darkness. They were at the far end of the room near the tree, which glowed and twinkled in friendly magnificence.

He took her wrist in a light embrace, turned it over and examined the palm. "I'm driving down to Hampshire tonight," he said, and her first reaction was acute disappointment.

"Where are you going?"

"I have a cottage in Hampshire where we spend Christmas. Everyone arrives tomorrow. The family who usually looks after the place for me is away, so I have to get down there tonight to turn the heating on."

In England a "cottage" could be nearly anything from a ten-bedroom Victorian rectory to a fifteenth century workman's two-room home with a modern kitchen attached. The one thing it would not be was a Canadian-style summer cottage. "Oh, it sounds lovely!" she exclaimed. She could imagine few things so pleasant as Christmas in a pretty country village, and Hampshire was certainly full of those. "Who is 'everyone'?"

"This year, my sister and her family, and my father, and a few friends. I have friends in the Foreign Service, and they join us when they can get back to England for Christmas. They'll be with us this year. They arrive tomorrow."

When the recording of "Frosty the Snowman" gave way to soft jazz, they danced again. He talked about the people he had mentioned. There was a curious undertone to what he said, as though he was describing people she was going to meet. He described the village, and talked about the local aristocratic family, still living in the "big house," and protecting the village from the uglier incursions of modern life.

There were several changes of music, none of which impinged very much on their conversation or their dancing. In one pause as the music changed, he asked, "Would you like to come for Christmas, Jasmin?"

"Oh, I'd love to, but I can't," she said in real disappointment. Across the room in the silence the sudden sound of a quiet dispute caught her ear. Dominic Parton was in conversation with Tamiko, the Ph.D. student in ancient Persian languages. Jasmin watched them for a moment. She had only introduced them half an hour ago, but they seemed to have made rapid strides in their acquaintance. She heard Dominic laugh and looked apologetically back at Ben. "My brother's coming to me for Christmas. He's in Europe at the moment and needs a break. Otherwise, I'd have loved to."

If he suggested that Jake could come, too, she would agree. She would be really disappointed not to go, and after months of photographing war a few days in a quiet

English village were probably much more what Jake needed than time in London.

But Ben's face had taken on a look she recognized of old—stern and remote. He was staring in Parton's direction, as though he had suddenly been reminded of a grievance. "You've been seeing a lot of Parton, have you?" he asked.

"Yes, I'm sorry, Ben, I should have mentioned it, shouldn't I?" she said. "But I..." She paused. The music started again, but he did not take her in his arms.

"No real reason," he said.

Except that he had said she shouldn't get involved with Parton's collection, and he was her supervisor. "I should have told you."

"Well," said Ben, "you're telling me now."

"I'd like to discuss it...not now, of course, but when term starts."

Ben's hand, as if involuntarily, came up to stroke the curve of her upper arm, and then for a moment his hold tightened. All the urgency that had not been there when they danced was there now, and Jasmin's blood rose in answer and rushed to be warmed by his touch. She closed her eyes, feeling light-headed. In this moment she had no mixed feelings about Ben. She only wanted him, and she felt that if he made love to her, it would, after all, come right. Taking a trembling breath, she said, "About Christmas, I...Jake...when I said..."

He shook his head. "It's all right, Jasmin. You enjoy your holiday, whoever you spend it with. I'll see you in the new term." His voice was cold, the detached voice she knew of old. Jasmin gasped, feeling slapped. Did it mean he would have found her brother's presence inhibiting, or was there something more? Abruptly, she didn't care. She wasn't going to bother to try to understand him. Perhaps he just liked giving her regular rebuffs.

"I hope you have a very good Christmas," she returned quietly. She followed him into the bedroom, where, with some difficulty, he extracted his coat from the bottom of the large pile. "Thank you for coming," she said, the pleasantly meaningless phrase a mask for a hurt bewilderment that she refused to feel.

"Thank you for a very nice party," said Ben, shrugging into his coat. Something fell noisily from his coat pocket and he bent and retrieved his car keys. At the door they looked at each other for a moment of awkward silence. There were no kisses now, yet she had the feeling that it could have been very different. "Good night, then," said Ben, turning away down the stairs. A minute later she heard the street door bang.

She had not wanted him to come. Much, much more painfully, now, she wished that he had not.

*Chapter 13*

Jasmin was almost asleep when the doorbell rang just before four o'clock. Struggling out of a half dream, her first thought was that it was Andrea or Shahdeen returning because they had forgotten something. Her second thought brought her upright. It must be Jake, arriving earlier than planned because he had had to grab some suddenly available flight unexpectedly.

She had not seen Jake for six months. She flicked on the bedside lamp and tossed back the duvet, and not bothering with slippers or a robe, ran into the hall. "Hello?" she called into the entryphone.

"It's Ben," she heard unbelievingly. "I'm very sorry to disturb you, but I seem to have—"

Jasmin buzzed without waiting to hear the rest, and then leaned against the wall, her heart pounding from the little series of shocks it had received. Why had be come back? What did he want at this hour? The front door closed downstairs and she opened the apartment door and watched him appear up the stairs, and in that vulnerable, drowsy state, Jasmin was suddenly face-to-face with the truth. She felt the heat of it begin in her heart and spread outward through her body with her blood. It was as though he had been away a long time, and was coming home at last. And it was here that he belonged.

He looked tired. "I am extremely sorry about this," he said, and she could see that he was. He looked as though he'd rather be anywhere than right here, right now.

"It's all right, come on in," she said, because she could not say what her heart wanted to say. What would he think if she said, Welcome home? "What on earth's happened? Have you..." She was going to say, had an accident, but that was ridiculous. He would hardly have come to her if he had.

She held open the door as he entered, belatedly aware that she was barefoot and in thin pajamas and her hair must be a mess. Normally she put her hair into one long plait at night, but after the party she had been just too lazy. She had fixed it in a loose bun, but that had come out in her sleep. She would pay for it tomorrow, she thought absently, getting the tangles out.

He would have stayed in the hall, but Jasmin led the way to the kitchen and turned on the light. Her breath hissed as her feet hit the cool linoleum. She always shut off the heat in the apartment at night, and when the temperature was low outside the rooms got cold. Her cream-colored pajamas were silk, and as silk will, it turned cold suddenly. She shivered.

"Don't catch cold," said Ben softly, entering behind her.

His voice was caressing, and she closed her eyes against hope. Why had he come? Had he changed his mind about inviting Jake for Christmas? "No," she agreed, bending to pull the oven door open and switching on the gas. It was the only way to get heat quickly at night. There was the small, familiar *whoop!* of igniting gas and then warmth began to percolate into the air. "Do you...would you like something to drink? Coffee? Brandy? You look shattered," she said.

He hesitated. "No, I've got to get going again. I drove down to the cottage and found I hadn't got my keys with me. My town keys are with them, so I couldn't get in anywhere." He grinned ruefully. "If they're not here, I'm in trouble."

She looked at him, thinking, *that's not why you're here, even if you don't know it.* Aloud, she only asked, "You're sure you had them when you came?"

"They were in my coat pocket when I left my apartment. They are not anywhere in the car."

Jasmin grinned sympathetically, because it was clear from his tone that he had taken the car to pieces looking for them. "They must be in the bedroom. That's the only place your coat was. We'd better look."

She turned off the oven and led the way down the hall. He entered the softly lighted bedroom a few seconds after her, glanced involuntarily at the bed, and then at her. She felt the tension go out of him and realized with surprise that he had expected to find someone with her. "Jake hasn't arrived yet," she said. "He's not due till tomorrow, but I thought you might be him, arriving early. He's unpredictable."

He was curiously still. "I see," he said.

Her bed looked soft and warm and inviting in the glow from the little lamp. The top of the duvet cover was a dark, exotic print, like a Persian carpet, and the underside and the sheet were pale cream. It was a powerful metaphor of the feminine—dark and secret on the outside, with warm and inviting inner depths, and both of them stared at it for a curious moment of immobility, and then glanced, irresistibly, at each other.

Jasmin tensed and turned away. "I'm sure you walked straight in here and put your coat on the bed, didn't you? You were the first, except that Andrea and Padma came early to help, and they hung theirs in the closet." She was nervous. She could look anywhere but at Ben, for fear of what she might see in his eyes, or he in hers.

"Jasmin," he said, and she turned away and squeezed her eyes shut. Her pajamas were like ice on her skin.

"I remember now!" she said brightly. "Your *car* keys fell out of your pocket. Don't you remember? You were standing just about... there." She pointed to a spot a few feet away from where he stood. He stood silent now, watching, as if waiting for her charade to play its course.

"I remember," he said, but his voice was rough on her skin and he seemed to be talking of something else. Jasmin was breathing through her mouth, the only way she could get air. Even at this distance, his heat reached her. She was frozen, and he would give her life. She knew it now, and it was momentous knowledge. It changed everything. In something not far off terror, she turned her back on him.

"They must be on the bed! The first set fell out on the bed, and the second set—" She grabbed the duvet and shook it once, and a small, shining cluster flew from its folds onto the carpet at his feet. She dived after it so quickly that she had the keys in her hand while he was still reaching down. He did not stop. He bent down over her so that she felt his breath in her hair, his hand closed deliberately over hers and slowly, slowly, he drew her to her feet. He carefully turned her hand over, and gently took the keys from her grasp. He slipped them into his coat pocket, and then she felt his hand on her cheek, her chin, her throat, and she was forced to look at him.

"Ben," she whispered hoarsely, wanting his touch too much to be able to bear it, and urgently then, as if afraid to hear a protest on her lips, he covered them with his own.

His skin was warm against hers. Warm, electric, his lips brushed her lightly, softly; his hand, firm on her throat, brought her face like a flower against his mouth. She pressed a hand to his chest, taking pleasure from the strong beat of his heart, as though it were her own source of life. After a moment his left arm encircled her back, while his hand moved into her hair, cupping her head, and then abruptly his control broke. He drew her tightly against him, her body curving back, her hair sweeping down as he bent over her and held her face up to his passionate kiss. She was lost.

"Jasmin," he said, lifting his mouth only to press it against her eyelids, her cheek, her throat, her mouth again. She was almost sobbing with the joy of it. Her arms curled around his neck, and she delivered herself into his embrace with an abandonment that made him wrap her even more tightly against him, and their bodies pressed close as though they must connect in every minutest measure of skin, in every cell.

"Ben!" she cried, when he let her mouth go. "Ben!" At last she knew she loved him, and she was utterly free. And then she was swept up, then falling, and the bed was beneath her and he was above, and the whole world was here.

When she awoke, the sky was dark, but she knew it was morning. The lamp was still on at her bedside, and she smiled lazily with a new sense of physical well-being. There was an unfamiliar weight on her hip: it was Ben's hand. Even in sleep he held her. Jasmin turned slowly, and his hand moved from her hip and encircled her waist, unconsciously drawing her against him.

He lay on his side, his head bright against the dark pillow slip. In sleep, he looked like a fallen god, his eyes shadowed, his mouth perfectly carved. He was naked, and his chest and half his body lay uncovered; in the night the duvet had shifted. She reached to draw it over him, and his hand tightened around her and he pulled her down firmly into the warm curve of his body. "Jasmin," he breathed her name out softly in her ear, "are you telling me that wasn't a dream?"

She giggled softly, and his body stirred against her. "I don't know," she said. "What was it about?"

His mouth covered hers in sudden possessiveness. "You," he said, lifting his mouth, with an urgency that thrilled her. "It was about you." He opened his eyes and raised himself on one elbow, drawing her under his body, and his mouth found hers again in a bursting passion that took her breath away. Her body, remembering the night just gone, melted instantly under his hands as he wrapped her upper arm in a grasp that was nearly painful, and lifted her helplessly against his mouth.

She opened her legs to his body, and unable to resist the temptation, he slipped into the cradle of her hips and thrust into her without warning, so hard she gasped. "Ah, *God!*" he cried, as though it was torn from him. "Jasmin, you're so..." He rose on his elbows above her, held her head and kissed her while he thrust into her and she moaned under his kiss. Then he lifted himself higher, on his hands, and he pressed into her, over and over, until she cried out with each thrust. It was as though they had never stopped; her body knew all the pathways it had learned in the night and eagerly followed them again.

How beautiful he was. She lifted a hand to stroke his arm, his throat, his chest, marveling in his strength, his austere beauty. He was watching her, and when their eyes met, pleasure rippled through her, the soul's embrace intensifying that of the body. She lifted a leg, and he caught it under the knee and pressed it against her shoulder, and then he looked down to where their bodies met and she heard the noise he made in his throat, and knew that the sight gave him pleasure, and her body took such pleasure from that knowledge that she trembled.

His face was firm in passion, all the skin drawing tight as though he were a high priest at an altar, so that he became amazingly beautiful; and suddenly sight and sound and touch all met in a high vibration that was all, and none, and something other; and as she cried out her answer to some unheard question her body shifted into the realm of pure sensation, and joy coursed through her as somewhere a river flooded its banks; and then there was love.

She said, "It's after eight. What time are your friends arriving?"

Ben stroked her hair and her arm. "Will you come with me?"

"Ben, I have to wait for Jake. I promised to spend Christmas with him. And I haven't seen him for six months, and I miss him."

"I'll come and pick you up," he said. "Do you know when he's arriving?"

"Tonight, with any luck. But with Jake I never know."

"Is he in a war zone?"

"Oh, yes. Jake is always in a war zone."

"Call me when you can. I'll come and get you both. If he's not here by Christmas Eve, leave him a note and say we'll pick him up when he arrives."

"I'll see," she said. "Maybe he'll phone."

"I've got to go," he said. "The Fishers have a newborn, and they are going straight to the cottage from an early flight. I've got to get the place warm before they arrive. Are you sure you won't come with me?"

"Look," she said, "when Jake comes we'll drive down. He hasn't got keys, and the people downstairs have gone abroad, and I don't want to leave a note on the door so he can't even get in. He may be completely exhausted by the time he arrives. Or broke. Or both."

"All right," said Ben. He leaned up to kiss her as she lay propped over him on her elbows, and then lifted her to one side and swung his body up. She smiled involuntarily. After five years it was no surprise to see him naked. It only seemed right, as though she had finally been drawn into the slipstream that was the truth of her life's course.

He touched her face. "If you smile at me like that, I'll never leave," he said.

"Don't tempt me," she said. "Do you want a shower?"

She had coffee waiting by the time he emerged, showered and dressed, and with his coat over his arm. He was looking particularly rumpled, and she realized that his clothes must have simply lain where they fell last night, coat included.

"I have got to go," he said, gratefully gulping the coffee. "Their plane will be landing in less than an hour." He set down the cup and she followed him to the door. "I've left the phone number and address of the cottage on the note-pad in the bedroom. Call as soon as you know what's happening."

"All right," she said.

He kissed her quickly. "Come as soon as you can."

And then he was gone.

Jake arrived late that evening, as expected. What was not expected was the way he looked. He was thin, gaunt almost, and his eyes were deep in his head. He was exhausted and looked as if he had been in hell, and Jasmin was in no doubt that he had. She asked no questions. She kissed him and led him straight into the spare bedroom, which was warmed by a bar heater, and slid a hot-water bottle between the sheets.

"You get undressed and into bed," she ordered. "We can talk in the morning."

He didn't argue, which was unusual for Jake. Jake always imagined he had superhuman reserves of strength and that any admission of physical or psychological weakness was unmasculine.

"Can you get me a drink?" he asked, pulling his jacket off and wearily letting it drop where he stood.

"What do you want?"

They were close; there was never any need for formality or even ordinary politeness between them. Their communications were often abrupt, but neither ever noticed. It was as though they were two halves of the same brain communicating.

"Whiskey if you've got it, brandy if you don't." His sweater and shirt followed the jacket, and there was a scar she had never seen before burned across his chest. It was fresh and only just past the raw stage. Jasmin gasped but said nothing. He had survived whatever it was, and he did not need her frantic worry about what might have happened. But the thought that it had been a bullet stayed in the forefront of her mind for hours after he slept.

He was in bed, wearing only shorts, when she returned. He hadn't bothered to unpack anything. "Thanks," he said briefly, taking the whiskey glass and downing half of it in a gulp. "It's hell, what they're doing to each other over there," he said. "Jasmin, it doesn't get much worse than what I've seen."

It was not at all like him, but Jasmin kept down her fear and smiled confidently at him. "You're here now," she said. "Everything's all right, and you're here."

"Almost didn't make it," he said, in a matter-of-fact tone that was much more his old self. Whatever had affected him like this, it was not fear of his own death. Jake figured life was for risking. He knocked back the last of the contents of the glass.

"I know," said Jasmin. "I'm glad you did."

He fell asleep then. He slept fitfully, muttering and tossing as though he were really sickening from something, but when she laid a hand on his forehead he had no fever. Jasmin left the heat on overnight and crawled into bed, more worried than she had ever been about Jake. She left both bedroom doors open, but he slept the night through and did not wake her.

She had half expected him to be up and about before her in the morning; that was Jake's way. He rarely went down for more than twenty-four hours with anything. But he was not up when she awoke at half past eight. She went into his room and found him just lying there, staring up at the ceiling.

"How are you?"

"It's the worst I've ever been in," he said, as though continuing a conversation they had begun some time ago. "The worst I've ever seen."

"I'm sorry," she said, sitting down in an armchair she pulled close to the bed. "Will you tell me about it?"

Jake shook his head. "No, I don't want to tell you. It'll be worse talking about it. Anyway, it always sounds cliché, doesn't it? It's always a cliché until it's happening right in front of you. I've got pictures of some of it, but I lost six rolls of film of the worst. They confiscated them. They knew where I'd been."

He crossed his arms under his head and breathed deeply. "This is nice. I always like coming here. Glad I made it out."

She had to remain calm. It would do no good to show her distress. But that calm "glad I made it out" chilled her to the bone. So casual, as if relaxing for a few days in her apartment was a good enough reason to stay alive, in the absence of any other. So Jasmin fed him, and chatted, and drew him out a little, but never about the details of what he had seen.

Later, she mentioned the invitation to Ben's cottage. "It will be really pleasant, I'm sure," she said. "Those little Hampshire villages can be the prettiest places on earth, and it'll be very peaceful with no traffic or anything." She chatted a little about the people Ben had said would be there.

He smiled wearily and shook his head. "You go, Jasmin," he said. "Don't let me keep you here, because frankly I couldn't care less whether it's Christmas or July first. I just want to sleep. Anyway, I couldn't stand to be around strangers right now. And all that loving Christmas stuff would just seem like hypocrisy to me. I've seen what I've seen."

"Oh, Jake, don't you think it would cheer you up? Bring you out of it and help you forget?"

"Maybe you're right, maybe it would. But, you know, Jasmin, I feel as though . . . it's not right to forget so soon. I've seen— Did you say they had a newborn baby, these people? Do you know what I've seen done to babies, Jasmin?" He heaved a sigh. "Well, no, you don't. And I can't tell you. But it would be . . . it would be a violation of some kind to go and be happy with some happy family when

I couldn't do anything about what was going on there except take pictures of it. Do you understand what I mean?''

She thought she did, but it was so unlike Jake that it terrified her.

"I can't leave him," she told Ben on the phone. "Even if it weren't Christmas, I simply couldn't leave him alone in this state. I'm very sorry."

"I'm sorry, too," said Ben. "When he's recovered a bit, perhaps he'd like to come down. Everyone will have gone early in the week, and I've got that conference in Berlin. You two could have the place to yourselves. Would he like that?"

"I don't know," she said, feeling suddenly near tears. "I just don't know him like this. Thanks, Ben, but I'll have to let you know."

Jake was restless and delirious that night, but still without showing any signs of fever. She sat up with him most of the night, because her touch and voice seemed to calm him when he was at his worst. She fell asleep in the armchair toward dawn, and when she awoke he was sweating and trembling.

"Should you put him in hospital?" Ben asked. He rang at ten, when her first worry had abated a little. Jake was awake, and he was not delirious, or he seemed not to be.

"He doesn't want to go," she said. "He says he's strong and it'll pass, and he hates doctors." She laughed, grateful for the chance to do so. "He always has, so at least I know it's Jake I'm talking to."

"Have you got food in? Do you need anything?"

"I'll go out this afternoon," she said.

"Take care of yourself," said Ben, as though that would be important to him, and she smiled as she promised, "I will."

A couple of hours later the doorbell rang. Jasmin wasn't expecting anyone, so she went downstairs. The face she saw through the glass was somehow familiar, and she opened the door. "Hi!" said the young man with a grin, standing amid a half dozen bags of groceries. "Ben sent me."

* * *

"I'm doing a master's in Area Studies, Central Asia," Jonathan explained a few minutes later, as he helped her carry the sacks of supplies into the kitchen. "Ben's supervising my thesis. He's really a nice guy, isn't he?"

Jasmin smiled. "Yeah," she said softly, hugging her secret knowledge. "Why did he call you, I wonder?"

"I think because I live so close. We're just down in Belsize Park, so it was easy for me." He looked anxiously at the bags and parcels. "I hope I've got everything you need. Ben just said get everything. My mother made a list for me."

Jasmin, surveying the contents of one bag, grinned. "Your mother must be used to feeding a very large family. How much do I owe you?"

"Nothing. Ben said to tell you he'd settle it with you when you have less on your mind. I'm afraid there's no turkey. My mother says if you don't book early there's no chance. But I got a chicken and a ham. I hope that's all right."

"Yes, it's fine," said Jasmin, feeling overwhelmed. "It's all terrific. Thank you very much."

"My mother says will you and your brother come for Christmas dinner tomorrow? It's at one o'clock. Here's the address." He handed her a piece of paper.

She explained that Jake was too ill to go out and she did not want to leave him.

"If you need anything, just phone," said Jonathan, as he left. "I can be around in five minutes. It won't be any trouble."

The bags held everything she could need for an invalid Christmas. In one bag she even found the latest Dick Francis and another new novel, three newspapers and a book of crossword puzzles. There were tangerines, chocolates and more importantly, as far as Jake was concerned, a large bottle of whiskey.

His demons wrestled with him again that night, but by Christmas morning Jake's natural strength had won through. They spent a quiet day, and although Jake only got

up to eat the Christmas dinner she prepared, it was clear he
was going to be all right. Their mother and sister phoned
from Toronto, and Jake summoned up the strength to sound
all right, if weary. Her friends phoned, too, but she invited
no one around. She talked to Jake, who read nothing, but
lay thinking for hours on end. He told her how he had got
the bullet wound, but he did not want to talk about what
horrors he had seen. She read the Dick Francis and did some
crosswords, and sat by the Christmas tree, and dreamed a
little.

She dreamed, and she remembered, and at last she understood. Of course she had been in love with Ben for a long
time. His rejection of her in her first year wouldn't have hurt
the way it had if she hadn't been some way along the road
to loving him, even then. And after that, each subsequent
step she made in her heart had had to be hidden from her
head, had to be disguised. She had disguised it first as indifference, then, when it grew too strong for indifference to
be an adequate cloak, she had hated him.

That day in his office when he had kissed her, the knowledge had tried to surface... but it was a difficult knowledge, and Andrea's words had been there to help her hide
from it again. But that day—she understood now—that day
she should have known. That frightening sense of everything being different from what she believed, everything
being stood on its head—that should have told her. Well, she
knew now, and so did he, even though they had not said it
yet in words....

Ben called her each day, and although they only talked for
a few minutes, she had a sensation of security, of belong-
ing, and each time she hung up with a little smile, and the
dreams got stronger. On the twenty-seventh he flew to his
conference in Berlin, taking the Fishers to the airport with
him. The cottage would be empty from that evening, but
Jake was already feeling restless: he would need no more
recuperation.

On the twenty-eighth Jasmin kissed him goodbye, sure that he should stay longer, but it was impossible to hold Jake when he wanted to be off. "For goodness' sake, take care of yourself this time," she urged. "Do you have to be right at the front line all the time?"

"The whole world is the front line, Jasmin. Haven't you noticed?" said Jake. He kissed her and stepped into the taxi. He closed the door and pulled down the window. "Oh— you'd better not mention this to Mom," he advised. "I don't want any third degree next time I see her, okay?"

Jasmin shrugged, a little disapproving of this. "Okay," she said. "Can I at least tell her you got shot at?"

He frowned. "Why?"

"Well, because she's your mother, Jake. She kind of has the right to know, don't you think?" Jasmin admonished, with some impatience.

"Hmm," he said. "Somebody else said something like that to me, not long ago. Maybe you're right. Yeah, all right, tell her whatever you think is best."

"Jake!" she exclaimed, in sudden insight. "Have you got a . . . Are you in love?"

He made a rueful face. "It shows, huh?" he said. "Yeah, well, don't start looking at crystal or anything. She wouldn't look at me if I were dancing on my head." He leaned out of the window and kissed her again. 'Bye, Jasmin, thanks for just being there. I'll probably be back sometime in January, if that's all right." He sat back. "Heathrow, please," he said.

She went out that afternoon and had a cup of coffee at her favorite café, reading the paper and getting back in touch with the world. When she got home, she had missed a phone call from Ben, and when she rang the hotel number he had left, there was no answer from his room.

When the phone rang at six that evening, she was in her study trying to get down to work, which seemed suddenly elusive. She had unplugged the phone here and taken it into

Jake's bedroom, so she had to run to the sitting room to answer it before the answering machine automatically picked it up.

"You sound breathless, my dear," said a half-familiar voice it took her a moment to place.

"Oh, Dominic! Hi," she said, and perhaps her disappointment was obvious, because he laughed lightly, and not in amusement.

"I do hate to bother you over the holiday, when I'm sure you have better things to do," he said. "But, my dear, something has arrived that I think you would very much like to see, and I will have it for no more than a day or two. If you want to see it, I'll be at home this evening until ten o'clock."

# Chapter 14

The housekeeper opened the door and took her coat, and Jasmin made her way to the sitting room, where Dominic Parton was sitting with a man she thought was probably an Arab, but might be Iranian. He and Jasmin nodded, but Dominic did not introduce them. "Hello, Jasmin," he said, "you were very quick. Hatim, I'll see you later."

He bowed the man out and returned to offer her a drink; they sat, as usual, in front of the fire. They chatted a little about Christmas, and Dominic asked, in an odd non sequitur, "And where is Ben tonight?"

Jasmin tried hard not to look disquieted, but there was no reason not to tell him. "He's in Berlin at a conference on Islamic art. He's delivering a paper."

"I suppose it's one way academics can avoid work over the holiday week," he said cynically. "And you didn't go?"

She shook her head. "Outside my field."

"You're a very naughty young woman," he said then, in a curiously flirtatious manner that was not at all like what she knew of him. He touched a fingertip to her nose. "You've lost me a bet."

"I have?" Jasmin asked in surprise.

"I thought you'd be the one to be different," he said. Then, abruptly businesslike, he said, "But let me show you this little treasure I've found! I think you'll be impressed. You may even be grateful you didn't go to Berlin!"

There was a bit too much subtext in all this for Jasmin, and she felt the best way of coping with it was to ignore it. She finished her sherry and stood. "Yes, please. Is it silver ware?"

He did not answer. Laying his finger aside his nose and giving a nod, he led the way to the Inner Sanctum. Inside, for the first time, he double-locked the door. Then he turned to a narrow cabinet that was fixed to the wall. Previously he had never opened any piece of furniture except one drawer, and the obvious implication was that this piece was too valuable to risk in the temporary drawer even for an hour. Against her better judgment, the atmosphere began to have its effect on Jasmin; she could feel her heart beating in her ears.

The cabinet opened to disclose a wall safe, and fleetingly Jasmin wondered if someone had stolen the great jewelled cup of Khosro and was trying to sell it to him. By the time he had opened the safe and withdrawn a velvet parcel, her pulse was jumping uncontrollably.

When he led her to the green baize table, it was all she could do to sit down. With a studied lack of ceremony, Dominic set the still-wrapped piece in front of her. "Open it, my dear," he said.

She carefully lifted the black fabric folds to one side and the other, and then there were two more, at top and bottom, and she lifted these. It was a silver plate, she could see that, but it was wrapped now in white silk. Jasmin lifted one fold and then it all seemed to slide away, and the piece was revealed.

She gasped—a long, hoarse noise that was almost horror—and her hands leaped to her breast. Her heart was kicking like a trip-hammer, and her mouth went dry, and she was deafened by the sound of her own blood. "Oh, dear God!" she whispered, when she could speak. Her hand pressed against her mouth. She leaned forward to look. "Oh, my God, Dominic, where did you get this?" She moved a hand to caress it, saying breathlessly, "Look at that nimbus! He's absolutely unmistakable." Distantly she noticed that her hand was trembling, as if with a palsy.

It was Mithra sacrificing the bull. It was the most difficult section of her thesis dramatically proved in one plate. It was an absolutely original piece. Nothing like it had ever been seen ... except in the niche of the underground room of the temple of Mithras at Dura Europos, and the other Mithraic temples of the Roman Empire. It was nothing less than the missing link between the Mithras cult of the Roman Empire, and the Mithra of ancient Persia. It was of unimaginable importance.

"Is it genuine?" she demanded hoarsely. "What's the provenance? Who brought it to you?"

"Well, my dear, it isn't going to be worthwhile to inquire too closely into provenance. I suspect it has recently been found in an unofficial excavation near Persepolis, and I have no doubt but that it has been brought out of Iran in defiance of antiquities export law. But, of course, that is not the story one hears."

Stroking the plate lovingly, she shook her head. If he was right, she was incredibly lucky to be seeing it. Things found in illegal digs might suffer any fate. "Are you going to buy it?"

"I am not. I can't afford four hundred thousand pounds for a piece that will inevitably be claimed by the Iranian government the moment its existence is revealed. But for your sake I have pretended to consider, and it is mine for the space of two days. If you mention it to anyone I shall, of course, deny all knowledge. However, I would advise you not to do so."

"But, Dominic!" she said helplessly. "It can't just disappear! It's—can't you see that if this is genuine, it's a landmark piece? It's quite different from anything that is known! Look! The face and the hands of the god are cast!" The casting technique, by adding a piece of cast-worked silver to the plate, gave a three-dimensional effect that was generally found only on pieces of the highest artistic merit. "I've never seen it done quite that way before, just the face and hands, and the nimbus. And they're gilded, too! It's stunning!"

But for historical purposes, the most astounding thing was the unmistakable shape of the figure's nimbus, and the sacrifice he was performing. Where on royal plates of a similar type each king's individual crown was pictured, this figure had the sun-ray shape of long, narrow triangles radiating from his head. It could be no one but Mithra, the god of light. It was unquestionable. Jasmin began to laugh in a kind of helpless joy. "Unbelievable," she said. "Absolutely unbelievable. If it's a forgery the artist is a magician."

"Is it a forgery?" Parton asked.

Jasmin carefully picked it up. "You'll need a better expert than me. I'm completely thrown. The problem with completely new styles like this is that there is nothing you can properly compare it to. Oh, I wish Professor Hazlett could see it!"

"I don't believe there's much chance of its being a forgery," the collector said. "The source that has offered it to me is ... shall I say, very reliable."

She was sure he meant that he had some corrupt Iranian government official in his pocket. Jasmin closed her eyes. Oh, if this were real! If this were the real thing! How could she let it disappear forever, being sold who knew where? She would have to notify someone. She would phone Ben in

Berlin when she got home. He would know what she could and couldn't do.

"Turn it over," Dominic ordered her softly.

Mesmerized, she lifted the plate and turned it over. On the centre bottom, just visible between the pockmarks of corrosion, was a line of squiggles. "That's Pahlavi," she whispered. "It's genuine. It's got to be. Dominic, the thing is worth a million pounds. In an auction..."

"It will not come to auction, or, at least, not public auction. These days the risks are too great. And I'm not going to risk that amount of money."

She bent over the inscription while he spoke. "Where's my magnifying glass?" she muttered, and realized then that, today of all days, she had left her bag in the sitting room. Even if he left her alone she could not photograph it. He handed her his own glass and she bent over the inscription.

"I didn't know you read Pahlavi," said Dominic, in some surprise.

"No one who studies with Professor Hazlett gets away without knowing something of everything," she said with a smile. "This is epigraphic, not cursive, and must have an early date...." She bent over the glass, carefully examining the letters, right to left. Aloud, she read out, "'...w...h...r...m...' two letters almost obliterated here...'d'...obliterated...'t.' These numbers below will be the weight of silver." She looked up. "Ohrmazd-dad, if I'm reading it correctly. It's a known name—it means, more or less, Gift of the Wise Lord. There's at least one Sassanian seal bearing that name."

Dominic looked at her admiringly. "I had no idea you had this skill. You really are something very special, Jasmin." He laughed. "I thought you'd be different from all the others, and you should be. But I suppose, when it comes to sex, brains just don't count."

"What on earth are you talking about?" she asked, frowning.

"Oh, my dear—" he lifted a hand "—ignore me. I'm just a little sore about my judgment. My money was on your *not* sleeping with Ben, but I should have known better. Of course, I suspected I was on a losing streak at your wonderful party, so when he rang me all cock-a-hoop, I shouldn't have been surprised, or disappointed. But I confess I was."

When he finished speaking there was a long silence in the room. Then, forced to make some reply, she said, "Are you telling me that Ben Bredon had a bet with you on whether I would sleep with him? I don't believe it!"

"No, no, no," said Dominic hastily. "No, my bet was with someone else entirely. We've watched Ben's career with his graduate students, you know, for a few years now. We make little bets with each other, that's all it is. The money's token, of course. I've always bet on Ben before, and I've always won. This time I took the negative, but my friend said Ben had too good a record by this time. She bet you would." He paused, and then said apologetically, as though made aware of it for the first time, "I'm afraid it doesn't reflect very well on either of us."

Jasmin had the sudden certainty that the friend he was referring to was Winifred Knowle, and in that moment she hated them both with a heat that was like fever.

"If Ben Bredon told you he slept with me, he was lying," she said with cold hostility. Everything hurt, down to her fingertips.

He raised his hands palms outward, to pacify her. "Good God, of course he didn't!" Parton exclaimed. "Ben has more style than that! He would never breathe a word about a lady! No, it was entirely my own guesstimate of his mood. He's always rather cheerful when...well...when it's someone new. Forgive me, my dear, for thinking it was you. Peace?"

She looked blindly down at the radiant face of the god on the plate. "Peace," she said flatly. She wanted to think of nothing, feel nothing. And, like an animal, she wanted to hide her hurt from his gaze. "Can I get to work, please?"

she said, fixing on the plate as her only spar in a deadly sea. "Would you mind if I took a photograph of this?"

He only laughed. Jasmin bit her lip. What a stupid thing to ask. Of course he wasn't going to let her photograph it. She said, "I must take some notes. Let me get my notebook." She looked up as Parton hesitated. "I've got to take notes, Dominic! I've got to know it existed! I've got to remember the details!"

"My dear," he said sadly, "I'm afraid that is precisely what you must forget. The people who are selling this would, shall we say, take it very amiss if they thought a record of any kind had been made of this plate before they got their money. As you said yourself, it is worth a very great deal. It has been offered to me for £400,000, but if a private auction can be arranged among a few important collectors, the price might go very much higher. If I were to show interest, I expect they would tell me to put in a bid. If word got out to the Iranian authorities in time to prevent any of this, my friends...well, let us say I value my skin and I hope you value yours."

She sat in stunned and battered silence. "Why did you call me? Why have you put me in this position?" Exactly the position, she reminded herself cruelly, that Ben had warned her she would get into if she associated with this terrible man.

"You're right. It was wrong of me. But it is, as you say, a landmark piece, and I was sure you would consider it very significant. I thought you would rather see it than not see it."

She must concentrate, or break down completely. "I can't use it, then? I can't even mention it in my thesis?"

Dominic examined his fingernails. "It would be unwise."

"And you thought I would want to be placed in this position," she said bitterly. Tears burned her eyes, but whether for the plate or for Ben she didn't want to think.

"Jasmin, for some people the most important thing is to *know*. Whether you feel it just now or not, you have that kind of mind. Consider a moment. If in five years' time I were to casually mention to you that I had had this plate in my hands and had not told you, what would be your reaction? Wouldn't you be terribly dismayed and angry?"

Maybe he was right. Her head was in turmoil; she had never felt so incapable of simple thinking. "All right, then, let me look at it properly, if I'm never going to see it again."

"You're being dramatic, my dear. There is every possibility that whoever buys it may be able to establish a secure provenance, and will publish it. It will probably be rather too late for inclusion in your thesis, but one never knows."

Ignoring this, she bent over the table and adjusted the lamp, but never in her life had she had such trouble focusing, making mental notes. Chased and engraved design, beveled edges of main outlines, *he doesn't love you*, mercury gilding of face, hands and nimbus, the eyes averted from the deed, just as on all the Roman statuary, *it was just another conquest for him, it meant nothing*, three . . . four different chasing tools of various sizes, but no calipers to be sure . . . Methodically, she turned the plate over again. Centering mark on the back, early Pahlavi inscription . . . Her eyes burning, her heart sick, as minutely as she could, Jasmin examined the treasure of a great empire now fallen—a treasure found by thieves, smuggled out of its proper home with the collusion of a corrupt official whose job it undoubtedly was to protect his people's heritage, about to be sold into the hands of some wealthy person who cared for nothing except possession and self. . . .

On that scale, a university lecturer who did nothing worse than screw around with his students just didn't measure at all. When you thought of it, it just didn't count.

# Chapter 15

Jasmin got the car halfway up Piccadilly before the tears came. The streets were jammed, there wasn't a parking place to be seen, but if she drove blind she would hit a pedestrian—in Piccadilly at this hour they jumped out anywhere. At last she was able to pull into a bus stop, laid her head and arms on the steering wheel, and the flood came.

If it had been only a week, it might have been less overwhelming. But these were the pent-up tears of five years, and it was as though a river ran out her eyes. "A fiery heart, tears flowing," as the Persian poet says, "night's sorrow, dawn's lament."

She didn't hear the tapping on her window, so the young bobby banged on the roof. "We've got a live one 'ere," he said to his partner.

Jasmin lifted her head and saw the face peering in at her. She rolled down the window. "Yes?" she said.

When he saw her face he changed his estimate: not drunk after all. "You all right, miss? 'Ere, Bella?" he called to his partner, standing on the passenger side. "She's crying," he said helplessly.

Bella strode around the car with feminine authority, and he made way for her. "What's the trouble?" she asked Jasmin, half sympathetic, half suspicious of being conned.

Jasmin shook her head. "Nothing," she said. She hiccuped. At least the interruption had served to halt the tears. She wiped her cheeks with her hands. "Nothing at all." She hiccuped again.

"Man trouble," said the policewoman to her partner in a succinct aside. To Jasmin, she said, "Right, look, you can't stop here, love, you're at a bus stop. Can you drive?"

"Yes," said Jasmin, "I'm all right now." Before they could say any more she rolled up the window, put the car in gear and eased past the two officers out into the stream of traffic. That was it, wasn't it? It might seem extraordinary to her, but to anyone else it was the same old story. It was just man trouble.

Inside her own apartment, in the comfort of known surroundings, her brain cooled a little. It might not be true. A mind that loved scandal was capable of producing scandal where none existed, or half the newspapers in London would be out of business, after all. Jasmin took off her coat, strode into the sitting room, and picked up the phone.

If she had got through to Ben immediately, probably she would have blurted out her doubts and questions without thinking, and so got her answer. But the hotel in Berlin didn't answer, and her confidence diminished with every second that she had to wait. What was she going to say to him? On what ground was she now going to demand an accounting of his past sexual history? And how could he answer her? If Dominic were right, it would be unspeakably humiliating, however Ben tried to put it. If Dominic were wrong…would he feel she was trying to force him into some kind of declaration?

"Hotel Stadts—" she heard, and hung up. She would wait until he returned. It wasn't possible to have this conversation over the phone.

Under her hand, the phone rang. A jolt of adrenaline made her heart race uncomfortably as she lifted the receiver, but it was Andrea. They had scarcely talked since the party, and Andrea wanted to discuss the party and Christmas—and, of course, Ben.

"So, you're getting serious with Ben," she said after a few minutes.

"They usually do, I understand," said Jasmin, unable to help herself.

"Who?"

"Ben's students." She didn't want to talk about it now, she wanted to think first. But she was not in control.

"Ahhh," said Andrea sympathetically. "Really?"

"You don't know anything about it, by any chance?"

"What has happened, Jasmin?"

"I've been told Ben makes a point of sleeping with his graduate students," she said, and felt tears start again. "People apparently already know I'm one of his successes."

Andrea swore. "That's terrible! Who told you this?"

Jasmin avoided answering her. "Do you think he...sleeps with everyone he supervises?"

"Who has he supervised?"

Jasmin had been asking herself that, and she didn't know the answer. As an undergraduate, she had had no idea who the postgraduate students were in the Central Asia Department, and over the past two years no one had been encouraged to talk to her about Ben Bredon. She remembered seeing a Muslim woman in a headscarf going in and out of his office from time to time. She was surprised now that she had noticed it, because she thought she was entirely ignoring Ben Bredon in those days.

"I have no idea," she said.

"Look," said Andrea reasonably. "It's just the kind of thing that happens. Probably Ben *has* been involved with other students before you. It would be surprising if he hadn't. That doesn't mean it meant anything. But you're different, aren't you?"

Jasmin found herself clutching at this straw. "Am I?" she asked.

"Well, look how much you hated him. You were so loyal to Professor Hazlett, and so suspicious of Ben."

She *was* remembering it, with a curious sense of shifting realities, as though she'd been dreaming and were now waking up. The reality was, she had always believed Ben disliked her. "What's your point?" she asked.

"Well, you two didn't just fall into bed, did you? I mean, he had to make it happen. You were always saying how much you hated him. He took a huge emotional risk. I think that means you're special to him."

Jasmin heard the words, but in her heart they said something entirely different from what Andrea intended. Suddenly, she saw it all with extraordinary clarity. Of course he had made it happen. She had been a challenge to his ego. She had hated him, and let the whole school know. Now she had slept with him, and no doubt the whole school would know that, too. No matter what the result of their intellectual differences, he had won their personal war.

Doggedly, her brain pursued this line. Maybe it was even worse than this. Maybe making love to her had been a deliberate attempt to get under her guard. She had no real idea how deep Ben's antagonism to Professor Hazlett went. Could she maintain her intellectual independence if she was involved with him? Would her loyalty to Professor Hazlett survive?

Jasmin began to shiver uncontrollably. What a fool she had been.

She refused to cry anymore. Instead, she went into her study, took out her notebook, and began to make a sketch

of the Mithra plate from memory. It wasn't easy, but she
was glad of that. She needed something to engage her mind
fully, to keep her emotions at bay. She made meticulous
notes of all the details of craftsmanship she could remember.

Then she sat back and wondered what to do. She couldn't
ask Ben about this now. Could she ask Daniel Hazlett? She
remembered how her own heart had beat when she saw the
miraculous plate, when Dominic had been telling her it
would be dangerous to cross the people trying to sell the
plate. Could she risk making her professor's heart beat like
that?

Should she call the police? Just phone Scotland Yard and
ask for the Art and Antiquities Squad? Did the Art and
Antiquities Squad even deal with cases of smuggling? She
could phone and ask; it would be easy enough to find out
who did.

Where was her duty? Having been put in the position of
knowing about the plate involuntarily, was she morally
obliged to risk her life by notifying the authorities? Her life,
and Dominic's, since it would be clear where the leak had
occurred. Was property ever more valuable than life?

What if the plate were not even genuine? She had seen
with her own eyes that Dominic Parton was routinely offered what she thought were forgeries. If it was a forgery
that couldn't be exposed, it would be better off in a private
collection, not messing up the record. Should she risk her
life to save some collector half a million pounds?

Oh, if only she could *think!* If only she could ask someone . . . if she could ask Ben . . . but she would not ask Ben.
She could not talk to Ben now.

The phone rang. Jasmin leaped for it, and then stopped.
She stood up and went out into the sitting room and stared
at the phone there with her eyes wide while the answering
machine picked up the call.

"It's Ben again, Jasmin. I'm sorry I missed your call. It's
eleven o'clock now, so I won't try again tonight. Ring when

you get in, if you're not too tired. I'll ring tomorrow morning, and if that fails, I'll be on the five o'clock into Heathrow tomorrow night." There was a pause, and then, "Goodnight," he said, as though he might have wanted to say something else but thought better of it, and hung up.

Jasmin put out the lights, turned off the heat and crawled into bed. She did not dream, but in the morning her pillow was wet.

She had to study the plate more fully, that was the answer. She had to decide as best *she* could whether it was genuine. Then she would know better what to do. Last night she didn't seem to have absorbed anything of what she saw. She had remembered the technical details, but her judging capacity had simply been in abeyance.

"Dominic?" she said. "Sorry to phone you so early, but you said you had the plate for two days."

"Yes," he said, as if he had been expecting her call.

"Can I come round again? I—if I'm never going to see it again, I'd really like another look."

For some reason she thought she felt him smiling. "Yes, that's all right, my dear. You come round for lunch. Shall we say, one o'clock?"

She didn't want lunch under his scrutiny, but she wasn't going to quibble. Jasmin put down the phone and then went and hunted up an old address book.

"Rena," she said, when she had dialed a long-forgotten number. "It's Jasmin Shaw. Do you remember me? I'm Jake Shaw's sister."

"Jasmin! Goodness, yes, of course I remember you! It's been an age. How are you? How's Jake?"

"We're fine. Jake was a bit ill over Christmas, but he's gone back now. He's all right. He had a narrow escape, but he thinks he's a cat."

"In November, right?"

"Pardon?"

"Did he have the narrow escape in November? The last few days of November?"

"I don't know," said Jasmin. "Recently, anyway."

"Yes, I had a dream . . . I nearly called you. Funny, isn't it?"

Jasmin thought, *Has the world always been full of broken hearts? I didn't notice till it happened to me?* Rena still in love with Jake, Jake, meanwhile, in love with someone else . . . and who was that unknown woman in love with? "Yeah, funny," she said. "Look, Rena, I need a favor. A big favor, and you might not be able to do it. Could I come and see you?"

"Sure, I'm pretty free this week. What day?"

Jasmin bit her lip, and pressed on. "Well, right now, if you could." There was a silence. "If you're busy, please don't worry about it."

"No. No, you come round. Do you remember the address?"

Absently, Jasmin nodded. "Thanks. I really appreciate it," she said. "I'll be there in half an hour, depending on traffic."


"Let me take this slowly. You've got to take a picture with someone sitting right there and your life's in danger if he notices," said Rena.

"It's not as cut and dried as that. That's only a distant possibility . . . if other people find out."

"Just out of curiosity, who might want to kill you? I mean, what group of people might find out?"

"Well . . . smugglers. Iranian smugglers. I think," Jasmin admitted reluctantly.

Rena closed her eyes. "Oh, fine. Oh, terrific. These are not, correct me if I'm wrong, but these are not incompetent people, right? I mean . . . Jasmin, I can't help you with this! I'm just a photographer. I have no idea how this kind of thing works."

"You must know someone, Rena. You've got to. It'll only be worse if you don't help, because my camera's too big."

Jake's old friend sat silently a moment. Then her eyebrows went up and she shrugged. "Well, at least you didn't say Libyans. There's some comfort in that, I guess." She shook her head, and smiled with a kind of grim humor. "Don't you ever tell Jake I helped you. That is, of course, if you survive."

"They don't make them any smaller than this," said Rena's friend. "In fact, they don't make them quite like this any more. This is the best spy camera made. Well, the best that was available publicly. I don't say Q didn't have something better for James from time to time." He grinned, holding it up, a small shape about a half inch square and two and a half inches long.

"Wow," said Jasmin. "They really exist."

"Oh, yes, they exist. They were manufactured pretty well throughout the Cold War, and very useful they proved, I'm sure. Do you want black and white or color?"

"What sort of detail will I get?"

"If it's detail you're after, I'll give you the real spy film." Rena's friend suited the action to the words, pulling a box from a shelf over his head, tearing it open and dropping a tiny 16 mm film in the little camera. "This is the film they use for documents." He flicked it into position, snapped the camera shut and wound the film on. "All right, you're camera ready, as they say. You've got eighteen prints there, so you can waste a few practicing. You've got an eight-inch focus. My best advice is not to get too complicated, coughing into a hankie or anything like that. You don't want to drop it. Just pull it out of your pocket when you get a chance, and fire away."

"Thank you," said Jasmin. "Is it...if I lose it, how much do I owe you?"

He smiled at her. "Don't worry about it. If you lose it, come and let me shoot you for a session or two." He touched her cheek and turned her head gently to the side, looking at her. "Fabulous face," he said.

There was a self-assurance in his touch which reminded her suddenly of Ben's. It had been passion, not professional expertise, that gave Ben that firmness, but it reminded her all the same. Passion, not love. Jasmin's eyes filled with tears, and she smiled. "Okay," she said.

"Please don't do it," said Rena. "It's too much of a risk, and you are no expert. Please, Jasmin."

"I'll see," said Jasmin.

"It's Ben," said the voice from her answering machine. "It's nine o'clock and I'm going down to the conference now. Try you later."

"It's Ben. It's twelve-thirty and I'll be leaving for the airport after lunch. I'll see you when I get in tonight."

*No, you won't,* thought Jasmin.

"You won't mind if I search you, I hope," said Dominic. He smiled without warmth. "Sorry not to be more trusting, but I really couldn't afford the consequences if such trust were misplaced."

She shrugged, smiling. "No, go ahead," she said. The emotional cold storage she was in gave her an air of bored innocence. She stood impassive while his hands ran over her body.

"May I look in your bag, my dear?"

"Sure," she said. "What are you looking for? A gun?"

Dominic grinned. "I must say, I didn't think of that. Perhaps I underestimated you. No, I'm looking for a camera."

"Oh," she said. While he pawed futilely through her bag she lifted a hand under her glasses and rubbed her eyes.

Dominic frowned. "Are you ill?"

"I have a bit of a headache," Jasmin said. "I think I'm coming down with the flu." The lie came easily to her. Or maybe it was true. That might account for the way she felt—some horrible new flu virus. "I hope you don't catch anything from me."

"Oh, I'm immune. Haven't had a bug for years."

She smiled coldly, reaching for her bag. "You're lucky."

"You won't mind if we leave your bag out here? I have searched it, but I feel..."

Jasmin shrugged. "Whatever you want."

She leaned an elbow on the table and her head on her hand, toying with her earring as she bent earnestly over the plate. "It really is fabulous," she said. *Whiiish.* It was soundless, like a whisper next to her ear. "I wish Professor Hazlett could see it, he'd be able to make a much better judgment than I." *Whiiish.* Eight inches. Was she measuring it correctly?

"So do I," said Parton insincerely. *Whiiish. Whiiish.* Absently she wondered why he didn't mean that. *Whiiish.* It was best while he was speaking: impossible that he should hear with his own voice in his ears.

"I wish you'd buy it, Dominic," she said. She turned it over. "And this inscription just puts the icing on it. Would you pass me the magnifying glass?" *Whiiish. Whiiish. Whiiish.*

Her heart was going like a ratchet at a football game. "If you get less nervous as you go on, you can keep taking pictures," David had said. "If you get more nervous, it's best to stop and stick with what you've got. It just depends on your own makeup, and with no experience, you'll just have to read it as you go." She was getting more nervous. *Whiiish.*

Jasmin lifted her head from her hand and reached for the magnifying glass. Her hair fell down over her shoulder. "Of course, if they cleaned this a little, they'd get a better reading, but a lot of people don't like to disturb the patina in any way. Probably this says *nafshu* and the weight, and those missing letters in the name might show up." She was even more nervous now she'd stopped, but he seemed to notice nothing unusual. "But I doubt it'll be possible without some disturbance of the patina."

He looked at his watch. "I'm sorry to give you so little time, Jasmin," he said, and she took the hint, laying down the glass and sitting back. She was relieved, but she made a move of disappointment.

"I'm very grateful, Dominic," she said. "It was really important to see it again when the shock had worn off, I think. Last night it was just too overwhelming."

"And what do you think? Is it genuine?"

She shook her head. "I still don't know. But if it is, another piece will certainly turn up someday, and then I'll remember this one, and be a better judge of *that* one." She grinned at him and got to her feet.

"If you'll just wait outside, my dear." He began to wrap the Mithra plate, and she glanced down at it one more time.

"Of course."

She went out, but she did not wait. She took her coat from the closet and picked up her bag and went out. She didn't care how rude he thought her. She was getting out while the luck was on her side.


"You did it?" shrieked Rena, doing a little dance. "Jasmin, that's fabulous! Let's have a look! Oh, I hope it worked!"

"So do I," said Jasmin feelingly. "I've never been so terrified in my life. I would make a dreadful spy."

"Take off your coat. Where is it?"

She meant the camera, not the coat. "Still in my ear," said Jasmin. "I drove straight here."

In the end they had hung it from a silver ear wire and she had worn it as an earring, pulling all her hair over that shoulder, as she sometimes did, and counting on no more than that for concealment.

"Careful, careful," cried Rena, trying to disentangle it. "Golly, I hope your hair didn't get in the way!"

"So do I," said Jasmin. "So do I."

"It's going to take awhile to dry, if we want to be sure of getting no spots on the film," said Rena, turning on a low light. "I don't have the fastest equipment."

"That's okay," said Jasmin, in sudden decision. "Could I use a phone?"

"Sure, just outside the studio in the bedroom. You can be private there."

"This is Ben Bredon," said his recorded voice. "I'll call you back if you leave a message. After the tone."

*Beeeep.* "Hi, Ben, this is Jasmin. Sorry I haven't been able to take your calls. Ben—I don't want to see you for a while. I think what happened was a mistake. I'll see you at SAES when term starts. Sorry to do it this way, but I'd really rather not talk to you just at the moment."

"Fabulous!" said Rena, holding up the negative over a lamp. "They're just fabulous. Look at that. The clarity is very good. Right, let's get some prints."

It seemed unbelievable, after so much stress and excitement, that she should be driving through town with a brown paper envelope beside her on the seat, in the most ordinary way. Jasmin felt nervous and apprehensive, as though it had all been too easy. As though she ought not to go home.

Rationally she knew there could be no reason for such nerves. She shook her head and took her hand off the wheel to pat the pictures. Rena had been right; they were good shots. She'd be able to study the thing properly now. She might even take the pictures to Professor Hazlett. She would ask Gillian. She'd explain it all and ask whether his heart could stand it.

It was after seven and a very dark night by the time she pulled up in front of her home. Jasmin doused the lights and glanced up and down the street before she picked up the envelope and got out. She knew there was nothing to be afraid of. No one knew she had taken the photos; no one would be tailing her. No doubt she would shake the feeling once she got safely inside. She always felt safe in her apartment.

She had climbed the steps and opened the door before the figure came out of the shadows and up the steps behind her. She turned and gasped.

"Good evening, Jasmin," he said, and then she understood what she'd been afraid of. It was Ben, and he looked furious.

# Chapter 16

"Ben!" she cried, in a faltering voice.

"What's going on, Jasmin?" he asked tiredly. "What's the matter?"

He was inside the door now. She had lost her chance of shutting him out. "There's nothing wrong," she said. "Why are you here?"

He absorbed that in silence, looking at her in a way that unnerved her. His hair was wet and slicked back and his coat looked damp; it must have been raining. "I picked up your message from the airport," he said at last. "Where's Jake?"

"Jake?" The abrupt change of subject confused her.

He said, "The last time we talked, you were very worried about your brother's health, or don't you remember? For two days you've been incommunicado. I thought you must have taken him to the hospital. I've been calling every hospital in London trying to track you down. Then I get home to a message saying you don't want to see me. What's going on?"

She should have waited till he was home before she rang him. She might have predicted this would happen. "Jake got better. He went back yesterday." Was it only yesterday? "Two days ago," she amended. Jasmin shut the door and started up the stairs. As she turned at the half landing, she looked down at him. He had not followed her. He was watching her, his face shockingly grim, and a little thrill of fright went through her. *He's really angry,* she thought. It hadn't occurred to her that he would actually be angry.

"Are you inviting me up, Jasmin, or am I coming up uninvited?" he asked.

She did not want him near her. She did not want to explain in person. She wished he had phoned. Her hand on the railing, she paused, looking down. "I'd rather not talk about it, Ben," she said at last. "But if you feel you must, you can come up."

For an answer he started up the stairs after her. Jasmin unlocked her own door, keyed in the number of her alarm, and shrugged out of her coat. Not bothering to hang it, she tossed it on the chair that stood in the hall, and Ben followed suit with his battered trench coat.

She hesitated at the door to the kitchen. "Do you want a cup of coffee?"

"No," said Ben. "Would you like to explain to me why I got that phone message?"

She couldn't look at him. She said, shrugging, "Ben, I've said it before."

He swore. "You've said what before?"

"I've said that I didn't want to get involved with you."

He looked at her, his eyes glinting. "That was the time before last, remember?" he said, and his tone stung.

She said quietly, "I don't deny that I find you physically attractive, Ben—"

"Good," he interjected, but she ignored it.

"—But I do think... but I don't want to get personally involved with you while we're working together on my thesis."

"Why not?"

She bit her lip. "Isn't it obvious?"

"Not to me."

"Ben, we're . . . we have enough trouble as it is, trying to get along. Don't you think personal involvement will just make everything more complicated?" She knew the argument was weak. But she would be damned before she'd confess the truth—that she had fallen in love with him.

"That depends on the nature of the personal involvement," he began.

That was too close to the heart of her argument for comfort. Jasmin interrupted hastily, "No, it doesn't."

"You're sure of that."

She felt angry suddenly. Who was he to talk of the nature of the involvement, when only one option was on offer? Her anger gave her the courage to look at him at last. "Whatever the nature of the involvement, two things stand to happen, right?" she said. "If we break up in the middle of my work, my thesis will suffer."

"And?"

"And—" she took a breath "—if we continue, the nature of a romantic relationship is such that I will be much less likely to . . ."

"Go on," he urged as she paused. But it was the urging of someone who knew what he was going to hear. "Tell me about the nature of a romantic relationship."

She raised her head defiantly. "I'm more likely to see your side of the argument if we're lovers, aren't I?"

He smiled briefly, but not in friendliness. "I don't know," he said. "That depends on you. Or are you suggesting I might play subliminal tapes under your pillow at night?"

"You know what I mean!" she said hotly.

His anger abruptly flared out. "No, I do not know what you mean, if what you're saying is that a relationship with me will undermine your intellectual integrity! What the hell are you talking about?"

Partly what she was talking about was that she would be at a disadvantage in the relationship because she loved him, and to him she was one in a string. And the desire to try to please him might become uppermost in her work. But mostly what she was talking about was her fear of getting hurt, the worst hurt of her life. She was not walking into that with her eyes open, not if she could help it. And she would tell him any lie, if it would convince him to leave her alone.

"Ben," she said, "it was Christmas and we'd both had a lot to drink."

"Speak for yourself. I'd been on the road for five hours on nothing but bad coffee," he said with a glint of humor.

"All right, I'm speaking for myself. I was drunk, or nearly." It wasn't true. She'd been clearing up with the help of Shahdeen and Andrea for well over an hour, and they had drunk only decaffeinated coffee. "And I was half-asleep."

"And so you fell prey to my wicked wiles all against your pretty will," he finished for her.

"I don't say that," she said, flushing at his tone. "I wasn't unwilling. I told you I ... don't find you unattractive."

He whispered an explosive curse, shaking his head. "There's a compliment! So you weren't unwilling. And they say the English have the monopoly on milk and water emotions! You weren't unwilling. You've just thought better of it since."

"That's right," she said. "I'm sorry."

"I could, of course, arrange to get you drunk first, and then wait till you were half-asleep," he offered dryly.

"Ben, please ..."

"On the other hand, you weren't drunk in my office. What's your excuse there? 'Oh, Dr. Bredon, this is so unexpected?'"

She flushed. "It *was* unexpected."

"By me, maybe. By you, I'm beginning to think, it was not."

Jasmin gasped. "What?"

He leaned over her. "That was all you wanted, wasn't it? Just to see if you could? That's been the goal of all the little games of recent weeks?"

"What games?" she demanded, in angry bewilderment.

He laughed. "You just wanted to know if you could get that response out of me, is that it?"

"I *never* wanted that response out of you!" Jasmin shrieked in indignation. "Who do you think you are?"

"I think I'm the only one who didn't do sufficient homage to your green eyes," he said, and if she thought he had been aloof and detached before, his manner now required a whole new adjective. He was arctic, and his eyes were blue ice.

"That's a lie!" she cried. This was even worse than what she had feared. He hadn't even been moved by his own desire—only what he imagined was hers. And what he felt for her was contempt, the kind of contempt you feel for... Her stomach shriveled and curled with humiliation. "How can you say—when did I *ever*...?" She was nearly incoherent, so desperate was she now to hide from him. "I don't even *like* you! I hate you!" she cried, and in that terrible moment it was the truth.

Ben cursed again, so forcefully she started. "Right. Well, now we know where we stand." He turned, picked up his coat, and opened the door. He reached out a hand and covered her throat. "You live in the wrong era," he told her softly. "You should have been a *hetaera*." He meant the famous courtesans of ancient Greece. "The highest intellectual achievement, exquisite sexual skills... and the heart of a tart," he finished brutally. He ran his thumb over her full lips with the air of a connoisseur tasting wine. "You'll go far," he promised, and then he was gone.

# *Chapter 17*

One of the great benefits of being an academic and not a model was that she didn't have to work out every day of her life anymore. But working out was a way to stop thinking, and the next day, after a futile morning spent trying to concentrate on marking some of her students' essays, Jasmin went down to the Students' Union building, where she swam for two hours and then got on the machines and worked herself nearly into oblivion. Jasmin went for burn first, and then she went for utter exhaustion.

By the time she staggered home her muscles were jelly, and her mind couldn't have focused if a land mine went off under her. She watched television without taking anything in, and then fell into a heavy, undisturbed sleep, but it didn't seem to refresh her. The next day she went back to the gym for more. That afternoon she slept for two hours, got up aching in every cell, bought a bottle of wine and went to visit Andrea.

"You look worn out," said Andrea, in some shock. "What's the matter?"

"I'm worn out," said Jasmin. "I need alcohol. Can we open that, please?"

Andrea stood looking at her for a moment. "It didn't work out, *ja?*" she said sadly.

Jasmin was too exhausted for surprise. "No, it didn't work out," she replied, sinking onto the bed. Andrea had a bed-sitting-room with a small sofa, but Jasmin always ended up on the bed.

Andrea shook her head. "I'm really sorry. You know, he seems like a very nice man, your supervisor. Ben. I talked to him for a while at the party. He's a little shy, but..."

Jasmin felt an extreme reluctance to discuss Ben or any part of what had happened. "Did you?" she asked, without interest. "Please don't talk to me about him. I would be quite happy never to hear his name again."

"I don't think one bottle of wine is going to be enough," Andrea observed sagely, as she pulled the cork. "You'd better get really drunk, that's the cure."

"Oh, good. I'm glad someone has these pathways all pegged," said Jasmin. "What's the recommended dose, then?"

Andrea handed her a glass of wine and eyed her expertly. "Jasmin, you really look like hell," she said, in sudden concern, seeing a pallor she hadn't noticed before under her friend's pale skin, and gray beneath the puffy eyes. "What have you been doing to yourself?"

"A little healthy exercise is all," said Jasmin lightly. She took a gulp of the wine. "Ah, yes, Doctor, I feel the cure is imminent. What are we doing tonight? Shall we just sit here and go quietly blotto, or are we going to go on a pub crawl?"

"We're going to Shahdeen's," Andrea said, surprised.

"We are?"

"It's New Year's Eve, Jasmin."

"Is it really? Oh, God, how wonderful! I can get absolutely blind, stinking drunk and it will be acceptable on seasonal grounds? What luck I do have! What a brilliant idea! I may patent this. Get into a mess at Christmas, and get it out of your system on New Year's! Pure genius, as the man says!''

Andrea was unmoved by this eloquence. She stood looking down at Jasmin for a moment, and said at last, "When did you eat last?"

"What do you mean?"

"Food, I mean food. When did you last eat anything that might be called food?"

"I haven't the least idea," said Jasmin airily. "Anyway, I'm used to not eating. Do you know how much a working model gets to eat on a daily basis? I gained ten pounds in six months after starting university, and that was just eating like a starling instead of a sparrow!"

Andrea went to the kitchen unit and buttered a piece of bread. Returning to Jasmin's side, she nipped the wineglass from her hand and gave her the bread. "Eat that first," she ordered.

"It wouldn't hurt me to lose a bit of weight," said Jasmin. But she obediently munched the bread.

"It will hurt you to get terribly drunk on an empty stomach and throw up all over Shahdeen's carpet," Andrea pointed out mildly. "I'm going to feed you, Jasmin. You can drink this now—" as Jasmin finished the piece of bread she handed her back the glass "—but I am going to make you something to eat, and you have to eat it."

"I'm sorry to be so much trouble," said Jasmin. She drank some of the wine and, dropping her head back on the mound of pillows, looked up at the ceiling. "He said I threw myself at him. He wouldn't have touched me otherwise."

Andrea swore in shock. "Did he really *say* that? What did he say?"

"He said he was the only man around not interested in me, and I couldn't stand that fact. He said I had the heart of a tart."

"God, what a bastard!"

"Yeah, well, whose fault is it? I knew he was a bastard before..." She shrugged. "I've got nobody to blame."

"He didn't have to say that."

"No, but that's men, isn't it? When they're crossed they go for the jugular."

"What do you mean, when they're crossed? How did you cross him?"

"You know what? I don't want to talk about it. I really don't ever want to talk about him or think about him or see him again."

"Jasmin, he's your supervisor. You have to see him again."

Jasmin nodded profoundly, and raised a forefinger. "That's why I'm getting drunk," she said.

The next day she was an utter physical wreck, as well as having the kind of headache only cheap wine can give, and she crawled home at noon to fall into a hot bath. In spite of the damage to her body, she actually felt human again. Her brain was suffering, but at least it functioned. And it was time she got back to work.

The flat seemed dusty and untended, and prior to settling down to marking, Jasmin opened windows, got out the vacuum cleaner and began dismantling the tree, packing away all the ornaments. When she got to the gold rings, she snorted. "Oh, no, you never made a move on me," she said aloud cynically, "oh, not at all." She nearly threw them in the trash, but stopped herself. By next year they would mean absolutely nothing to her. They meant nothing to her now. So she packed them away with the rest.

When she came to the little silver plate, she held it up by the window to examine it in daylight. It really was lovely. Suddenly Jasmin gasped and lowered the plate, looking toward the hall. "Oh, my—!" she whispered. She ran out into the hall, looking around.

Her trench coat was still lying on the chair where she had dropped it days ago. She had been wearing her tracksuit and a bomber jacket since. Jasmin snatched up the coat, and breathed with relief as the paper envelope fell from the chair underneath it and dropped to the floor. The black-and-white photos slipped out and fanned across the polished, stripped-pine floor: the Mithra plate.

How could she have forgotten so thoroughly? Jasmin dropped her coat and bent to pick up the pictures. They had come out well, considering the conditions she was operating under. What an amazing piece it was.

But she had left it too late. Dominic would have given the plate back to whoever had been offering it to him over forty-eight hours ago. By now they'd have approached someone else, perhaps even sold it.

Whatever had happened, the Mithra plate might now be anywhere. Anywhere in the world.

"I'm afraid it's gone, my dear. Did you want to see it again?"

"Yes. Do you think it's possible?"

"Not at all," he said firmly. "I don't intend to tell anyone I showed it to you, and if you are wise, you will adopt the same course. However, I do have something new which you might like to see. Nothing so world-shaking as the plate, of course."

"If it's stolen property, I'd rather give it a miss," she said dryly.

"My dear, you mustn't let it make you bitter."

"Goodbye, Dominic."

"And he told you the item was stolen," said the well-spoken voice at the end of the phone.

"He as good as said it had been taken out of the ground and smuggled out of the country with the help of a corrupt official," said Jasmin.

"Well, in that case, to answer your question, it will depend on what the country was, and what that country's antiquities laws are. If all antiquities still in the ground are considered the property of the state, as is the case in some countries, then the item is stolen under the laws of that country and is considered stolen under British law.''

''Oh, God.''

''However, what often happens in such cases is that the country doesn't even know yet that the item has been taken. In which case it will not figure on the Art Loss Register, and unless it surfaces somewhere, will never be claimed by the government,'' said Detective Sergeant Stephen.

''And what is my position, then?'' asked Jasmin.

''Well, it's possible you might be guilty of what is called assisting in the retention or disposal of stolen goods. However, if only one person knows that you saw it, and you no longer know where the item is, it's your word against his, isn't it?''

''Should I come and see you?''

''You can certainly send us the details of the item, if you like. But if it hasn't been reported stolen, and you don't know where it is, there's not much we can do, is there?''

Sometimes she felt like a motherless child. To be abandoned by her male guiding figure twice in the space of a few months was, psychologically, very reminiscent of the abandonment she had suffered as a nine-year-old, when her father died. Jasmin felt raw and sore, empty and alone. A terrible responsibility for which she was unprepared seemed to fall on her from a great height. When she was nine, it had seemed to fall all the way from heaven—*why* had God taken him away? Now it was only from the fourth floor of the SAES building, but she responded with the same aching misery. She was not really unprepared for responsibility; many people, she knew, completed their Ph.D. work with far less supervision than she was used to. And she knew she could do it without the weekly or twice-weekly meetings she was used to with Ben Bredon. It was just that the transition period hurt.

And, of course, that picture of her state also provided a very good rationale to explain why she had imagined she was in love with Ben in the first place. She had been looking for a replacement father figure, and sex had simply intruded into the equation. Naturally she had confused all that with love.

The logic was impeccable, but sadly, it didn't stop her missing him. And she did not merely miss him during those hours, twice a week, when she would have been seeing him. She missed him twenty-four hours a day. She missed him over morning coffee. She missed him when she came out of her study after an evening's work, as though he had always been there to talk to. She missed him in bed, sometimes waking deep in the night because she had turned over and reached for him, and he was not there.

All this, perhaps, went unaccounted for in the "father figure" explanation of her life, but Jasmin, in defiance of good scholarly method, was sticking to her theory in the teeth of the evidence.

It was made worse by the fact that she could have gone to see him at any time. She knew Ben would not refuse to work with her. In the second week of the new term, she had been caught in the same elevator with him. They were not alone, but still Jasmin would have stepped out when he got in if she hadn't been squashed in a corner by the press.

Ben didn't see her at first. When he did, a look of indifference amounting almost to distaste came over his face. She knew he had to remind himself he was her supervisor and therefore had a certain responsibility to speak to her. Over the heads of the people separating them he observed, "I haven't seen you since term started."

"No," she agreed, trying to sound indifferent.

"When will you be coming?" he asked.

When circumstance forced her, not a moment before, but she couldn't say that. Or when she could look at him and not want anything more from him than academic opinion. "Can I, uh, let you know when I need to see you?"

"All right. How are you getting on?"

"It's going well," she said.

He was utterly self-possessed. He was even more indifferent to her than in her first year. No one in the elevator would have guessed there had been anything at all personal between them. No wonder she'd heard no rumors of his liaisons with his other postgrads during the past five years. But, of course, the case was not the same, Jasmin reminded herself; presumably he had wanted to sleep with the others. But she had thrown herself at him.

She knew she would be forced to go and see him soon. She was lying when she said it was going well. Her chapter on Mithraism had been well advanced before Christmas, and even with all her emotional troubles she should have been able to get it into some sort of order for her seminar early in February. But the Mithra plate had completely thrown her. She could not use the plate in any way in her work, and yet, knowing it existed, and that the theory of Mithraic symbolism had such support, she was determined to find this kind of evidence elsewhere. It *must* exist. If plates such as the Mithra plate had been made—and such an artifact could not have existed entirely on its own—somehow, somewhere, there must be a resonance of it, something she could use.

It disrupted the entire course of her work to date, destroyed its focus, like an avalanche falling across the path of a river and forcing a hundred little rivulets to search for a way over inhospitable terrain. She knew this, knew it would have been better for her never to have seen the plate, and yet she could not do what she knew she ought, and simply pretend that she had never seen it, that it did not exist.

At last she went to see him.

"I'm not going to be ready for this seminar, Ben," she said, standing just inside his office door.

There was a moment of stillness as they looked at each other, which she could afterward never be certain had happened. "Come in and sit down," Ben said at last.

Leaving the door open, she crossed the office and sat. Ben glanced over her shoulder at the door, but the expression on his face didn't change in any way.

"Now," he said.

"I won't be ready to deliver this chapter next week," she said. "I'd like to cancel."

He paused a moment as this sank in. "Jasmin," he said, "you were over halfway there a month ago."

"I know, but there are things I still haven't found, and it hasn't come together."

"It doesn't have to be in final shape, you know. You're expected to present a work in progress."

"I can't do it. It's not there yet."

Ben took a breath and rubbed his cheek. "You'd better bring it to me and let me have a look at it."

"That's what I'm telling you! There's nothing to show you! I need more time!"

"Jasmin, it had a rough shape to it a month ago. Even if you've done nothing since, hard work over the next ten days will bring it up to a level where you can read it as a working paper.'

"I've thrown away that shape. I didn't like it. I'm telling you, Ben, I don't have anything."

"You've thrown it away. What have you put in its place?"

She sighed. "Nothing. That's what I'm telling you. I've gone back to..."

"To what?" Ben asked, mystified. "What did you have before?"

"It's not anything I had before. I mean, I've gone back to square one. I'm redoing the whole chapter."

"Why?"

"I'm not sure. It wasn't right. It didn't go far enough."

At this, his eyebrows went up. "As I recall it, much of the substance of our discussion of this chapter centered on the fact that I thought it went too far for the evidence you had. What new evidence have you found that makes you think you can go further?"

There was the rub. She should have known he would put his finger right on the problem. "Nothing," she said. "I just feel . . ."

"Are you telling me you've thrown out two months of solid work for nothing? For a chimera?"

"It didn't feel right," she said mulishly.

There was a long pause. At last, in a tone of great reluctance, he asked, "Has this anything to do with what has happened between us?"

"No," she said. "I knew you would think so, and that's why I left it so long to tell you. No. It's something else entirely."

"What, exactly?"

She couldn't bear to leave him thinking what he thought. To hell with it. "I've . . . come across something that supports the theory, but it's . . . I have to find other ways of showing it."

"Goddamn it. Dominic Parton," said Ben, in level tones. "What did he show you?"

"I can't say. Anyway, you're wrong," she said, caught out like a child.

"Jasmin, I warned you this would happen. The man is not to be trusted, and neither is anything he shows you. You don't know what you're getting into. What the devil was it you saw?"

She sat silent.

"And you're not going to be allowed to publish it. That's it, is it? So now you're on a wild-goose chase after something that will give you the same support." He swore. "I don't know what game he's playing, Jasmin, but I know that you had better keep out of his way. You are now in a nearly impossible position. However, the way out is clear—you've got to throw it away. You have to operate on the basis that you have never seen whatever it was, at least for the present, and get this chapter in order."

"I've tried that. My brain won't work that way."

He snorted. "For a woman who wants to be told she's brilliant, you seem to have an extremely limited idea of your own capacities. Of course your brain will do whatever you tell it," he said roughly. "It's called discipline. Now go and put that chapter into some kind of shape, and come and show me something in two days." He pulled his diary toward him. "I'll see you Thursday at two," he said.

It was in that moment that the hope died. In truth, since the holiday, Jasmin had been nursing a secret hope that it really had meant something. Now, suddenly, she saw the strength of his indifference, and her heart began to search out the pathways of defense that it had used before. She must learn to hate him again, or die.

*Chapter 18*

"Have you looked at the Sotheby's catalog?" asked Professor Hazlett.

Jasmin shook her head. She knew there was an auction of Iranian antiquities coming up, but she had other preoccupations at the moment and had forgotten. She was a little surprised that it was happening so soon.

"I get an advance copy of any catalog of this type," Daniel Hazlett explained. "It's on the table behind you. You might take a look at page thirteen. I think you'll find it interesting."

"Oh," said Jasmin, as she flipped through the glossy pages and stopped at the photo of a silver plate. "It's that Bahram Gur plate Dominic showed me."

"Yes, I thought it must be. The chances of two plates substantially the same surfacing at the same time is rather remote. But you see that the vendor has found someone to accept it as genuine."

Jasmin suppressed a pang of guilt. She had warned Dominic he should get another opinion. "It's a very dark photo," she commented after a moment, holding it to the watery sunlight that was, with some difficulty, forcing its way through thick cloud to give London some semblance of daylight. "Why is it so dark? You can hardly see the engraving."

"It's the way the patina sometimes photographs."

Jasmin, reading the descriptive text, shook her head. "Oh, how strange! It can't be the same plate, Professor, because it says this one has an inscription. There was no inscription on the plate I saw."

"Of course, it's not always easy to see an inscription, especially where there's a heavy patina like that one. You may have overlooked it in one examination."

But she was sure she had not. "It just can't be the same plate," she said, frowning and trying to make out the design.

"It's possible they cleaned a little of the patina and revealed the inscription, of course."

"The patina is all wrong, too. The one I saw just didn't have a patina heavy enough to conceal any inscription...and yet, as far as I can see, the design is nearly identical."

"Well, it might be worth your while to go down and have a look at it," said Hazlett. "I usually go and view any major auction before the sale date, and no doubt, arrangements could be made for you to go on my behalf." He said no more, but Jasmin could see his mind ticking over behind the level gaze.

Jasmin met the look, and returned it. "Yes, all right," she said.

"Dominic," she said. "Have you seen the Sotheby's catalog?"

Parton shrugged. "Possibly, my dear. Which one?"

"The auction coming up in Asian antiquities. Have you looked at this?"

He set down his glass, reached for the catalog, and looked obediently at the picture she was indicating. Then he looked back up at her, and not for the first time, she was struck with the peculiar metallic shallowness of his gaze. "Yes?" he asked.

"That's the plate you showed me back in October. The first plate I looked at for you."

"Is it, my dear?"

"Dominic, I've been down to have a look at it. It's the same plate, and it's been changed. The patina has been— improved. The shape has been altered slightly. And there's an inscription on it, in Pahlavi, that was never there before."

"It begins to sound as though it's not the same piece at all," said Dominic.

"I've seen it. I've held it. It's the same piece. But someone has altered it, and they've done so bearing in mind the criticisms I made to you that night."

"My dear, it has always been my understanding that patina is produced by great age." He handed her back the catalog. "If this plate has a patina that makes the experts accept its age, how can it be the same piece you condemned as being too young only a few months ago?"

She looked at him for a long, considering moment. "Well, for a start, they might have put it in a bucket of urine," she said baldly. "That's a pretty good way to falsify a patina."

He raised his eyebrows. "But, my dear, if it were so easy, why did you yourself cite the lack of patina as a feature tending to prove lack of age?"

She was getting more and more certain. His manner was entirely too casual, too cynical, as though they both knew some dirty secret. She said slowly, "Because, whereas the *presence* of patina doesn't necessarily prove age, not many people are stupid enough, in this day and age, to clean the patina off an antiquity. Therefore, the *lack* of it is evidence of a recent date."

He sipped his drink again. He was completely unmoved. "And why are you telling me all this, my dear?"

"I think that's obvious."

His eyebrows went up for a moment of suspended animation. Then they came down. "Ah, perhaps it is."

"So, what's going on, Dominic?"

He set his glass down very carefully, watching it as he did so. "My dear," he said at last, and that strange, flat gaze met hers firmly, "you are faced with a choice. You may now choose to know, or you may carry on in pretended ignorance. Which is it to be?"

She nearly screamed in astonishment. "What on earth are you talking about?"

"What you may not do is carry on in this tone of high moral outrage," he continued, as if she had not spoken. "Now, choose wisely."

She could hardly breathe. "Are you telling me that you know this plate is forged and that . . . that . . ."

"Ah, you choose to know. Perhaps that is the wise choice, after all. Yes, I do know that the plate is forged. What's more, so do you. You have very kindly given me the kind of advice my silversmith needed to make a workmanlike job of it. That is why the item can be sold at auction, instead of privately, and it will almost certainly fetch a much greater price because of that. Your cut, my dear, will be two percent. I hope you find that sufficiently generous."

Jasmin was on her feet, staring at him as though he had turned into a Martian in front of her eyes. She had never experienced a moment of such utter and confusing horror. "Are you out of your *mind?*" she demanded, her voice coming out in a curious growl. "Are you pretending you think I . . . I *agreed* with this?"

"It is certainly what I will tell the authorities, if you should be so foolish as to approach them," Dominic said softly.

"You tell them what you like!" said Jasmin. "I'm not going to be a party to this!"

"Aren't you, my dear? I think you are."

Jasmin turned without bothering to notice that, and strode toward the hall. "Perhaps you'd like to listen to this," he said, and she heard the click of a button being pressed. Then suddenly the room was full of the sound of her own voice.

"An inscription is usually considered pretty conclusive," she was saying. "Pahlavi has been dead for a thousand years, so it would take the piece back at least that far." *Click.*

"Do you need to hear more, my dear?" he asked quietly. "There is quite a lot of it."

She turned slowly to face him. "What does that prove?" she asked haughtily, but she was afraid.

"Well, it proves that your reputation, if not your actual freedom, lies in my hands, as mine may be in yours. It would be rather an unsavory contest, don't you feel? Two criminals pointing the finger at each other in accusation? Whatever the outcome for me—and, of course, you might actually get me put in prison, although it seems unlikely, given the state of your evidence…" He smiled. "Your word against mine, my dear, though I hate to be cliché. The outcome for you is certain—repudiation by the academic community, and the utter destruction of a very promising career."

She was staring at him, motionless, her brain taking in all the information, but finding no solution.

"Look," he said, in a conciliating tone. "I know you're having financial difficulties. Suppose, just this once, we say ten percent? It may not realize more than fifteen thousand, but if there's no challenge to its authenticity, Jasmin, your ten percent could amount to anything up to twenty thousand pounds from this one sale alone."

From somewhere deep inside her, her blood rose, and the proud fury of some distant ancestress flamed at him out of the green eyes. She made a noise of contempt she had never even heard before, and spit. The spittle landed on his shoes.

They stared at each other for a moment of curious astonishment. Then whoever was running her body at that moment turned and walked out.

"Ring me when you've thought it over," Dominic called after her, but his voice was not entirely steady.

"I see," said Daniel Hazlett. He put his elbow on the table and his chin in his hand and thought for a moment. "Yes, this is difficult. Well, I had no idea there was anything questionable about Parton. I wonder what we can do?"

"It sounds like a police matter to me," said Gillian. Jasmin had told the professor's wife first, and together they had presented it to him as carefully as possible. But the professor showed no signs of any relapse. He even seemed to be grateful for the excitement.

"Yes, it may be, as far as the criminal element in it is concerned. What we're going to do about tracking down the forgeries the man has put onto the market is rather a different problem."

Gillian advised gently, "Perhaps the criminal part of it ought to be looked after first."

He frowned, as if unsure why criminality should have a higher priority than the historical record that had been tampered with. "Do you think so?"

"Yes, I do," said his wife firmly. "Jasmin has got to go to the police and tell them what has happened."

"He'll tell them I'm involved," she said. "Couldn't we do something to stop him just on our own?"

"I think what we want to do at this juncture is get Ben over here," said Hazlett.

Jasmin jumped. "Dr. Bredon?" she asked in surprise.

"He warned you against Parton, didn't he?" said Hazlett. "I remember being surprised by that. It's likely he knows something, and information always helps."

She couldn't protest, but there wasn't anyone whose help she wanted less. Because to ask for Ben's help meant telling him how much of a fool she had been.

"Do we have his number handy?" asked Professor Hazlett.

The two men shook hands as though there had never been hard feeling between them. Jasmin wondered if there ever had been. Perhaps he had been forgiven for the book review. Fifteen years was a long time to bear a grudge, and she had never known Professor Hazlett to bear any grudge. She realized suddenly that she had never had any evidence that Professor Hazlett and Ben Bredon disliked each other. It might all have been her own imagination, her own need to find an excuse for hating Ben.

Ben looked at her thoughtfully from time to time as he heard the story, sitting in an armchair with his elbows propped on the arms and his face resting against his clasped hands. "Well," he said when, between them, they had finished telling the story, "I think Gillian is right. It's a police matter, and the sooner we get down there the better."

Jasmin looked at him. *We?* she thought. Addressing him directly for the first time, she said fiercely, "He's going to say I was involved, haven't you understood that?"

His level gaze rested on her for a moment. "Yes, I understood that. You have a choice, Jasmin. You can decide to submit to blackmail and be tied to him for the rest of your life, or you can destroy his hold now by facing the consequences of what you have already done. Which shall it be?"

She fired up. "What I've already done? What have I done that any specialist doesn't do every day? I gave him advice about antiquities!"

Daniel Hazlett said, "There is certainly nothing dishonest in what you did." But Ben just looked at her, and she knew what the look meant: he had warned her, and she had ignored the warning.

"I need time!" she cried. "Suppose we go to the police and they can't do anything? Suppose he starts to drop hints to people? He can destroy me!"

"He cannot destroy you unless you give in to him now," Ben said. "Otherwise, whatever happens, the truth will eventually come out."

His sense of honor was an almost physical presence in the room, and Jasmin, feeling shamed by her own weakness, reacted with anger. "I suppose you've never done anything you regretted!" she said. "You've never done anything mean, or low, or self-serving, so you've never had to face the truth of what you are! Well, for the rest of us, it is not—"

He looked at her, and she simply broke off. "On the contrary, I have done a great many things I regretted," he said softly. "As well as my share of what you call the mean, low and self-serving. It is not possible to be without regret, and human. But we need not be defined by our errors unless we choose. You have a chance to put things right. If that is the decision you make, I can and will help you in it."

He didn't *say* he wouldn't help her otherwise, but she knew it. She glanced at Daniel Hazlett and then at Gillian. "My dear," said the latter, "it's never as hard as it seems."

"No, I guess not," said Jasmin tiredly. Anyway, the worst was over. The worst had been Ben finding out what a stupid, dishonest person she really was. Because whatever they said about it, *she* knew that in her heart she had known there was something wrong about Dominic Parton. But she had wanted to see his collection. She was not innocent. She was getting what she deserved.

"Let's go through some of the detail again," said the detective sergeant. "How many items have you seen altogether, do you think?"

"About fifteen. Ten or eleven of them were plates, and the rest were seals, rings and figurines."

"And of those, how many did he say he was considering buying and asked for your detailed comments?" He had been very quick to understand Jasmin's outline of events, and the significant points. Jasmin had a peculiar feeling of unreality, as if she were in some detective story, where Scotland Yard had finally been called in, and would fix everything.

"Six—seven," she said, adding the Mithra plate.

The detective whistled softly. "Seven plates over a couple of months? And of those, how many did you think were forgeries?"

"I said three or four—one I wasn't sure."

"Could the others have been forgeries? Of the ones he asked you to estimate?"

Jasmin shrugged. "In this field—" She stopped. They all nodded. Metalware forgery, if it was done with care, was very difficult to detect. The officer made notes.

"And—I don't suppose you happened to make a mark on any of these items as you examined them? Something that would let you identify them, if necessary?"

She looked at him, smiling. "No, I didn't. It's considered rude to mark or damage any antiquities you're offered a look at."

"Yes, of course."

"I expect you've got detailed notes, though, haven't you, Jasmin?" Ben suggested.

"Oh, yes, I wrote each of them up while I was examining them, and drew sketches."

"That'll be very handy, if you don't mind letting us have a copy of your notes," said the detective sergeant.

"I took photos, as well," she said. "I haven't had them developed yet, but I've got three rolls of film I took whenever he left me alone."

The detective paused in his writing and his eyes moved to Ben's. He nodded and smiled. "Right," he said. "Well, we were wasting our time with you, weren't we, Ben? We should have put Miss Shaw up to it from the beginning. I expect we'd have him by now."

Jasmin said, "You're working for Scotland Yard? Isn't that a little unusual?"

He was driving her home to pick up the films. "Jeremy's an old friend. We did our first degree together. He went and taught at Leeds, and a few years ago, when the Art Squad was revived, he joined Scotland Yard. I was just doing him a favor."

"Which was what?"

He paused. "Letting Dominic Parton make a friend of me," he said.

Jasmin gasped. "Is *that* why—?" Why he had told her to keep away from Parton, while keeping close himself.

"Jeremy has suspected Parton for some time. But they couldn't catch him in anything, mostly, he thinks, because the people he cheats are private collectors who willingly buy something they believe to be stolen or illegally removed from the country of origin. It's hard for them to complain if they think they've been cheated. I don't think Jeremy had any grounds for suspecting him of actual forgery until today. But it all makes sense."

"And how did you get close to him?"

"It wasn't difficult. Collectors of that sort always like to have a few academics in tow. It lends them credibility. That part was easy. We met at a few sales or lectures, and I simply fell for the bait."

He was in complete control of himself. Never by a look, a move, did he suggest that he found it difficult to sit beside her without reaching for her, nor that he remembered what had happened between them with regret. She was just a student in a little trouble.

"I see," she said.

* * *

They collected the films, her notebooks and the prints of the Mithra plate, and returned to Scotland Yard.

"Good," said the detective. He handed the rolls of film to an assistant. "Jill, get those down to Ray and tell him we want prints as soon as possible, please. Tell him we're waiting for them. Greg—" he handed a young man the notebooks "—a copy of every page, please."

Then he turned his attention to the envelope holding the prints. "Right. What have we here?" He shook the envelope, and the glossy photographs slid out in a rush, and spread out over the desk. "Uh-huh. When did you see this?"

"Over the holiday. The twenty-eighth and twenty-ninth of December."

"You saw it twice?"

"Yes, I went back the second time to take the pictures."

Silently, Ben reached out a hand and picked up a photo of the front of the plate. He looked down at it for a moment, and then up at her. "I see," he said. Jasmin nodded.

"You think it genuine?"

"I don't know. It wasn't like the others. It's got cast-worked pieces, and none of the others do, and it's gilded. I'm still examining it in detail."

"It's very significant, if it's genuine."

"Yes. Almost worth the trouble."

"If it's genuine," Ben repeated.

"You wouldn't want it to be, would you?" she said tiredly. She hated being in the same room with him, hated talking to him as if nothing had ever happened, hated his cool indifference.

"I wouldn't want you to be made a fool of, Jasmin," he said. "The man is going to be uncovered as a forger. Anything he's touched will now have questions asked about its authenticity. And certainly anything as controversial as the subject matter of this piece will come under great scrutiny."

"The others were copies," she protested. "More or less. All the silversmith had to do was look at a book of photographs. So far there's been nothing like this design ever found in any Sassanian piece. Where would he get the information from? How would he know what to copy?"

Ben raised his eyebrows. "From you, I suppose," he said. "Hasn't it occurred to you that this plate is exactly what you wanted?"

She closed her eyes. She didn't know who she hated more. Him for being right, or herself for being wrong.

"Right, let's have them," said the detective, reaching out a hand for the newly made prints.

Jill handed them over hesitantly. "Ray says it's not damage to the camera, or the lens cap left on. It must have been some kind of deliberate sabotage—the film was exposed to bright light, either sometime before or sometime after actual pictures had been taken."

"What?" Jasmin whispered. "That's impossible! Nobody ever touched my camera but me, and—"

She broke off as the prints slithered down onto the table from Jeremy Stephen's hand. They were all black, every one. The detective raised his eyebrows expressively, and pursed his lips. "He's fast," he said. "How did he know you were taking pictures?"

"He couldn't have! I only took the pictures when he left me alone, and I always—even the Angel Cup?" she cried in despair. "Are there no shots of the Angel Cup?" She pawed through the prints, but she knew that it was hopeless. One print showed the faint edge of a round shape at one corner, but the rest were completely black.

"Where were you when you were taking the pictures?"

"In the Inner Sanctum—that's what I called the room he had everything stored in. The room I told you about."

The two detectives exchanged glances. "He must have that room under surveillance."

"'Do you mean . . . he was *watching* me when he went out and left me alone in there?''

He shrugged. "Or got you on film."

"But how did he get to my camera? Some days he wasn't even in the apartment when I went there!"

The detective picked up one of the black prints and gazed at it. "You were using what—twenty-four-print film? He probably substituted a preexposed film when you weren't looking and took the risk that you wouldn't use up the roll before he had time to do it again." He turned the print the other way up. "You were using a special camera, I imagine, not something you'd be likely to take to the park to get pictures of your dog. So the risk was calculated." He looked at the print with the faintly visible line of a curve. "Perhaps with the first film he was unprepared, so he just opened the back of the camera when you weren't looking."

"Except that he failed once," said Ben, picking up a picture of the Mithra plate.

"Yes, I wonder how those got by him?"

She had not mentioned the little camera. She had said only that she had returned the next day and taken pictures. "It was a different camera," she said. "I borrowed a spy camera and hung it from my earring. I forgot to tell you that part. I had to do that because I knew he wouldn't leave me alone that day. He even searched me to make sure."

There was a short silence as Ben and the two detectives exchanged glances again. "I think we'll have this one from you, Ben," said the detective. He smiled at Jasmin. "Ever thought of joining the police?" he asked.

# Chapter 19

"I want ten percent of anything that sells privately and twenty percent if it sells at auction," said Jasmin.

Dominic swallowed and set down his fork. He had insisted on feeding her to celebrate her return to the fold. He reached for his wineglass and took a drink. He was perfectly trained to his class. Nothing ruffled the surface. "My dear, those figures are rather high," he said smoothly, as though his wife had been spending too much at Harrod's.

She said, "If my analysis allows a plate that would otherwise only have been sold privately to pass muster at an auction, you stand to make ten times the money."

He opened his hands as if he admitted her point. "But I'm afraid I can go no higher than five and three percent."

Jasmin laughed and reached into her jacket pocket. She pulled out a pocket calculator. "Let's say a plate goes on auction and opinion is divided as to authenticity. What do you think it's likely to raise?"

He shrugged. "It's very difficult to say. So much depends on the economic mood and the artistic merit of the piece."

"Give me a ballpark figure," she said.

"Fifteen thousand pounds would not be unreasonable."

"And if you sold it privately?"

"Substantially the same," he said.

"And if there was no division? If it was generally accepted as genuine? You'd be sure to put it on auction then, wouldn't you? How much would it get?"

"Two hundred thousand, perhaps. A hundred, certainly."

"So, if I do my job properly, you stand to gain up to one hundred and eighty-five thousand pounds of pure profit—because the cost of making the plate remains the same. Isn't that right?"

"My dear, you take to it like a duck to water, if I may be permitted such an expression. I am all admiration. Do go on."

"And of this sum, which would simply not exist but for me, you expect me to be happy with—" she punched in the figures "—nine thousand, two hundred and fifty pounds. That means you clear...one hundred and seventy-five thousand, seven hundred and fifty pounds." She set down the calculator, speared a bit of steak on her fork and popped it into her mouth. "Of course," she went on, snatching up the calculator before he could reply, "you have to pay your Pahlavi expert, too, don't you? So, is the deal what you offered me? Five percent?"

He did not reply, and she blithely carried on. "Let's assume it is. Take off another five percent, and what have you got?" She glanced smilingly up at him. "Dominic, your take-home pay is still a very healthy one hundred and sixty-six thousand, five hundred." She took another mouthful. "I think twenty percent is a reasonable demand. It's not greedy, is it?"

It was likely that she might have made it as an actress after all. The mantle of a cheerfully grasping, hardheaded woman had seemed to descend on her, even as they had agreed, in the detective's office, that this was the line she should take. If she were greedy rather than totally unwilling, she could ask more questions.

Dominic was watching her, and his eyes were slate. "What makes you think there's a Pahlavi expert?"

It was the first sign of weakness she had ever seen in him. He should either have ignored the comment or pretended to assume she would know. Instinctively Jasmin refrained from showing triumph. She lifted her hands. "Show me a modern silversmith who can write Pahlavi, and I'll show you someone who's copying it from somewhere. I've noticed that the names you've used on the plates so far are attested on seals, but seal inscriptions generally have more than the name. A silver plate with an inscription beginning *This seal is from* wouldn't pass muster very long, would it? Someone has to be able to sort out the name from the rest of the inscription. Right? Elementary. You have a Pahlavi expert."

"Ten percent," said Dominic. "Seven for private sales."

"Fifteen. That's as low as I'll go. And ten. And I want it retroactive, to cover all the plates I've commented on already."

"My dear," he said, by way of capitulation, "it's an education to be dealing with you."

"And one more thing," she said. As she paused, he looked up, and she met his eye firmly. "I want to know if that Mithra plate was genuine, or just another forgery."

"That plate? You will have to use your own judgment on that, I'm afraid. I can't tell you anything that I haven't already told you about that one."

Her heart kicked a little. "Are you telling me it wasn't one of yours?"

He opened his hands. "It's very different from anything I've done, isn't it?"

Was it possible that in all this mess she had found one glorious, fabulous thing, a genuine contribution to ancient history?

"I wish I could buy it," she said.

"Well, my dear," he said softly, "if you do your job well, I will inquire if it is still available, and I will take the risk for your sake. Who knows? You might even be able to publish it."

"I can't do it on Friday," she said. "It's just not possible."

"If that's really true, we can postpone," he said, and she heaved a sigh. "But I would like to see your work before we make that decision." In the excitement of recent days she had neglected that appointment they made.

"It would be such a relief!" she said, scarcely hearing that. "If I can just put it off for a while, I know I can..." She faded out. He was looking at her steadily. "What's the matter?" she asked.

"Is this something to do with that plate?"

Jasmin felt herself blushing. She shouldn't have tried to avoid telling him. "Dominic says that plate wasn't one of his forgeries. I want to wait with this chapter and see if I can find anything that will let me get the information in without using the plate."

"Why do you believe him, Jasmin?"

"Why should he lie about it?"

He laughed in real amusement. "I can think of several reasons. Has he by any chance held out to you the promise of your being allowed to publish the plate?"

She was outraged. "If he has, do you imagine that that would tempt me to anything?"

"No, I don't." He spoke levelly, but the strain of doing so was evident. "But I imagine that Dominic imagines it would. Think, for God's sake! He must know your alliance with him is a precarious thing. He's looking for ways to keep you on the leash when the inevitable moment comes that you balk at something he wants to do."

"And how will this do the trick, Ben?" she asked.

He swore in impatience. "If he let you publish that plate, and then threatened to reveal it as a forgery, and to say you knew it was when you published it, he'd have plenty of evidence to back him up, wouldn't he? He thinks that would keep you in line for life, and if things were what he imagines, no doubt it would."

"I don't believe it *is* a forgery. It's not like the others."

"You don't believe it because you don't *want* to believe it." He was losing his temper, and hers wasn't far behind. "Can't you see that your judgment is impaired here?"

"And yours isn't, I suppose!" Jasmin snapped.

"What is my judgment being impaired by?" he asked in a hard voice.

"You haven't even seen the plate, except in photos!"

"I don't need to see the plate. I have seen the man, Jasmin, and as I have told you before, he is not to be trusted."

"And I don't trust him! I know he's a forger and I know he buys and sells things dishonestly! But that doesn't mean he's lying about this! The two don't necessarily follow!"

She was nearly in tears. Ben stared at her for a moment. "Are you falling in love, Jasmin?" he asked quietly.

She looked at him, her heart beating in absolute terror for what seemed like a full minute before she realized what he meant. Then she laughed. "Well, that really crumbles the cookie! Are you accusing me of falling for *Dominic Parton?*"

He looked at her in silence. She wanted to kill him. "You really imagine I could fall for that kind of—ignoble creep?" she said.

"Women have been known to."

For two cents she'd have told him what kind of miserable, coldhearted, cold-blooded, detached bastard she had really fallen for, but her restraint held. "So have men," she said bitingly. "I am not *women*."

"Well, then, you are being blind for other reasons," he said, but she could hear the relief in his tone, though he tried to disguise it, and she stared at him as the truth swept over her. He wanted her. She knew it with blinding clarity. He wanted her; it hadn't been just a response provoked by her imagined flirtatiousness. He didn't care about her, but he damned well was attracted to her, and how *dare* he blame it all on her, the way he had?

"At least it isn't sex that's blinding *me*," someone said with level intent. She was only a little surprised to realize it was herself speaking. It caught him off guard. She stared at him for a long, accusing moment.

"Well?" he said, at last.

"You're a hypocrite," she breathed.

"Am I?"

She stood up suddenly and walked around the desk to him. He watched her without a movement. A force field struck her as she drew close, and in spite of herself, she felt her body thrum into powerful awareness. "You don't fancy me unless I'm deliberately being provocative, is that what you said? You wouldn't have touched me if I hadn't aroused your indiscriminate male desire?"

She was standing over him, so close they were almost touching, but although she was desperate for it, she did not allow herself to touch him. "Is that true?" she said. "You're not attracted to me just standing here? I'd have to blink seductively or throw myself at you before you wanted—"

He moved then, standing up abruptly, his chair shooting back behind him. "No, it is not true," he said, and with a shock that sent all the air out of her body, he pulled her into his arms and smothered her mouth with his own.

When he lifted his mouth they were both shaking. He set her away from him. "Right," he said. "Now you've proved

your point. Bring me your paper tomorrow. It's time I saw
where you were, exactly."

"I know who it is," Jasmin said later, at Scotland Yard.
"It just came to me as I was driving over here. It's a student doing ancient Persian languages research at SAES.
Tamiko. She was at my Christmas party, and I *thought* I
introduced them. But later on, they seemed to be arguing."
Jasmin turned to Ben. "Do you remember that? It was while
we were dancing." She felt the heat invade her cheeks and
dropped her eyes.

"I didn't notice any atmosphere between them," Ben said
after a moment.

"Well, there was one. I just didn't put it together until
now. Shall I try to talk to her?"

She was looking at the detective. "Not if it means telling
her what you're doing," Ben interposed firmly. "You don't
know under what conditions she's working with him, and
there's a lot at stake here. We have no idea to what lengths
Dominic would go to avoid being exposed."

Jeremy Stephen was looking at him, but Jasmin kept her
eyes on the detective. "That's true," the detective said reflectively. He turned to Jasmin. "Don't forget that your
position may be precarious. Maybe we haven't emphasized
that enough. Remember your own safety comes first."

Jasmin thought of the slate-gray eyes, and shuddered ever
so slightly. "I will," she said. As if compelled, she looked
at Ben.

"I'm taking that as a promise," he said. That sounded as
though he cared for her, and it moved her in spite of herself. Then she reminded herself how far his caring went.

"Sure," she said.

No one had seen Tamiko at the School since the Christmas holiday. She had been working at her regular place in
the library right up until the day it closed, but in the new

term she hadn't returned. None of her friends had heard her mention that she expected to make a trip home, and she had financial problems that made that seem unlikely.

"Her father went belly-up last year," said a young American undergraduate whom she had been tutoring in spoken Japanese. "She was charging me a lot, but she was worth it. But—" he shrugged "—well, she just hasn't been here this month." He looked at Jasmin. "Do you think she's in some kind of trouble?"

Jasmin pretended surprise. "No, why?"

"Somebody else was asking about her a couple of weeks ago."

Jasmin's pretended insouciance went out the window. "Who?" she demanded.

He shrugged. "Some guy who said he wanted to find someone to teach him Japanese. Everybody in the department knows she's tutoring me, so anyone could have given him my name, same as you."

"What did he look like?" Jasmin asked.

"She's in trouble, isn't she?"

"She might be, if the man you spoke to finds her before I do. What did he look like?"

"Ah, you know, a business type. He said he had an important trip to Japan coming up and wanted to know when she'd be back. I wouldn't have thought anything about it if you hadn't asked about Tamiko, too. Now that I think of it, he really wanted me to think they were just casual questions. But they weren't. Where could he get in touch with her, things like that, you know?"

"Did you tell him anything?"

"No. I don't know where she is. I wish I did." He looked at her. "Are you a friend of Tamiko's?"

"Yes. She's in my graduate seminar."

"She's been really worried for the past couple of months. She didn't say anything, but I knew. Once she just started crying in the middle of a lesson and ran out."

Jasmin said, "Here's my number. If you think of anything else, or see her, or find out anything, will you phone me? Or ask Tamiko to?"

"All right," he said. He stood looking down at the paper with her number on it. "If you find her and she's in trouble, will you—" he coughed and cleared his throat "—will you tell her she can count on me? Tony. Tony Blair."

"All right, I'll do that."

"She always says, 'Brail.'" He grinned at Jasmin, but his eyes were serious. "If you need any help or anything, will you let me know?"

Love. The whole damned world revolved around love. She couldn't understand why she had never understood this simple, obvious fact before.

And, as far as she could see, it made everyone suffer.

# Chapter 20

"Let's have a look," said Ben, gathering up the untidy sheaf of paper she laid on his desk, and quickly leafed through it before returning to page one and settling in to read more closely. He read through the first ten pages or so of computer printout, then came to one that was handwritten, rough notes of her thoughts on how to connect two themes, and frowned in concentration as he read. "What's this?" he asked, pointing to a phrase.

Jasmin slipped one long, black-stockinged leg beneath her and pushed up, leaning sideways over his desk as he turned the page halfway round to her, his finger marking the spot. She groaned. "I can't read that myself!" Her eye glanced up to the previous paragraph. "What am I talking about here? The cosmogony of—"

Her long hair, hitched up over one shoulder, came cascading down without any warning, covering the sheaf of paper and his hands, forming a curtain behind her that closed them in, and delicately scenting the air with her perfume. It startled them both. Jasmin's audible breath matched a little grunt of surprise from Ben, and her scalp prickled with sensation. For a moment she heard her heartbeat. Her head bent, her lips parted, she watched his hand move convulsively under the mass of black curls that had tumbled across his palm, and her hair translated that movement into a caress for every nerve ending in her body.

She looked up at him. His eyes were deep blue, and the skin of his face was drawn tightly over the bone. Her gaze locked with his, while excitement and desire chased themselves all over her system. Never had her feelings been so confused. She dragged her eyes away and waited for the storm to break.

At last he lifted his hand, brushed her hair aside and picked up the page again. She knew that the action had taken all the control he could muster, and that knowledge was like heat on her skin. Fighting for control of her own, Jasmin swept her hair behind her and sat back. "Sorry," she said, in a choked voice. "What's the context? I'm not sure where you are."

Ben glanced at the page and set it down in front of her. She swallowed and reached for it. His hand moved away. She knew he had to force that movement.

"I see what it is," she said. It was a lie. She could scarcely focus. She picked a legible line at random. "'In a similar way...'" she began. She put her hand up to her throat, swallowing over the lump she felt there, and the touch of her own fingers on her bare skin rippled in a wave across her neck, her arms, her back, her breasts. "Ben," she whispered.

"Go on," he commanded roughly.

"'In a similar way, the images of the lions killing their prey on the walls of the palace of Darius may have been some reference to this myth of creation...'" she read.

Her own heartbeat was choking her, the pressure of the stuff of her shirt was burdensomely heavy on her forearms. But Jasmin kept reading blindly on, not taking in the sense of what she read. "'Here, too, certain elements are...'"

He reached forward and slowly pulled the paper from her hand. "Look," said Ben, "I'll cancel your seminar. There's no point in forcing you to deliver it if you don't feel ready. In the meantime, leave it with me, and I'll look through it and see what advice I can offer."

She looked up. His face was naked, stripped to the bone. Her mouth was dry and she licked her lips. "Thank you," she said.

"I'll see you again Thursday," he said.

"Ben, I . . ." She stopped, feeling choked.

A muscle moved in his jaw. "Just get out, would you?"

"Is that Jasmin Shaw?" said a male voice in soft urgency.

Jasmin's hand clenched on the receiver. "Yes. Who's that?"

"Tony Blair. Do you remember talking to me? I—"

"I know who you are. What is it?"

"Uh . . . I can't talk on the phone. Can you meet me somewhere?"

"Yes," said Jasmin, her heart going like a war drum. Ben's detective sergeant friend might think she made good police material, but Jasmin knew she was far too excitable to last for long in such an occupation. "You say where. Or would you like to come here?"

She heard the mouthpiece being covered momentarily. Then he said, "Yes, that might be best. If you promise you'll be alone. Shall I come now?"

It was midnight. "Come now," said Jasmin.

She did not put the porch or the inside light on when she went down to answer the bell, and she was not surprised to see the diminutive figure of Tamiko move out of the shadows beside Tony Blair when she opened the door.

"Quick, up the stairs," she whispered, and then, as the girl slipped past her, said aloud, "Hi, Tony. Come on in."

She glanced up and down the street as she closed the door, but saw nobody.

They sat down in the sitting room with all the drapes pulled, but even so, the Japanese girl was clearly terrified. Jasmin brought her a glass of sherry, and her teeth chattered against the glass.

Tony Blair sat protectively on the arm of her chair, his arm around her. He looked older than a few days ago, as though maturity had fallen on him suddenly. "We're going to get married," he said. "I don't care what she's done. She came to me to ask for money, but I wouldn't give her any. I don't care what she's done, but if she has money she'll go away. I told her she had to come and talk to you."

Tamiko smiled tremulously up at him, but her eyes were grave as she looked at Jasmin. "I don't think you can help," she said.

"Tamiko," Jasmin asked quietly, "how well do you know Dominic Parton?"

The Japanese girl burst into tears.

"Basically the same method he used with me," Jasmin said. She was sitting in the Art and Antiquities Squad office again, with two detectives and Ben. "A little nastier, perhaps. Tamiko's family lost a lot of money in the market about a year ago. Her father stopped short of committing suicide, but there was no more money for Tamiko's education. Tamiko applied for emergency grants to complete her degree, and among the bodies she applied to was the Parton Foundation.

"She didn't get the grant, but Dominic came to see her. He said all the foundation's money was already dispersed for the year, but she was a very worthy cause, and he would support her from his personal finances until next year, when she could apply for a grant from the foundation again.

"One day Dominic asked her if she would read a line of Pahlavi for him and tell him what it said. It was a seal inscription she recognized, and he wanted a detailed breakdown of it. Then it happened again. One day there was an old man there, an Iranian, and she gave him a lesson in the Pahlavi alphabets, both early and late. Several times Dominic brought her a weight and asked her to translate it into the Attic weight system used by the Sassanians and write it out in Pahlavi.''

"Does she remember the weights she translated?" asked Jeremy Stephen.

Jasmin smiled. "I asked her that. As far as she remembers, they ranged from about four ounces to eight or nine ounces." She lifted her hands. "That's about the range that most silver plates fall into."

The detective grunted.

"She said it took a long time to sink in. She's not used to questioning men in authority, but finally she asked him what he was using the information for. That was in November. Her December check never arrived.

"When she saw him at my party at Christmas she asked him about it, and he told her if she asked any more questions she would never get it. He knew she would have to drop out of her course soon if she didn't have the money to carry on, and threatened to report her as an illegal immigrant, because she's on a student visa. She couldn't bear the shame of going home like that. She's been working illegally as a chambermaid in a hotel on Bayswater Road. They fed and housed her, but kept putting off paying her wages. Yesterday they finally paid her a quarter of what she was owed and said that was all the wages she was getting. So she went to Tony."

"Tony?" asked Jeremy Stephen.

"A student. They're getting married, apparently."

"And where is she now?"

"They're both at my place. She's afraid to go out, and he's not leaving her."

Ben looked over at her. He didn't say anything, but she blushed, anyway.

The other detective spoke for the first time. "Who's the old guy she was talking to? She have any idea?"

"Something he said—they could speak Persian together, that's what she did her first degree in—made her think he was some sort of artist or artisan."

The two detectives exchanged glances. "She met him here in London?"

"That's right."

Jeremy Stephen said, "Have you ever seen this man, Ben?"

Ben lifted his shoulders. "You know I tried to meet as many of his friends as possible, but he liked to keep people in groups. I know he has contacts in the Iranian community, because my own Iranian friends tell me so, and he told me himself he supported a family of Iranian refugees here. But that is as far as I got."

"Well, we'd better see Tamiko and find out if she can give us a detailed description of the guy. If he's got his silversmith right here in London, we've got him." He picked up the phone and pushed the intercom button. "Jill," he said, "can you pull all those surveillance reports we've got on Dominic Parton?"

Jasmin sat over the pictures of the Mithra plate with a magnifying glass, examining it inch by inch, making notes. It was a cross between the bull-slaying of the Roman Mithras temples and the royal hunting plates of the king on the back of a stag, stabbing it with a dagger. The god was not riding the bull, but nor did he have his foot in the traditional position on the back leg of the animal. Although he used a dagger on the bull's throat, he wore a quiver on his right hip, like the kings.

The intricate designs of the quiver were chased with three different tools. Jasmin bent closely over it, trying to make out the design. A pointed tool with which the artist had made straight lines and diamond shapes; a small circular tool, about one sixteenth of an inch in diameter, with which he had trimmed the upper and lower edges of the quiver, and a... Jasmin gasped as though one of the god's arrows had pierced her breast, her unconscious taking in what she had seen before she was fully aware of it. Her heartbeat shifted into a quick, horrified rhythm. She pushed the glass closer to the photo, adjusted her own glasses, and examined the chasing design for a long, frozen moment; then stopped and wildly looked to see where else the tool had been used. There! Across the breast of his costume, a double row of them. Jasmin bent over the glass again, and then straightened. There could be no question. Whatever she wanted to believe, she must accept this as the truth.

The artist's chasing tool was slightly damaged. She had seen the tool before, on two of the plates she had condemned to Dominic Parton as forgeries.

"Well, if you're sure you want to take the risk," Jeremy said, "what we'd like is to establish an incontrovertible link between a piece Parton shows you and that same piece later on the market. Is there some way you could mark the piece?"

"I think it could be done, but if it's going back to his silversmith, won't he recognize it and remove it?"

"Or tell Parton about it," Ben added. "It's too dangerous, Jeremy. You can't ask her that."

"Ben," she said, "he's got to be stopped. He's screwing up the historical record, and I've helped him do it."

"A half-dozen copies hasn't done very much damage to the historical record," he said irritably. "If he finds out what you're doing we don't know how he'll respond."

Ben's bias was toward written history, and it was natural he should not care as much as she about the physical record from which history was also deduced. "You're forgetting the Mithra plate. I could do it in Pahlavi," she said, turning to the detective. "The silversmith wouldn't notice that, because he doesn't read Pahlavi. He's only copying what Tamiko gave him. That won't be dangerous."

The detective said, "You'd have to be very sure about the mark you made."

"Do you mean so I can testify in court?"

"We wouldn't want the defense to be able to confuse you about an alphabet you weren't very familiar with. There are genuine plates and seals with poor inscriptions." She knew it was true. Even in the ancient world, artisans had often copied inscriptions in languages they didn't understand, and made mistakes. Jasmin thought a moment.

"I could add a figure to the weight of silver. Tamiko could tell me what to write. The silversmith doesn't know about Attic weights, Tamiko said so. Probably he has to measure and figure it out every time, so he wouldn't notice if a change occurred afterward. I could just add one figure that made nonsense of the weight." She smiled at him. "Would that do? Then even if the defense confused me, you could always get someone to testify to the actual weight."

Ben said impatiently, "There's no way of telling if the silversmith is getting the weights correct in the first place. Suppose he's misunderstood Tamiko's instructions? Suppose he's copied them to the wrong plate?" He turned to his friend, and it was clear he was angry. "How's she supposed to do it, anyway? She'll need to take in some kind of tool, and you already think that room of his has a camera in it."

"That's true," said the detective. "Maybe we'd better give it up as a bad idea."

But she had the bit between her teeth now. "I can locate the camera and get out of its way," she said. "And I don't need a tool any bigger than a pin, do I?"

"It's not worth the risk, Jasmin," Ben said.

"I think I should try it," said Jasmin stubbornly, and his eyelids dropped and his face closed against her.

She despised Dominic Parton now with a cold passion that seemed utterly foreign to her nature. He had done it deliberately; there could be no question of that. He had asked his tame silversmith to make the plate that she wanted for her thesis, not caring what it might one day do to the record, as long as it got Jasmin where he wanted her. She would get him if it killed her.

"It's good," said Jasmin. "He's improving, your little man." She held it up. "The shape of this is very good." She turned it over, examining the bottom and then all around the edge. "Where is the inscription?"

"My dear, we wouldn't want to become predictable."

"It won't fetch the price," she warned. Her heart fell. How could she mark it when there was no inscription to begin with? Tamiko had shown her a simple stroke to add to the weight. But she had not expected there to be no inscription at all.

"If every plate that passes through my hands has an inscription, the fact will eventually be noticed."

That might be the reason, of course, or it might have something to do with the fact that, as far as Dominic was concerned, Tamiko had disappeared. She said, "You could have just the weight, no owner's name. That would give you variety and authenticity at the same time."

"My dear, you seem anxious."

"Dominic, it's much more likely to be condemned as late without an inscription."

Somewhere in the flat the phone rang. After a moment there was a tap on the door of the Inner Sanctum. "Sorry to disturb you, Mr. Parton," said the housekeeper. "But it's that call you were waiting for yesterday. I thought you'd like to know."

Dominic stood up smoothly. "My dear, you'll excuse me a few moments," he said. He leaned forward and touched her cheek. "Greed has been the downfall of too many otherwise intelligent people, Jasmin," he said kindly. "It is a very common failing among criminals—the unsuccessful kind. Try to cultivate detachment and patience."

He went out. She would have done well to listen to this very sound advice. But Jasmin was not detached, and she was impatient, and it was her only chance. She might never get another. When the door had closed behind him, she picked up the plate from the desk and walked over to the door, at the same time slipping off her ring. A piece of the ring's ornate design had been filed to a point, and facing the door, her back to the room, Jasmin pressed the point close under the outside rim of the plate and carved two tiny cursive marks, so quickly she might only have been fumbling for the lock. Then she pulled open the door and stepped through.

Instantly a loud alarm went off, and she jumped, dropping the plate, and sliding her ring back onto her finger. She snatched up the plate and examined it in concern, rubbing it with her handkerchief where perhaps it had hit the floor.

The little black smudge on the corner of her handkerchief transferred easily to the bright silver of the fresh scratch she had made, dulling it to the shade of the tarnished silver of the rest of the bowl.

"Sorry, Dominic," she said in contrition, "I completely forgot about the alarm. I wanted to ask you . . ."

"Yes?"

She laughed. "Whatever it is, it's gone completely out of my head!"

He looked at her. "Has it, my dear?" he said.

## Chapter 21

"Thanks," said Ben, as she pulled up outside a large converted warehouse near the river. They had been at Scotland Yard, and he had asked her for a lift home. "Will you come in for a drink? I'd like to talk to you."

Jasmin turned her head. Even something as simple as that could shake her out of her fragile control. "Now?" she asked stupidly. She wished he would get out of the car. Half an hour in such a confined space with him was more than enough.

"Now," he said.

She opened her door. "I have a date in half an hour," she lied.

He led her into a small hallway, where he hung her coat and then through to a gigantic room that overlooked the Thames through a window that covered most of one long wall. "Oh, fabulous!" breathed Jasmin, forgetting her nerves and moving to the window to gaze out at the lights. "I didn't realize we were so close to the river. You're right on it!" On the right was a fireplace with a sofa in front o

t, and the floors were polished strip pine, with Afghan car-
pets scattered around apparently at random.

"Yes, it's very nice in summer," he said, as if he were
thinking of something else. "What would you like to
drink?"

When he had gone to pour the drinks, she unlocked the
glass door that led to the balcony and slid it open. A cool
wind blew off the water, but the day had been mild. She was
wearing only a white cotton shirt, rolled up at the sleeves,
and a short black pencil skirt, but Jasmin stepped out into
it. She leaned on the rail and watched a barge sail by beneath her, the wind rippling her hair and caressing her forehead, and blowing away a headache she hadn't realized she
had.

Behind her the door slid open, and Ben came out to join
her, passing her a glass of red wine. It was nearly five
o'clock, the sun was setting somewhere behind the cloud
that smothered the city, and the barge was covered with
lights. She sipped the wine and turned again to cross her
arms along the railing, her body slanting away from it in an
unstudied pose. "It's lovely here," she said. "I love the
river."

He came to stand beside her, and instinctively she put up
an arm to draw her blowing hair down over her other
shoulder, out of his way. "Let it blow, Jasmin," he said, and
there was an intimacy in his tone that jerked her upright.
Suddenly she felt in too close proximity, felt her skin prickle
into awareness of his nearness.

"What did you want to talk to me about?" she asked.

He took a long drink, then stood by the rail, looking
down at his glass. "Philip Harding and I have been talking
with Daniel Hazlett," he said. "He seems to have recovered his health a good deal faster than his doctors expected.
His heart function is very good."

Jasmin smiled with pleasure at this news. "That's wonderful news! I've thought he was looking good! He just

seems to be...raring to go now, where in the fall he seemed tired.''

"He is raring to go. He's reversing his retirement and taking back one of his classes from me.''

"It's great, just great! I'm so...!'' She couldn't put it into words. "Oh, it's fabulous!''

Ben drank again. "He doesn't say it outright, Jasmin. He is far too polite to make the suggestion, but I know that he would like to have you back.''

It was completely unexpected. It was something she had never allowed herself to hope. Jasmin's jaw dropped. "Are you...is this...you're certain?''

He looked at her as if she were protesting too much. "Come on, Jasmin, what do you think?''

Of course he would. Of course her professor, her mentor, her intellectual father would want her back, provided he felt he had the strength to take her on. Jasmin smiled, hugging herself. "Did he say so?''

"He wouldn't want to force you, if you felt happy with me.''

Jasmin's smile died. "What do you think about it?'' she asked softly, stupidly wanting to hear that he did not want her to go.

Ben finished his drink and set the glass on the brick edge of the balcony under the railing. "On the whole, I think it would be for the best. You and Daniel have a meeting of minds on your subject that is sure to contribute to your thesis in a way that I won't be able to. And, of course, he is a great expert in the field. I am not.''

Jasmin laughed lightly. "And you'll be glad to get rid of such a troublesome responsibility.''

"I will be glad not to supervise you any more,'' Ben admitted, and there was nothing to do but swallow that.

She was thrilled and yet disappointed at the same time. Of course she would prefer to work on this subject with Professor Hazlett. Yet on a strictly personal level she would miss Ben desperately; she would have no right, now, to visit his office whenever she liked. She was angry with him, but still she would miss him. Jasmin did not try to sort the contradiction out. She looked out over the river. Night was falling, and she could see the lights from a long way away.

"You're sure he feels strong enough?"

"I think he would welcome an inquiry from you."

She finished her wine and set down her glass, then turned and leaned her elbows against the railing. The room behind them was softly lighted, and a fire was burning in the grate. It looked inviting. A gust of wind blew her hair wildly about her face, and again she put an arm up to contain it. "All right," she said. "You can consider yourself rid of me."

Ben turned, his eyes dark as they watched her profile. "Good," he said firmly. "Will you stay the night?"

She jerked around to look at him in amazement. "What?"

"Will you spend the night with me?"

"What are you talking about?" Jasmin whispered in shock. Her skin was suddenly alive everywhere, as though the wind carried electricity.

"I want to make love to you," said Ben, with a kind of ferocity. "Did you have any other objection besides the fact that you didn't want to get involved with your supervisor?"

"Ben!" she whispered in hoarse protest. He watched her, but though she opened her mouth again, no words came out.

"Good," he said, and reached for her. As his arms encircled her, the shock of his touch exploded through her body, and instinctively she put her hands up to hold him off.

"What are you doing?" she whispered.

Gently he stroked a strand of hair off her forehead, but she could feel an urgency in him that made her tremble. "Jasmin," he said softly, "don't fight me." Then he held her head and kissed her, and she could not prevent her lips parting under his, or stop her body melting. She could not stop her hands slipping up to encircle his neck, her fingers threading through his hair.

She could not stop him when, his mouth pressed to hers, he lifted her up against him and carried her through the open door into the welcoming room beyond.

She lay on the sofa, her hair streaming down in the firelight, spilling onto the floor, trembling as her body trembled. He was fierce, and tender, and passionate, knowing exactly what he wanted from her, what he wanted to give her. He was beautiful, and his eyes and hands were deeply and completely possessive. She gave herself up and was lost.

Jasmin lifted an arm lazily up in the air and watched her bracelet tumble down from her wrist to lodge at the swell of muscle at her elbow. It glinted in the firelight that bathed everything in a warm glow. They lay on a sofa that collapsed down into the biggest and most comfortable bed she had ever seen. "So," she said, in some satisfaction, "you are attracted to me, after all." She was giving in. She no longer cared how many other students he had slept with, nor how long it would last. It was stupid to try to turn her back on something that meant so much to her, on the ground that it did not mean enough to him. The world was full of people who loved and were not loved in return: Jake, and Rena, and if not Tony Blair, then probably countless others. Why should she be any different?

Ben laughed in soft amusement. "I have been attracted to you for longer than I care to remember."

She propped herself up on one elbow over him. "How long?" she challenged softly.

He looked up at her as though the sight gave him pleasure, one arm under his head, lazily playing with a strand of her hair. "Are you aware that it is a breach of school law for a lecturer to get involved with an undergraduate?"

She raised her eyebrows. "Really? No, I—" She stopped. "With an *under*graduate?" He nodded, tickling his lips with the end of a curl. "Are you . . . from when I was an *undergraduate?*"

"Why does that surprise you?"

"But . . . that's two years ago."

"It is nearly five years ago, to be precise," said Ben.

"You have fancied me for five years without doing anything about it?"

"What should I have done?"

"I don't know. Didn't you want to tell me, at least?"

"I wanted to do a lot of things. But of the real options open to me, half were stupid, and the other half weren't fair to you. I didn't want to ask you to lie, to engage in deceit. The rules exist for a good reason. I thought I could wait."

"This rule only relates to undergraduates?" she asked.

"Once a student has a first degree, the School assumes a certain maturity, and allows for self-determination."

"But I graduated two and a half years ago."

"Yes, and long before that time I couldn't turn a corner at the School without hearing you telling someone or other how much you hated me. It didn't occur to me then that you might dislike me yet still be sexually attracted to me, I am sorry to say."

"I'm sorry," she said feebly. She couldn't explain those contradictory feelings without giving away far too much.

"I can't think of any reason for you to apologize."

"Is that why you got so cold with me?"

"When was I cold with you?"

"In my first year, you told me to stop bothering you or something. I thought it was because you thought *I* was after *you.*"

"Were you?" he asked.

"Not as far as I know," she said. But perhaps she had been on the edge of it, without realizing. Perhaps that was why it had hurt so much when he made it clear she was unwelcome in his office. It was all too confusing to know when it had begun.

He said, "I have never needed control the way I needed it around you. I remember thinking that I had to keep you out of my office, and I knew that if you ever showed me the least encouragement I'd be making love to you on my own desk. Perhaps that came across as coldness. Whatever it was, by the time I realized what effect I was having, the damage was done."

"Damage?"

"I drove you out of my field, didn't I? In fact, I couldn't have affected your career any more negatively by following my instincts with you than by what I did do. I'd have been better telling you what I felt. Then, at least, you could have studied what you wanted to study. But by the time I understood all this there was no drawing you back. You hated me, and loved Daniel Hazlett."

"Yes," she said reflectively, as he began to stroke her back in long, strong strokes, pulling her down to within range of his lips. She could not tell him what she believed, that her hatred had grown up as a defense against what must have been love. He was talking about sex, not love.

"Anyway," she affirmed with a smile, "I'm glad I went to him. He'll be retiring for real soon, and I wouldn't have missed what he gave me for the world. I can always expand into your field, can't I?"

"No reason why not," he said.

"So I had my consolation. You had yours, too, didn't you? I mean, you didn't exactly die on the vine."

His mouth trailed across her shoulder and rested against her throat, taking in the heartbeat there. "Didn't I?"

"Haven't you been having affairs with most of your graduate students over the past few years?"

Ben was silent for a moment. Then he lifted his head and looked at her quizzically. "What?"

"Didn't you?"

"Where did you get the idea that I'm bisexual?" he asked. "I assure you, I'm not."

"What are we talking about?" asked Jasmin, frowning. "I mean the women, of course. Lots of people know."

Ben laughed. "As chance would have it, in the last four years the only woman graduate I've supervised was Muslim, and married, and it would have been more than my life was worth to lift a finger in her direction. She came to every one of our meetings with a chaperon. So who are these women everyone knows I've been bedding?"

# Chapter 22

"We've got the place under surveillance now," Jeremy Stephen told them. "A man who fits the description Tamiko gave us comes and goes. But we can't be certain it's the workshop, and if we make a move and it's not, we may lose everything."

"Would you like me to ask Dominic to take me to see the workshop?" asked Jasmin.

"No," said Ben firmly. "You're taking this too far. Let Jeremy do his job. That's what he's paid for."

The detective looked from one to the other. "Ben's right," he said. "You've done your part. Don't worry, we'll have him soon enough."

"And she should stop seeing Parton," Ben added.

"There's no advantage anymore in having you on the inside," Jeremy agreed. "It's just police work now, and patience. If that's not the address of the workshop, we'll find it."

Jasmin said nothing. It wasn't personal with them. With her, it was personal.

"By the way, we've traced purchases of old coins by Parton, going back two years. He's doing a very serious job of forgery. He means never to be found out."

Jasmin knew what he meant. Old coins had been melted down to make the plates. Modern silver, when analyzed, would instantly signal a forgery. But if he was melting ancient coins, silver analysis would show that it came from the right period. The forgery would be that much harder to detect.

"He's very thorough," said Jasmin. "And he's patient. And he's determined not to be greedy."

Ben rolled over as she entered the room, and she crossed to the sofa and sat within his arms. She stroked his mouth. "You ever read Anthony Trollope?" she asked absently. *Mouth of a god.*

"Not lately," said Ben. "Why?"

She recollected herself. "Oh, no reason. Just something you remind me of."

"Something you remind me of, too." His hand caught at a sleeve. "*Venus Robed.* Why are you wearing these pajamas?"

"They're yours. I found them in the bathroom."

"I know they're mine. Why are you wearing them?"

"I like them. They're very old and comfortable." She stood up and modeled them in a catwalk strut, lifting the collar to her chin. "And now, Jasmin is showing us the pajamas Ben has worn since he was twelve," she said in husky tones. She stopped and grinned. "Don't you like them?"

"Very much," said Ben. "How would you like to take them off?"

"No," she said, smiling provocatively.

Lifting one arm, Ben caught her and brought her down full length beside him. There was the small sound of a tear.

"Now look what you've done!" she said reproachfully. Where the pocket was stitched to the jacket, the fabric had given way, and pale skin gleamed through the faded navy.

"Do I have to do it myself?" he asked, with a smiling threat in his eyes that made her shiver with expectation. Jasmin just looked at him.

With his eyes on hers, Ben slipped his hand into the pocket and pulled, and the aged cotton gave way down the entire front of the jacket, electrifying them both with the high moan of tearing fabric. "My God, you're beautiful," he breathed. His hand slid up her rib cage to cup her bared breast, and then his mouth was on her skin.

She gasped in deep sexual excitement. "Ben," she whispered. "Don't."

For an answer he leaned up over her, grasped the waist front of the pajama bottoms and in one powerful motion tore the cotton halfway down one long leg. Then, in a contained fury of passion, he continued until her body lay revealed to him amid the tatters of cloth and they were both shaking with desire. He clasped her chin in one strong palm and kissed her ruthlessly on the mouth, so that her body yearned to his.

"Tell me," he commanded against her lips. His body was fiercely hard against her. "Say it."

"What?" she whispered.

"Tell me what you want," he said.

She could hardly breathe from sheer need. "Oh, God, Ben," she begged.

"Say it, Jasmin. Tell me."

She said it, and the next moment he was inside her, passionate, out of control, making love to her with a violence of passion that was utterly new to her. In response, the tiger of her own passion arose within her, handsome, sleek, powerful and fierce, and growled out its demands and satisfactions.

It was a mating of the perfectly physical. Afterward, they lay shaken by what had passed between them, and it seemed long before the ordinary world returned. Then she remembered that when he said, "Tell me," she had nearly, nearly said, "I love you." Just for a moment she had imagined it was what he wanted. She would have to be careful.

"Hello, my dear."

"Dominic! What on earth are you doing here?"

"Just a little business. May I come up?"

She was afraid to say no, though it might have been wiser to be afraid to say yes.

"My dear," he said when he had sat, "you are aware of where your own advantage lies, are you not?"

"I hope so," she said lightly, handing him a glass of sherry.

"What are the letters you have inscribed on the edge of the plate you were last examining?" he said.

Well, here it was. Jasmin took a sip of her own drink. "My initials," she said. "In late Pahlavi."

He smiled. "You are never stupid," he said. "And you never underestimate an opponent. Did I ever tell you how much I admire you for that?"

"I don't think so."

"I wonder if spies in the ancient world marked suspicious items with their initials at all," he said.

"Perhaps," she said. "Much of the population would have been nonliterate, of course."

"But not the police," he said. "Or whoever supervised the king's treasury."

"I suppose not. They had seals with their names and functions, and perhaps they could read them."

"You are working for the police, are you?"

She said, "It's personal, Dominic. You shouldn't have forged that Mithra plate. Copies are one thing. Forging something that interferes with our understanding of history was something else."

"But, my dear, it wasn't only that. You'd have done it for the copies, too."

She nodded. "Perhaps. But without malice. That plate made me hate you."

He smiled ruefully. "Well, I'll tell you a curious thing. When I went to Hassan and described the sort of plate I wanted, he had no trouble coming up with the one you saw. He told me he had seen such a plate as a boy, in his father's workshop. He said it was very, very old, and it had been in some wealthy family for generations. There were troubles with the king—it was in the time of the deposed Shah's father—and the head of this family was arrested. His wife came to her local silversmith—Hassan's father—and asked him to hide the plate, hoping that in a silversmith's shop it would pass without remark, and that if things got very bad, she would have something left from the wreckage. Eventually the man was released from prison and the plate was returned. My silversmith saw the plate then, as a young boy, and he did his best to reproduce it for me from memory. God knows where the original is now, of course. There have been two revolutions since then."

She didn't know whether to believe that story. "What do you want from me, Dominic?"

"I scarcely know, my dear. Of course, I made a mistake with you. You capitulated too easily, and I should have realized that. But your greed was so convincing, I thought I had you."

"Well, I am greedy, Dominic, if it's any consolation. I'm just not greedy for money. But I only had to transfer the feeling."

"I suppose greed for money is the least admirable kind," he said.

"I'm not so sure," said Jasmin. "Someone told me once—I forget who, isn't that funny?—that greed for knowledge was still greed. Maybe that's true of everything. Maybe even greed for love is greed."

"Perhaps. My own greed is not primarily financial, although I certainly have enjoyed the money."

"What was it?"

"Just to think myself more intelligent than anyone else, perhaps. To fool a lot of foolish art experts who pretend that they know a forgery from the real thing. Or perhaps I was merely bored."

She made a face. "It wasn't really much of a challenge, though, was it? Antique silver forgery is only too easy. A good forgery can always get past some expert or other, especially if he has something to gain. And then someone is sure to buy it, really."

"Ah, my dear, you put it so baldly. Do you mean that it was no proof of my talents, after all?"

"Well, when it all comes out, you'll certainly have destroyed the confidence of the experts in Pahlavi inscriptions. Up till now, most people have imagined that an inscription would go a long way to prove a plate genuine. But you've shown that all you have to do is read a book, or ask an expert."

"And how *is* Tamiko?"

"She's very well. She's staying with her fiancé at the moment, I believe."

He finished the sherry in his glass. "Well, my dear! And I can't even say we would have made a great team, can I? There was a very peculiar lack between us of the sexual chemistry necessary to a great criminal couple."

"Yes, I noticed that."

"But your interest was elsewhere. You would not have welcomed any... approach from me, and I find it hard to make one in such a circumstance. A failing, perhaps."

"Where was my interest?"

"Oh, you mustn't get coy now. If ever I saw anyone capable of drawing the earthiest of responses out of Ben Bredon, it was you, my dear. I kept expecting to see him throw the food off the table and put you down amid the plates. And although you had a certain edgy quality, I can't suppose there was ever any doubt of what your response would be."

She gasped. "Is *that* why you talked about my film that night?"

"Ben is sometimes rather holier-than-thou, isn't he? I confess I thought he might not know, and I would have the pleasure, having seen your face in sexual ecstasy, of describing it to him before he saw it himself. But he does sometimes surprise. I suppose you'll find he has a video of that film, and watched it from time to time when he could no longer resist the temptation."

"And why did you tell me about his affairs with his students?"

"Oh, not at all for the petty, malicious reasons you're now imagining. It was clear at that party of yours that things were moving along in a way he would like. But I preferred, at that point, for you and Ben not to be in that sort of proximity. Bedroom conversation can be so thorough, can't it?"

She laughed. "Dominic, I take it back," she said. "I can't hate you in person, whatever you've done. You're far too...amusing."

He smiled. "Well, my dear, that's very kind. I wonder if perhaps we might...negotiate a little."

Jasmin raised her eyebrows.

"I must suppose that your testimony will be rather damning, even without the photographs you were taking. I see now how naive it was of me to imagine that you were only operating from scholarly interest when you did that," he added in aside. "Perhaps you would accept a little something from me to forget anything material that you know."

She made a rueful face. "You know, I won't enjoy testifying against you, if it comes to that, Dominic, because I feel guilty myself. But if they ask me to say what I know, I'll have to tell them."

"I thought you might like the Angel Cup," he said.

Jasmin closed her eyes and involuntarily her head moved from side to side. The Angel Cup. "You really know how to make it tempting, Dominic. I don't suppose you could have offered me anything I want more." She grimaced regretfully, and chose to put it out of her power to choose. "Frankly, I don't think my testimony will be all that critical. You shouldn't waste the cup on me."

"Ah, you think they have enough evidence even without you?"

"I think they might."

She got up to pour him another sherry, and he took it gratefully and sipped thoughtfully. "Well, perhaps you'll deliver a message for me, then."

Jasmin inclined her head.

"I am willing to donate the Angel Cup to the British Museum, and perhaps one or two other pieces, and, ah...go out of business, shall we say?...if your friends are willing to save Her Majesty the expense and bother of further investigation and a trial."

Jasmin took a deep breath. "Well, I'll pass it on."

"Thank you, my dear. I am a sailor, you know. Prison would not suit me at all. I must go down to the sea again, and all that."

She said, "I suppose the Angel Cup is the genuine thing?"

He finished the sherry and stood up. "Its provenance is impeccable," he said. "But you knew it yourself."

"I thought I did. All of this has made me doubt whether it's possible to judge anything."

He touched her cheek. "A little humility in a scholar, my dear, is no bad thing. I'll leave you now."

She stood and led him into the hall. "I guess we won't b
seeing each other."

He shrugged into his coat. "You never know, my dear
We do have interests in common, after all. When it's al
over, we might be friends."

"Do you remember writing a review of *Themes in Sas
sanian Art* when it came out?"

"I do," said Ben. "A very unpleasant piece it was."

Jasmin gasped a little. "You mean you regret writing it?"

"I can't regret something from which I learned so much
But I have sometimes wished I didn't have so much t
learn," Ben said dryly.

"Why—what did you learn?"

"How a real scholar deals with opinion with which he
disagrees."

"And how did you learn that?"

He touched her nose and smiled. "Your professor—he
wasn't professor emeritus then, of course—mentioned the
review to me next time he saw me."

"Oooh."

"No, he was entirely gentlemanly. And that was when I
realized how far from gentlemanly I had been."

She grinned in embarrassment. "You mean he was never
angry about it?"

"He never said so to me. I was very young, you know
He'd have seen that sort of thing before."

"Ah, well, I was angry enough for both of us."

"Quite right, too. You were angry about my questions at
a seminar, too. I heard about that in the halls."

She winced. "I was pretty horrible about it, wasn't I?"

"You certainly made your feelings clear. But it served me
right. I think I was hoping to wean you away from your
professor intellectually. I shouldn't have done it."

Jasmin heaved a sigh. "Life would be a lot easier if people were either all good or all bad."

"But a good deal less interesting," said Ben.

"Well, we can't do anything about an offer like that," said Jeremy Stephen. "When we've got our case together we'll send it to the Crown Prosecution Service, and if there's sufficient evidence to go to trial, it'll go to trial. That kind of thing looks too much like corruption. If he wants to donate his collection to the British Museum, his lawyer can ask for that to be taken into consideration when it comes to sentencing, but he'll want to keep away from anything that looks like bribery."

"I've brought something to show you," said Jasmin. She opened the clasp of her bag and carefully extracted the package, all wrapped in tissue and velvet, and set it on the desk in front of him. She sank into her familiar position in front of the crammed bookcase with a sigh of satisfaction.

"I'm to open it, am I?" said Professor Daniel Hazlett, rubbing his hands in a characteristic gesture. He took the package in an authoritative grasp and unwrapped it.

The Angel Cup caught a ray of sun that shone through the window over his shoulder, and glowed like the Holy Grail. In spite of herself, Jasmin breathed audibly.

"Ah," said her professor in satisfaction, and for a moment, they let it sit there and simply gazed at it. Then he put his hand firmly around its base, lifted it, and looked down at the dancing girl inside. "The Angel Cup. It's a very fine piece, I see. Brundweiser wasn't exaggerating." Brundweiser was the Victorian who had described it and made the sketches that were, until now, all the world had known of the cup.

"Dominic Parton is donating it to the British Museum. He asked me to deliver it," said Jasmin.

Daniel Hazlett raised his eyebrows. "That's rather unusual."

"He's an unusual man, very unpredictable."

"Is he going to keep out of prison?"

Jasmin shrugged. "I don't know. Naturally, the police don't tell me anything anymore, and I haven't spoken to Dominic except when he called me and asked me to deliver this. It's going to be a complete surprise."

"You're going to walk over and drop it off, are you? Rather a valuable item to be carried through the streets. most unusual man." He was still examining the cup, turning it over and over. He set it down and pulled open his drawer. "Let's just take a picture while we've got the chance," he said.

"Always take pictures," Jasmin agreed, smiling.

"Perhaps you'd like to ring Dr. Maxwell at the museum," he said, closing the window blind. He set the cup under a bright lamp, then focused his camera over the Angel Cup. "He might prefer to send someone around to pick it up."

But Jasmin had been asked to deliver it. A few minutes later, she stepped out into the bright springlike sunshine, ran down the steps, and strode confidently in the direction of Russell Square and the north door of the British Museum. Inside, she dashed up the staircase she knew so well and along to Western Antiquities.

"I've got a delivery to make," she said at the door to the keeper's offices. "Is Dr. Maxwell in?"

"Was he pleased?"

"He was absolutely gobsmacked," said Jasmin in satisfaction. "He says he'll always remember the day the Angel Cup walked into his office on two legs."

"The legs are worth remembering even without the Angel Cup," said Ben, running an appreciative hand along one of them.

She smiled. "You'll remember them, will you?"

He was quiet for a moment. "All my life," he said. "Are they going somewhere?" His hand on her hip tightened, and then, as if by force of will, relaxed again.

'Would you miss them?' she asked, smiling so that he would not guess how much the answer meant to her.

His hands were urgent as he rolled her onto her back and bent over her. "Jasmin, don't play games with me," he said.

"I'm not playing," she said. "Would you miss me?"

"Are we assuming that I could let you go?"

Her heart thumped. "I . . ."

"Do you just want to hear me say it? I love you, Jasmin. It would kill me to let you go." He bent down over her, as though the admission had released powerful feeling in him, and his arm wrapped her tightly and drew her against him as he kissed her. "I love you more than I have ever loved anything on this earth, more than I ever expect to love anything again. And I'm tired of not saying it! I love you."

Her wide green eyes stared into his. "Ben," she whispered. Her heart was going to explode. "But why didn't you tell me?"

"Did you want to hear it?"

"Yes," she breathed. Feeling choked her. "Oh, yes." She couldn't get another word past her throat.

He placed a hand against her cheek and looked down into her eyes, and she could see in those depths that at last he understood. "Why did you want to hear it, Jasmin?" he demanded softly.

"Ben, I . . ."

"Tell me. I want to hear it."

"Ben, I love you so much, I think I—" But his mouth covered hers, urgent, possessive, drinking the words in.

"When did you fall in love with me?" she asked.

"When it happened, I'm not sure. I know when I finally admitted it. Or, at least, when I could no longer disguise the truth from myself."

"When?"

He kissed her. "The night of Dominic Parton's party, when I looked up and saw you standing there like something out of a dream."

She remembered the moment, remembered the look in his eyes. Should she have recognized it for what it was? "You always seemed so detached, so controlled."

"I lost count of the number of times I nearly broke."

"But you said—you said you didn't even fancy me. You said you only made love to me because I deliberately provoked you."

"I was very angry. I thought you knew I loved you and had just been proving something."

*"No,"* she said.

"No?"

"You see, I thought—Dominic as good as said you had bragged to him about . . . having slept with me. He said you slept with all your graduate students. And, of course, that's pretty common, isn't it?"

"Ah, we have Parton to thank for that little stay in hell, do we? I might have known." He stroked her cheek. "I suppose he was after you himself."

She grinned. "No, it was purely political. He was afraid you'd smell a rat if I told you too much of what I was doing."

"So you told me you disliked me but were physically attracted to me."

"It was a lie. Did you believe me?"

"I thought that you believed it."

"Did you think I was lying to myself?"

"I thought that your response to me meant that there was some hope that you didn't understand your own feelings."

"Oh, I understood them by then. It was yours I was hiding from."

He picked up her left hand and stroked her ring finger with his thumb. "Are you going to want a big wedding?" he asked.

She took a breath. "Are you going to want a wedding?"

He smiled slowly. "Oh, yes. You're my wife, and I intend to tell the world so."

"What on earth is it?" Jasmin said, unwrapping the bulky parcel. "It feels like...it can't be! Ben, it's a plate! What—ahhh!" She gasped in astonishment as the last tissue came off to reveal the Mithra plate, with a little card.

"Oh, how...! 'A memento, my dear.' Isn't that crazy! Oh, but isn't it beautiful! I do wish it were real! I suppose it's evidence, isn't it? I suppose I'll have to turn it over to your friend Jeremy."

"You'll get it back."

She bent over the plate. "Such perfect workmanship. Better than anything else the artist did, as if he were really inspired. And all that cast work must have been impossibly difficult." She looked up. "It might have been accepted, you know. If it hadn't been for that damaged tool, how could anyone have known?"

Ben laughed. "Don't sound so much as though you regretted it."

"Yes, but Ben, Dominic told me that the silversmith said he had seen a plate like this one when he was a child, and that he had copied it from memory. And when Jeremy Stephen questioned the silversmith, I asked him to ask about it, and he repeated the same story to Jeremy. So it wasn't just another of Dominic's lies."

"It doesn't prove very much, my darling. Memory is a tricky thing."

"But it might, mightn't it? I mean, if he really saw something even a little like this, it would be tremendously important! If he only remembered the nimbus and the fact of the bull being sacrificed, it would be enough to—"

"Jasmin, the evidence is so frail it's effectively nonexist
ent."

"But I might use it, don't you think? I might put in
picture of this and say the forger was copying something b
had seen as a child. I mean, if it's true, even the forgery is
terribly important piece. Don't you think?"

"Do you want to know what I think?" asked Ben.

"Yes, I do. Don't you think it's possible?"

"What I think, my darling," said Ben slowly, "is that yo
should discuss this with your graduate supervisor. He'll b
able to advise you."

\*    \*    \*    \*    \*

# HE'S AN

## AMERICAN HERO

January 1994 rings in the New Year—and a new lineup of sensational American Heroes. You can't seem to get enough of these men, and we're proud to feature one each month, created by some of your favorite authors.

January: CUTS BOTH WAYS by Dee Holmes: Erin Kenyon hired old acquaintance Ashe Seager to investigate the crash that claimed her husband's life, only to learn old memories never die.

February: A WANTED MAN by Kathleen Creighton: Mike Lanagan's exposé on corruption earned him accolades...and the threat of death. Running for his life, he found sanctuary in the arms of Lucy Brown—but for how long?

March: COOPER by Linda Turner: Cooper Rawlings wanted nothing to do with the daughter of the man who'd shot his brother. But when someone threatened Susannah Patterson's life, he found himself riding to the rescue....

AMERICAN HEROES: Men who give all they've got for their country, their work—the women they love.

Only from

**Silhouette Books
is proud to present
our best authors,
their best books…
and the best in
your reading pleasure!**

Throughout 1993, look for exciting
books by these top names in
contemporary romance:

**DIANA PALMER—**
*The Australian* in October

**FERN MICHAELS—**
*Sea Gypsy* in October

**ELIZABETH LOWELL—**
*Chain Lightning* in November

**CATHERINE COULTER—**
*The Aristocrat* in December

**JOAN HOHL—**
*Texas Gold* in December

**LINDA HOWARD—**
*Tears of the Renegade* in January '94

When it comes to passion,
we wrote the book.      BOBT3

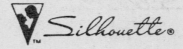

# ROMANTIC TRADITIONS

Paula Detmer Riggs kicks off
ROMANTIC TRADITIONS this month with
ONCE UPON A WEDDING (IM #524), which
features a fresh spin on the marriage-of-
convenience motif. Jesse Dante married
Hazel O'Connor to help an orphaned baby,
underestimating the powers of passion and
parenthood....

Coming to stores in January will be bestselling
author Marilyn Pappano's FINALLY A FATHER
(IM #542), spotlighting the time-honored secret-
baby story line. Quin Ellis had lied about her
daughter's real parentage for over nine years.
But Mac McEwen's return to town signaled an
end to her secret.

In April, expect an innovative look at the
amnesia plot line in Carla Cassidy's
TRY TO REMEMBER.

And ROMANTIC TRADITIONS doesn't stop there! In
months to come we'll be bringing you more
classic plot lines told the Intimate Moments way.
So, if you're the romantic type who appreciates
tradition with a twist, come experience
ROMANTIC TRADITIONS—only in

SIMRT2

**INTIMATE MOMENTS**

*Silhouette*

Southern Alberta—wide open ranching country
marked by rolling rangelands and roiling passions.
That's where the McCall family make their home.
You can meet Tanner, the first of the McCalls, in
BEYOND ALL REASON, (IM #536), the premiere book in

**JUDITH DUNCAN's**

**WIDE OPEN SPACES**

miniseries beginning in December 1993.

Scarred by a cruel childhood and narrow-minded
neighbors, Tanner McCall had resigned himself to a
lonely life on the Circle S Ranch. But when Kate Quinn,
a woman with two sons and a big secret, hired on,
Tanner discovered newfound needs and a woman
worthy of his trust.

In months to come, join more of the McCalls as
they search for love while working Alberta's
WIDE OPEN SPACES—only in
                    Silhouette Intimate Moments

WIDE1

**INTIMATE MOMENTS**®

*Silhouette*®

**CONARD COUNTY** continues...

Welcome back to Conard County, Wyoming, Rachel Lee's little patch of Western heaven, where unbridled passions match the wild terrain, and where men and women know the meaning of hard work—and the hard price of love. Join this bestselling author as she weaves her fifth Conard County tale, LOST WARRIORS (IM #535).

Vietnam veteran and American Hero Billy Joe Yuma had worked hard to heal the wounds of war—alone. But beautiful nurse Wendy Tate wouldn't take no for an answer, staking her claim on his heart...and his soul.

Look for their story in December, only from Silhouette Intimate Moments.

---

He staked his claim...

# HONOR BOUND

by
*New York Times*
Bestselling Author

Sandra Brown

previously published under the pseudonym Erin St. Claire

As Aislinn Andrews opened her mouth to scream, a hard
hand clamped over her face and she found herself face-
to-face with Lucas Greywolf, a lean, lethal-looking
Navajo and escaped convict who swore he wouldn't hurt
her— *if* she helped him.

Look for HONOR BOUND at your favorite
retail outlet this January.

Only from...

Silhouette

where passion lives.  SBHB

*Christmas Classics*

Share in the joys of finding happiness and exchanging the
ultimate gift—love—in full-length classic holiday
treasures by two bestselling authors

## JOAN HOHL
## EMILIE RICHARDS

Available in December at
your favorite retail outlet.

Only from 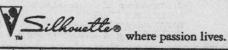 *Silhouette*® where passion lives.

## SILHOUETTE.... Where Passion Lives

Don't miss these Silhouette favorites by some of our most popular authors!
And now, you can receive a discount by ordering two or more titles!

### Silhouette Desire®

| | | | |
|---|---|---|---|
| #05751 | THE MAN WITH THE MIDNIGHT EYES BJ James | $2.89 | ☐ |
| #05763 | THE COWBOY Cait London | $2.89 | ☐ |
| #05774 | TENNESSEE WALTZ Jackie Merritt | $2.89 | ☐ |
| #05779 | THE RANCHER AND THE RUNAWAY BRIDE Joan Johnston | $2.89 | ☐ |

### Silhouette Intimate Moments®

| | | | |
|---|---|---|---|
| #07417 | WOLF AND THE ANGEL Kathleen Creighton | $3.29 | ☐ |
| #07480 | DIAMOND WILLOW Kathleen Eagle | $3.39 | ☐ |
| #07486 | MEMORIES OF LAURA Marilyn Pappano | $3.39 | ☐ |
| #07493 | QUINN EISLEY'S WAR Patricia Gardner Evans | $3.39 | ☐ |

### Silhouette Shadows®

| | | | |
|---|---|---|---|
| #27003 | STRANGER IN THE MIST Lee Karr | $3.50 | ☐ |
| #27007 | FLASHBACK Terri Herrington | $3.50 | ☐ |
| #27009 | BREAK THE NIGHT Anne Stuart | $3.50 | ☐ |
| #27012 | DARK ENCHANTMENT Jane Toombs | $3.50 | ☐ |

### Silhouette Special Edition®

| | | | |
|---|---|---|---|
| #09754 | THERE AND NOW Linda Lael Miller | $3.39 | ☐ |
| #09770 | FATHER: UNKNOWN Andrea Edwards | $3.39 | ☐ |
| #09791 | THE CAT THAT LIVED ON PARK AVENUE Tracy Sinclair | $3.39 | ☐ |
| #09811 | HE'S THE RICH BOY Lisa Jackson | $3.39 | ☐ |

### Silhouette Romance®

| | | | |
|---|---|---|---|
| #08893 | LETTERS FROM HOME Toni Collins | $2.69 | ☐ |
| #08915 | NEW YEAR'S BABY Stella Bagwell | $2.69 | ☐ |
| #08927 | THE PURSUIT OF HAPPINESS Anne Peters | $2.69 | ☐ |
| #08952 | INSTANT FATHER Lucy Gordon | $2.75 | ☐ |

|  | AMOUNT | $ _____ |
|---|---|---|
| *DEDUCT:* | 10% DISCOUNT FOR 2+ BOOKS | $ _____ |
|  | POSTAGE & HANDLING | $ _____ |
|  | ($1.00 for one book, 50¢ for each additional) | |
|  | APPLICABLE TAXES* | $ _____ |
|  | TOTAL PAYABLE | $ _____ |
|  | (check or money order—please do not send cash) | |

To order, complete this form and send it, along with a check or money order for the total above, payable to Silhouette Books, to: *In the U.S.*: 3010 Walden Avenue, P.O. Box 9077, Buffalo, NY 14269-9077; *In Canada*: P.O. Box 636, Fort Erie, Ontario, L2A 5X3.

Name: _____

Address: _____ City: _____

State/Prov.: _____ Zip/Postal Code: _____

*New York residents remit applicable sales taxes.
Canadian residents remit applicable GST and provincial taxes.

SBACK-OD

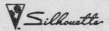